SISTERS
OF THE
NEVERSEA

Don't miss this anthology edited by
CYNTHIA LEITICH SMITH!

SISTERS

OF THE

NEVERSEA

CYNTHIA LEITICH SMITH

Heartdrum

An Imprint of HarperCollinsPublishers

Heartdrum is an imprint of HarperCollins Publishers.

Library of Congress Control Number: 2021932059
ISBN 978-0-06-286997-5

Typography by Catherine San Juan
21 22 23 24 25   PC/LSCH   10 9 8 7 6 5 4 3 2 1
❖
First Edition

In memory of Lillian, AKA Great Aunt Sis

CHAPTER 1

Tick tock. Tick tock. Each *tick, tick,* ticking second brought Lily and Wendy closer to the end of their time sharing a home as stepsisters. Not that they were on speaking terms anyway.

You see, Wendy's father, Mr. George Darling—that's him in the trim, navy suit—he had already accepted the assignment on Wall Street. And Lily's mama, Ms. Florene Roberts-Darling—that's her in the bright blue calico—she had flat-out refused to quit her job with the Tribe and move away from Oklahoma. And this, in turn, had created a rift between the girls over their own summer living arrangements. But that evening the whole family was still together, surrounded by community, celebrating big brother John's high school graduation.

Gripping her rolled-up ceremony program, Lily exclaimed, "He's next, John's next!"

Flashing a brilliant smile, John strode across the stage

in a flowing black robe with a beaded eagle feather dangling from his mortarboard.

His parents and siblings proudly rose, cheering. His grandparents, aunties, uncles, and cousins proudly rose, cheering. Great Auntie Lillian had done the beadwork herself.

"He looks so grown-up!" Wendy exclaimed as John raised his diploma high.

"Way to go, John!" Lily sang out, as if he could hear her from the arena bleachers.

In that joyful moment, Wendy Moira Angela Darling never would've muttered that John was merely her *step-*brother, and Lily Maria Roberts never would've boasted that John was her *real* brother. Instead, Wendy blinked back tears because *everything* was changing, while Lily gave her mama and daddy bouncing high fives. Meanwhile, Mr. Darling lifted the siblings' four-year-old baby brother, Michael, onto his shoulders for a better view of John's big moment.

"John, John, John, John!" Michael chanted, clapping. "John, John, John, John!"

Michael shared a mama, Ms. Roberts-Darling, with Lily and John.

Michael shared a father, Mr. Darling, with Wendy.

Michael would be staying with Lily, John, and their mama in Tulsa rather than boarding tomorrow's red-eye flight with Wendy and their father for New York City.

Or so they all assumed at the time.

* * *

The stepsisters' silent truce had lasted all the way through the very, very, very, very long speeches and graduates' roll call and ceremonial fanciness. It had survived a few scathing looks and a couple of turned-up noses in the expansive leather back seat of Mr. Darling's sedan.

What's more, the girls had managed to mostly avoid each other at the boisterous potluck reception in their backyard. On the wraparound wooden deck, Lily and Wendy helped serve sherbet fruit punch and chocolate-raspberry sheet cake without exchanging a word.

"You girls must be so proud of John," Auntie Lillian said, accepting a plated serving.

"*I'm* proud that he graduated with academic honors," Lily answered.

"*I'm* proud that he got a baseball scholarship," Wendy replied.

Which was silly because they were both equally delighted with John all around.

Wiping chocolate icing from Michael's chin, Auntie Lillian remembered a time, not long ago, when the girls were inseparable and every third word out of their mouths was "we."

High in the night sky, a cluster of curious, twinkling stars gathered to observe the festivities. As the crowd of party-goers thinned, the stars watched John exchange a round of hugs and handshakes. They watched Mr. Roberts, who was John's tall, jovial daddy (and, to be perfectly clear, also Lily's daddy), swing an arm around his son's shoulders and walk him to his pickup truck. They watched John hop behind the wheel, wave goodbye, and drive off to meet up with his school pals.

Then the stars turned their attention to the younger children of the family. The ones who hadn't grown up yet. The stars knew what was coming, who was lurking. They always did. They'd seen it all before, countless times, across vast, green oceans and ethereal night skies. They recognized the tiny, sparkling glow, nearly hidden in the wise old oak tree sprawling above the Roberts-Darlings' backyard. They recognized the crouched, shadowy figures within its branches. The stars weren't the only spectators closely observing Lily, Wendy, and Michael.

CHAPTER

2

The family cat, Spot, was—as her name suggested—a tawny, spotted tabby with a rhinestone collar, known for her perpetually alarmed expression and a tendency toward thievery. She dozed with one eye open on the padded window bench in the stepsisters' shared bedroom. A navy-blue dress sock, swiped from Mr. Darling, was hidden beneath her furry belly.

"Um, Lily . . ." Wendy slipped a fantasy novel into her overstuffed, clear backpack, zipped it up, and propped it against the doorframe. (Wendy aspired to be a wizard.)

"Yeah?" Lily was stretched out, flat on her back, on one of the two matching twin-sized canopy beds with puffy sky-blue comforters. She didn't so much as glance over from her nonfiction book about large sea reptiles. (Lily aspired to be a zoologist.)

"Never mind," Wendy said, reaching for her last travel bag.

Both girls were wearing lightweight cotton nightshirts with matching ankle-length bottoms—Lily's in a heart print and Wendy's in a star print—and house slippers with rubbery soles that offered a little grip on the hardwood floors. Auntie Lillian had given the girls the pajamas last Christmas.

Wendy rolled socks and folded undies to tuck inside her bag. Lily turned page after page of a book that she was mostly pretending to read.

Both stepsisters were quietly reflecting on family and loss.

Wendy's earliest memories arose from her mother's funeral back in London. Wendy had been only four, the age Michael was now. She didn't remember much—a gray day, a gray dress, her father's gray expression. As much as she loved Ms. Roberts-Darling, Wendy had said "no, thank you" to her stepmother's offer of adoption, which had been extended almost a year ago on Wendy's twelfth birthday. The idea of saying "yes" had felt somehow disloyal to the long-departed mother she knew largely through stories, old photos, and video.

Lily's clearest memories from her preschool years were of Skittles the classroom hamster, and her mama and daddy's divorce. At first, it had felt confusing, overwhelming, but both had stressed that they'd always be her parents. That would never change.

This current family crisis was far more fraught with

uncertainty. Only last year Wendy had said "no" to being Lily's legally adoptive sister. If Wendy had said "yes," then they would officially be sisters forever, and that would never change. But she hadn't.

At first, Lily tried to understand Wendy's tender feelings. It must have been horrible to lose a parent, even if you could only faintly remember her. Perhaps that inability to remember made the loss even worse. But now the marriage that had made them stepsisters was in jeopardy. For the past several months, Lily had rationalized away the warning signs, refusing to believe the split would really happen, but suddenly, here they were.

What if this summer's trial separation became a permanent one? What if Lily's mama and Wendy's father split up for good? The girls would be ex-stepsisters. What would that mean?

Wendy was already moving away, starting a new life without Lily. There was nothing Lily could do about that, but Wendy could. Wendy could still say "yes" to officially being Ms. Roberts-Darling's daughter and, therefore, Lily and John's legal sister, and *so why didn't she*? Didn't Wendy love them all enough?

Alas, Wendy, having agonized to make her initial decision—the hardest thing she'd ever done—had closed her mind to the possibility and put it behind her. So, Lily did her very best to swallow what felt like rejection. She did her very best not to dwell on it. Lily always did her very best, but sometimes a wisp of frustration slipped out.

That night both girls were trying—and failing—not to focus on their immediate futures, about the fact that, come morning, Wendy and Mr. Darling would leave for New York City.

New York City was more than 1,300 miles away.

"Mea culpa, mea culpa!" Mr. Darling's voice boomed from the far end of the long hall. "Really, love, do we have to bicker on the night before I leave?"

Straining to eavesdrop, neither girl could quite make out Ms. Roberts-Darling's reply.

Then Mr. Darling said, "I can't seem to . . . Blast this tie!"

"It's a clip-on, remember? And pipe down. The kids will hear you."

How sad it was that their marriage had tumbled into disarray! They'd originally met as students at business school in Chicago. Ms. Roberts-Darling had enrolled with the goal of returning home to work in economic development for a tribal government. Mr. Darling had enrolled with the goal of clocking a few years on Wall Street before returning to England.

Eventually, they had agreed to set up household in Tulsa, which was a big city by Oklahoma standards. Ms. Roberts-Darling commuted to her job at the Muscogee Creek Tribal headquarters in Okmulgee. Mr. Darling was a rising star at the US southwest regional office of an international financial firm. Or at least he used to be. Within hours, he would be off to the New York office with Wendy in tow. "It's the opportunity of a lifetime! Besides, there's talk of closing the Tulsa branch, and then what would we do?"

"We'd get by! What with John leaving for college, we don't need such a big house."

"With John leaving . . . ?" Mr. Darling countered. "In case you have forgotten, university in the States is terribly expensive. Florene, we're still paying off our own degrees."

"Not everything is about money, George. And it's not like living in New York is cheap."

That was enough bickering for the girls, who'd overheard it all before. Wendy zipped her last travel bag and shut the door. Lily sat up on her bed, hugging her knees.

In their distress, neither stepsister noticed the three colorful leaves on the hardwood floor. Neither sensed the danger lurking outside the open window.

"I changed *continents* for you," Wendy pointed out, crossing the room to scratch Spot beneath her furry chin. (Wendy was seriously tempted to take the cat with her.) "Why can't you spend this summer in New York with me?"

It was to Lily's credit that she resisted the urge to point out that Wendy and Mr. Darling had relocated to the US *before* their parents had met in Chicago. "I'm happy right here." Lily rocked slightly in place. "This is home. Our friends, our cousins! We're all supposed to go fishing on Lake Tenkiller next weekend. You could stay here in Tulsa this summer instead."

It was to Wendy's credit that she resisted the urge to point out that all of their cousins in Tulsa were on Lily's side of the family. All the cousins on Wendy's side of the family lived far away in England. "But think of it, Lily— New York City! Broadway! The Statue of Liberty!" Wendy seized on Lily's interest in biology. "The Natural History museum!"

Lily had a distinct fondness for dinosaur exhibits, mixed feelings about Native-themed exhibits (depending on their quality), and she felt vaguely unsettled by animal taxidermy.

What she said was: "I'm not always a fan of natural history museums."

"Lily, please! You could at least come and stay for my birthday." It was only a couple of days away, and it was a sore subject. Mr. Darling's employer had been sympathetic to his waiting to begin the new job until after John's high school graduation—that was a once-in-a-lifetime event. But apparently, birthdays, which came around every year, didn't rate the same consideration. Even if it was the birthday that officially made you a teenager. Even if it was the birthday that meant that you were really growing up.

The stars peered at the girls through the bay window.

They were better translators than the stepsisters. The stars understood that what Wendy was *really* saying was that she didn't want to leave Lily behind. And she was nervous about the summer, the possibility of starting her whole life over in New York. The stars also understood that what Lily *wasn't* saying was how much she'd miss Wendy. And how home wouldn't feel like home without her.

What's more, Lily was terrified of flying on airplanes. Every winter, right after Christmas, Lily had been invited to come along to London to visit Wendy's side of the family, and every winter, Lily had declined and stayed in Tulsa with Auntie Lillian instead.

"Dad bought you and Mikey plane tickets to New York," Wendy reminded her stepsister. "They're paid for. You know Dad doesn't simply toss money around like that. Do you want them to go to waste?" Wendy was echoing what her father had exclaimed about purchasing the tickets ("I don't simply toss money around like that!").

"That's not my fault," Lily said. "I've made it clear from the beginning that I won't go." It went unsaid that if Lily turned down the trip, then Michael was out, too. He was too little to fly back home by himself, and John couldn't come because of his summer job at a nearby steakhouse.

I know what you're thinking. Yes, it's true that another cat might've noticed the intruders lurking outside, but Spot was self-occupied. Vexed that Wendy had stopped paying attention to her, the tabby stood, stretched, leapt off the window bench, and scampered out of the room to go sleep with Michael instead. She took Mr. Darling's navy dress sock with her.

"How about two weeks?" Wendy implored, never quick to give up. "What if you come along to New York for the first couple of weeks." She crossed the star-shaped throw rug. "It'd be an adventure. You could hurry and pack right now. I'll help—"

"*Your* adventure, not mine." Lily slipped under the covers. "You could celebrate your birthday here, just as easily." She clicked off the lamp on her nightstand. "If you want to leave home, fine. But don't expect me to make it any easier for you."

Wendy threw up her hands. "Why do you have to be so . . . boring all the time?"

Lily made a show of turning her back on Wendy. "Why do you have to be so . . . flighty?"

The girls quieted a moment, struggling to compose themselves. Their parents were still at it. Even with the door closed, the stepsisters could hear the muffled adult voices.

"They'll wake Mikey," Lily said, sitting up again. "If he's not up already."

Wendy replied, "Don't strain yourself. I'll check on him."

"Fine. You do that." With a sigh, Lily got up from her bed, followed Wendy out of the room, and stomped off down the hallway in the opposite direction.

* * *

"Auntie Lillian, I didn't know you were still here," Lily said, entering the country kitchen. "I thought you caught a ride with the Halfmoons."

Auntie Lillian, for whom Lily was named, was a formidable, fashionable elder with stylish purple eyeglasses and big hair who loved to socialize. She lived in an adorable cottage only five or so minutes away, depending on traffic, but had difficulty seeing well enough at night to drive. "I stayed to help your folks finish cleaning up." Using the sink faucet, Auntie sprayed barbecue sauce off the white porcelain serving platter. "They're supposed to take me home any time now."

Lily shifted her weight from one foot to another on the checked tile floor. She fretted that her squabbling parents had forgotten about Auntie. Then Lily fretted about whether she should interrupt their argument to remind them. Truth was, she fretted more than most people.

"Yeah, well." Lily blew out a long breath. "Nothing's the way it's supposed to be." She studied the poster—*Congrats, John! We love you!*—hanging on the wall above the kitchen table. It showcased photos of her brother in his baseball uniform, with his girlfriend, Gracie, at prom, spinning in fancy-dancer regalia, and splashing with his siblings at the water park.

"You fall asleep over there?" Auntie Lillian tilted her head toward the dishwasher. "I sure could use another pair of hands to hurry this up."

"On it." Lily began loading freshly rinsed plates in the bottom rack.

Once that was done, Auntie Lillian wiped the granite counters, the kitchen island, and the tabletop as Lily swept the floor. Meanwhile, on the other side of the ranch-style house, Mr. Darling and Ms. Roberts-Darling called a truce in their bedroom suite while Wendy read the second-to-last chapter of *Ella Enchanted* to a spellbound Michael on his bed.

In the sky above, the stars monitored the glowing intruder inching closer to Michael's window. Alas, they couldn't sound an alarm, being only stars after all.

The grandfather clock in the family room chimed eleven times. Auntie Lillian's voice was gentle, but she wasn't afraid to nudge. "Hon, you and Mikey could still fly to New York in the morning and return with your mama when she goes up to visit in July."

"July? Mama's going in July now?" That wasn't welcome news to Lily, who was torn between not wanting to go and despising being left behind. "I expect she's taking Mikey with her then?"

"I expect so," Auntie Lillian replied. Unbeknownst to the stepsisters, at the party that evening, Ms. Roberts-Darling had floated the idea of her making the trip when it became clear that Lily wouldn't change her mind about going. It had been quickly agreed that Michael couldn't spend the whole summer without his father and sister

Wendy, and Mr. Darling had been pleased that the flight tickets he'd purchased would be used after all.

"I'm so sorry, hon," Auntie added. "I thought you girls knew. What with all the excitement around John's graduation, your folks must've forgotten to mention it to y'all."

Lily shook off the broom bristles and emptied the dustpan. "You know, Wendy's *choosing* to leave this summer. It's not like she even knows anyone in New York City." Actually, Mr. Darling's whimsical, free-spirited cousin, Samantha, lived in Brooklyn and would be looking after Wendy while he was at work, but no one had mentioned that to Lily either.

Returning the cleaning utensils to the laundry closet, Lily added, "What's she going to do by herself all summer?"

"All the more reason for you to fly up and keep her company for a while."

Lily had heard enough talk of flying. "On a plane? At over *thirty thousand feet* in the sky?"

Auntie chuckled. "You two could have grand adventures in a city like that!"

There was that word again: "adventure." Lily didn't care for it.

In the too-bright kitchen, Auntie Lillian added, "Sometimes we get caught up in adventures whether we want to or not, and, sweet girl, I get the feeling you're overdue." She wrapped Lily in a comforting hug. "Remember to breathe, hon. In and out, slow as you please. Just breathe."

CHAPTER

3

Side by side, Wendy and Michael leaned against the headboard of his bed, which had been painted to resemble an antique treasure map. She wouldn't have admitted it, even to herself, but Wendy appreciated Lily giving her some quality alone time with their little brother.

He looked adorable in his oversized space-themed pj's with their colorful pattern of rockets, comets, and planets. Wendy worried about Michael, how he would handle the many changes to come. Since the tension in the family had kicked up, he had begun exhibiting more babyish behavior. At the moment, though, he was distracted by Spot, who was pawing at the oddly flickering shadow protruding beneath the denim beanbag.

"I won't be here in person to read to you tomorrow night." Wendy slid a bookmark into *Ella Enchanted* and held up her phone. "But I'll only be a video call away. At bedtime, we'll pick up where we left off, okay?"

"You're going away?" Despite his parents' best efforts to prepare him, Michael hadn't wrapped his young mind around the fact that his father and Wendy were moving to New York.

Wendy's breath caught. "I'd never leave you, if I didn't have to. Mikey, if it was up to me, I'd take you everywhere I went." That declaration was a bold overstatement, though it felt true in the moment. In any case, those listening outside the open window took Wendy at her word.

She cocked her head at the *clack-click, clack-click* sound of Mr. Darling's and Ms. Roberts-Darling's footsteps on the hardwood floor as they passed by Michael's bedroom.

Did those normally attentive parents notice the light spilling out from under his door? No, not that night. Both had pressing matters on their minds.

"What's that?" Michael asked, pointing toward his compass-rose throw rug. Like Wendy, he was fascinated with mermaids. Like Lily, he was fascinated with marine animals (with animals in general, actually). His parents had split the difference and chosen a nautical theme for the room, which had evolved into a pirate theme, complete with glow-in-the-dark stars stuck to the vaulted ceiling. Which did nothing to explain the glistening leaves on the rug.

Wendy hopped down from the bed, swept one up, and held it in the moonlight streaming through Michael's open bay window. As she studied the intricate pattern of the leaf veins, the gold particles clinging to them made her fingertips tingle. "Did you make these at preschool?"

Michael climbed down after her. "Don't think so."

Wendy could imagine him gently brushing away leaf pulp. Sprinkling gold . . . it wasn't glitter. What was it? Sparkly, brighter . . . finer, like dust. It shimmered.

Lily strolled in, and the departing glow of Mr. Darling's headlights caught her eye. "Auntie Lillian says 'good night.' Mama and Papa George left to drive her home." Yes, Lily called Mr. Darling "Papa George" (as opposed to "Daddy," which is what she called her own father). Wendy called Ms. Roberts-Darling "Mom," as opposed to "Mum," which she reserved for the mother who'd borne her. No, it wasn't like their parents to leave them home alone so late, but it had been a life-changing day soon to be followed by a life-changing morning. Auntie lived quite close by, and the girls were going into seventh grade now. Surely, with a phone handy, they could look after themselves and Michael for five to ten minutes.

"It's way past your bedtime, Mikey," Lily said. "Let's take off your bedroom slippers and tuck you under the covers."

Michael yawned. His eyelids fluttered. Wendy took off his slippers and put them away. Then a radiant light the size of your fist—a thousand times brighter than any night-light—swooped through the window and zigzagged across the room, trailing a fading stream of golden sparkles. The Roberts-Darling siblings froze. Michael perked up. "What's that?"

Spot's eyes dilated. Like a tiny tiger, she slinked from the cushy beanbag, intently watching the brilliant aerial display. She wanted very much to trap, kill, and eat it.

"It's . . . It's like a firefly and a hummingbird had a baby," Lily observed, eager to identify the luminous insect. She noted its speed, the radiant wings, and the fact that it didn't seem attracted to Michael's nightstand lamp or his cheerful night-light, shaped like a pirate hat.

"It's a Fairy!" Wendy countered, delighting her brother, annoying her sister, and, most importantly, flattering said visitor by adding, "Have you ever seen anything so beautiful?"

"Do you have to be so dramatic?" Lily asked. It wasn't that she thought science had all the answers. Certainly not. But, in her opinion, Wendy's enthusiasm could be a bit much. And now Michael was wide awake, bouncing on his knees, just when he'd settled down for the night.

Basking in the attention, the Fairy—yes, Wendy had been spot-on—hovered over the rug, quirked an arched brow, and, in midair, executed a confident pirouette to show off her wings and attire. Taking her time, she modeled a formfitting bodice and flaring skirt comprised of turquoise-and-forest-green leaves, set off at the waist with a tiny, red tropical bloom. Her chiming voice mimicked, "Do you have to be so dramatic?" The Fairy added, "You should know better than to talk to another girl like that! She has every right to express her appreciation!"

Lily staggered back. Was she dreaming? Hallucinating?

Should she seek medical attention? Lily breathed in deeply, breathed out as if blowing through a straw.

If the creature was real, it might be dangerous. Lily considered grabbing her siblings, rushing out of Michael's bedroom, and slamming the door behind them. But the creature was fast—so, so fast. Supernaturally fast? Lily doubted they could outrun it. "Who are you?"

It had been tempting to say "what" instead. To ask, "What are you?" But that would've been terribly rude, intrusive, and presumptuous. Lily knew better than to ask anyone "what" they were.

"Good evening, Wendy, Lily, and Mikey," the Fairy said in a tinkling voice. "My name is Belle." She clasped her tiny hands together under her pointed chin. "Poor dears. I couldn't help noticing that you've been abandoned by your parents."

Resisting the urge to roll her eyes, Lily circled Belle, keeping her distance. "It talks. It speaks English with a British accent." An accent not unlike Mr. Darling's, Lily thought. In case you were wondering, Wendy's accent had faded considerably, though it arose again each winter after she visited her grandparents in London.

Wendy shook her head. "It does *not* speak with a—"

"I am not an 'it.'" Belle landed on the footboard of the bed. "I am a 'she.' A Fairy 'she.'"

"Told you so," Wendy whispered, dropping the leaf.

"Neat!" Michael simply accepted the situation. The whole world—with its infinite wonders great and small—was a source of constant fascination to him. "Hello, Fairy."

"*Belle*. My name is Belle."

"Belle," he repeated with a quiet conscientiousness the Fairy found endearing.

Meanwhile, Lily had positioned herself between her little brother and the mysterious creature. She grabbed Wendy's wrist to keep her at a distance. "How do you know our names?"

"We listened to you through the open window," Belle explained. Why were they bothering her with all these questions? *She* was the one with questions.

Belle had tasked herself with quickly categorizing human children so they could be properly distributed, but this family confused her. Yes, of course Belle had studied Peter's old storybooks as a guide. But the illustrations never matched up with real-life humans.

"What do you mean by 'we'?" Lily asked. "Who's with you?"

Belle replied with a question of her own. "What are you, Lost or Indian?"

Not surprisingly, the question struck Lily as terribly rude, intrusive, and presumptuous.

"We're Creek!" Michael exclaimed. "Muscogee. Muscogee Creek."

"Is that a 'yes' for Indian then?" Belle inquired.

"Yeah." Pointing to Lily, Michael said, "Me and that Sissy." Pointing next to Wendy, he added, "Not that Sissy."

Normally, these statements of fact wouldn't have bothered Wendy at all. She fully understood that she and her father were white, while Lily and Michael were Muscogee Creek, as were John and Ms. Roberts-Darling. And, for that matter, Wendy adored her stepfamily and the intertribal community. But she was already mourning the loss of her home and everyone attached to it. "I'm not Native," she clarified, twisting her wrist free of Lily's grip. "My father is Mikey's father, and he's British. My mother was British and . . ." She didn't like to use the word "dead."

Lily didn't care for this line of conversation either. "Why do you want to know?"

Based on his *yo-ho-ho*-heavy room décor, Belle had already deduced that Michael was a pirate, and once she made up her mind about something, it tended to stick. So, regardless of how he'd just explained himself, it was the question of Wendy and Lily that puzzled the Fairy.

Belle zipped over to the dresser. "But *you two* are not sisters?" She gestured wide. "You share a bedroom, two brothers. One small and"—she wrinkled her pert nose—"one big."

Time was, Wendy and Lily would've linked arms and proclaimed their sisterhood. Never mind that Wendy was petite and freckled with coppery red hair and the strength and grace of a ballet dancer. Never mind that Lily was tall and lanky with dark brown hair and possessed the reflexes and team skills of a volleyball player.

As you should well know, plenty of loving families have children who don't look alike or share much in common.

"We're stepsisters." Wendy stopped short of adding that they were also best friends.

Spot crouched, her tail swishing. She sprang into the air—jaws open, claws outstretched. Spot nearly snagged one of Belle's slippers. The Fairy screamed, twisted, and punched Spot smack in her pink triangular nose. With a yowl, Spot flipped in midair, landing with most of her dignity on all four paws. "You vicious, wretched, awful creature!" Belle exclaimed.

Undaunted, the tawny cat hissed and sauntered to curl up on the beanbag.

The Fairy warily watched Spot settle in. What lucky children these were to have been chosen! Poor things— left home alone with a homicidal cat. Belle called, "Oh, there you are!"

You might be wondering who she was talking to. So were the Roberts-Darling siblings. It was then that they noticed the arrival of yet another visitor, perched in the center bay window.

He appeared about the same age as the girls, maybe a little younger. About Lily's height, maybe a little shorter. The girls noted the lithe form, the forest-green and brown garments, the sword at his hip and his smug, self-satisfied smile.

"Oh, great. There's another one," Lily said. "Who're you? What do you want?"

He'd positioned himself with nonchalance, confidence, and a bit like a praying mantis.

"Hello," Wendy said. "I'm Wendy Darling. What's your name?"

"You may call me Peter." He hopped down from the windowsill and bowed with a flourish. "Peter Pan, Captain of the Lost." Fisting his hands on his hips, he peered around Michael's bedroom. "Now, what have you done with my shadow?"

CHAPTER

4

Lily Roberts considered herself too sensible to believe in sparkly Fairies or wayward shadows. She briefly reconsidered the possibility that this was all a dream. She'd fallen asleep reading with Wendy and Michael before, and *Ella Enchanted* was an inspiring and imaginative story. "Shadow?" Lily quizzed the newcomer. "What are you talking about? Who's lost?"

After a glimpse at Peter, Michael's bedazzled gaze returned to Belle, who was preening in front of the portholestyle mirror hanging above his door. Wendy took in her brother's rapt expression, his openmouthed grin. Now *that* was an appropriate reaction to the appearance of a Fairy! Wendy considered this clear evidence that Michael was more like her than Lily.

Indeed, Lily was beside herself. She asked Peter, "What are you doing here?"

"Where are your manners?" Wendy scolded Lily. "Do

you have to pick at everything?"

Belle smoothed her leaf-skirt. "Peter is a human boy. Human like you." Though she had had her quarrels with Peter—*plenty* of them—it irked her to hear Lily question him so suspiciously. You see, Belle loved Peter, though she didn't always like him, and however tested, a Fairy's love is a lifelong bond. She explained, "He is seeking playmates. Children need playmates to be happy, healthy, and whole."

Peter spun in place and winked at the stepsisters. "I understand that you can't help staring. All the girls like me. Everyone likes me. I project a manly presence."

Lily folded her arms across her chest and muttered, "That's optimistic."

Wendy repressed a snort-laugh. "When did you last see your shadow?"

"I'm not sure exactly." Peter marched to Michael's toy box, which resembled a treasure chest, and opened the lid. "It used to follow me everywhere." Rummaging inside, Peter tossed out Black Panther, Thor, Spider-Man, and Wonder Woman action figures. A red rubber ball followed, bouncing three times on the hardwood and nearly knocking off the nightstand lamp.

Michael retrieved the ball and pitched it onto the floor, where it rolled past the cat. It was a credit to Spot's fixation on Belle that she didn't chase the ball or pounce on the Spider-Man figure that had landed only inches to the right of the beanbag.

Still searching, Peter said, "My shadow keeps wandering off. The last time we visited Kensington Gardens, it spent hours hiding in the Elfin Oak." He flicked his wrist. A Frisbee sliced through the air and into Lily's quick hands.

Peter added, "I'm beginning to take it personally."

"Why would your shadow be *here*?" Lily asked. "In my brother's bedroom?"

"In *our* brother's bedroom." Wendy recalled that Kensington Gardens were counted among the Royal Parks of London, which was located at least two plane rides from Tulsa.

Michael's lower lip quivered. "I'm everybody's brother."

"Not mine," Belle scoffed, launching from the porthole-style wall mirror to search behind the long, blue curtains, mindful to stay beyond Spot's leaping range. "We've been listening to your story, Wendy, the one about Ella. We've been listening at that window!"

Ella Enchanted was written by Gail Carson Levine, not Wendy Darling, but she beamed at the compliment anyway. She had, after all, put a lot of emotion into reading aloud.

Peter held up Michael's favorite plush toy. "Hm, who's this?" It was medium brown, wearing an orange polka-dotted dress. Normally, it traveled with Michael or stayed on his bed, but was stashed inside the box when the house was cleaned for company.

"Nana Bear!" the four-year-old shouted, scrambling

off the bed and past his sisters.

"Mikey!" Lily called, dropping the Frisbee to the floor as her little brother slipped beyond her grasp. "Come back here!"

Michael grabbed his teddy and hugged it tight. Nana Bear was a wonderful listener and secret keeper, especially these past few months as tension in the family had escalated. Michael had loved Nana Bear his whole life. It had been a baby gift from Lily and John's daddy, Mr. Roberts, who you remember from earlier that night.

"Shadow!" Peter got on his hands and knees and crawled over to peer under Michael's bed. "Not there!" It would have behooved Peter to ask Michael where to find the shadow. Four-year-old children know practically everything, and don't begin forgetting it until they turn seven. Instead, Peter tried to lure the shadow out of hiding. "Come out, come out! Are you homesick? Near fear, Shadow! Show yourself, and off we'll be to Neverland."

"Neverland?" Wendy radiated excitement. "Is that where Fairies come from?"

Peter hopped to his feet and strutted around the room like a ringmaster. "Of course it's where Fairies come from! Fairies, Merfolk, wild beasts, pirates, Injuns, and the Lost!"

"Fairies come from all over the world," Belle muttered, peeking behind the headboard.

"Merfolk?" Wendy exclaimed at the same time. "You mean, mermaids?" Just the word made her skin quiver.

"Pirates!" Michael echoed, swinging Nana Bear in one hand. "Yo ho ho!"

"I keep telling you, the word is 'Indians,'" Belle corrected with a sigh. "Not 'Injuns.'"

Michael and Wendy had never heard the term "Injun" before—as the Roberts-Darlings certainly didn't watch old Hollywood Western movies. Lily wasn't familiar with it either, but it wasn't a term Native people used. It struck her as deeply disrespectful.

While Lily had to admit that these strange visitors didn't seem dangerous, they were annoying, and they put her nerves on edge. She picked up her little brother—who was still clutching Nana Bear—and dumped him back on the bed. Lily wasn't sure if Peter had meant Native people or people from India, but neither should've been lumped into the same category as villainous pirates or make-believe creatures like mermaids or Fairies . . . though she suddenly felt less certain about the latter. And what was a wild beast anyway? An animal or a monster?

Across the room, an aloft Belle was using all her might to pull open Michael's lowest dresser drawer in hopes of finding the shadow in there. Working his way down from the top, Peter tossed aside socks, undies, T-shirts, shorts. "This isn't fun anymore!" he declared. "Let's make a game of it. I hereby order all of you to help me search."

Lily was seated at the foot of the bed. "You can't tell us what to do in our own home."

"I'm not home," Wendy put in. "I don't even know where my home is anymore." That earned her an angry scowl from Lily and a thoughtful head tilt from Belle.

Wendy wasn't the type to wallow in self-pity. She embraced the challenge, rushing about the room, regarding every object from every angle. "Look out, Shadow. You can't hide forever!"

Charmed by Wendy's enthusiasm, Belle lit her way. Perhaps Peter had been right about the girl. They did need a storyteller, and Wendy might have spirit enough for Neverland.

"Be careful," Lily called, putting a staying hand on Michael's shoulder.

"I want to help, too!" he exclaimed, checking behind the pillows.

Wendy located a wiggly, dim foot shape sticking out from beneath the beanbag. "There you are! Peter, I've found it!"

He rushed to her side. Leaning over Spot, Peter threw out his arms. "Scat, scat!"

The alarmed cat sprang from the beanbag and scurried under the bed, where she continued to intently observe Belle, who was hovering above the frenetic boy's shoulder.

Peter yanked up the beanbag, revealing men's dress socks, colorful hair ties, a couple of catnip toys, broken crayons, random bits of construction paper, and a Peter-shaped shadow. The shadow's arms were tucked where

Peter's were straight. Its legs were folded where his stood tall.

Lily could hardly believe what she was seeing. It made no sense at all. Her logical mind knew that a shadow was a darker lit area in the shape of whatever object blocked it from a light source. Consequently, the shadow of a person (or anything) should mimic it.

Instead, though Peter towered menacingly above, the newly exposed boy-shadow scrambled backward like a crab and rolled to the right, darting away.

Crowing, Peter gave chase. Gravity-defying chase. Up the walls, down the walls, across the wood floor. The shadow launched itself to grasp the ceiling fan in a flailing spin, and then it dropped and slid under Michael's little craft table without so much as knocking off any crayons. Coming up fast from behind, Peter crashed into it, sending art supplies flying.

Wearing a bored expression, Belle retreated to the windowsill as Michael applauded like it was all a circus show. "Magic," Wendy whispered. "Peter is magic."

Lily noted that the shadow wasn't entirely without substance. It had girth enough to hold on to something, to move solid objects like the fan. What's more, as it sprang about the room, the shadow clearly possessed a will of its own. And very little interest in reattaching itself to Peter, who was floating near the vaulted bedroom ceiling.

Peter, who—wings or not—could *fly*.

CHAPTER

5

Peter's shadow eluded them at every turn, twist, and side step. It moved like a dancer only faster, utterly silent and far more slippery.

"Don't let it out of the room!" Peter called as it flitted away.

Wendy yelled, "Lily, shut the door!"

"Don't tell me what to do," Lily groused, glancing at Michael's ship-wheel wall clock. Where were Mr. Darling and Ms. Roberts-Darling? Had they gotten held up at Auntie Lillian's?

Belle was glad Wendy was the storyteller, not Lily. Even little Michael swung his stuffed toy bear at the shadow, while Lily sat there like a stump.

With a full-speed flutter of wings, Belle managed to slam the door herself. She stuck out her tongue at the foiled shadow before addressing Lily. "Some good you are!"

"Think about it." Lily folded her arms. "It's a *shadow*.

It can slip into tiny spaces—"

"Stop giving it ideas!" Belle buzzed over and yanked Lily's long hair.

"Ow, let go!" Lily tried to bat her away, but Belle was fast and stayed out of her peripheral vision. Meanwhile, Wendy was running to and fro. Peter was flying, skipping, tripping this way and that. Michael laughed, clumsily copying Peter's movements.

The shadow seemed to be everywhere yet barely escaping each outstretched hand. It was chaos—Lily despised it, and Wendy found it all rather thrilling.

"Help us, and I'll let you go," the Fairy replied, tugging extra hard on Lily's hair as the shadow dived, spinning around them with cheeky panache.

"Ow! Stop that!" Lily replied. "Fine, fine—I'll help already."

"Our cat is under the bed," Wendy reminded Peter. "She can help us catch the shadow."

Belle let go of Lily's hair, and Peter gestured for the siblings and Fairy to come closer. After a brief hesitation, Lily told Michael, "Stay right where you are." The last thing they needed was for Peter to barrel into Michael like he had the art table.

"No!" he replied, verging on a fit from exhaustion and overstimulation.

"Mikey," Lily said. "We need you to hide under the covers with Nana Bear."

That sounded much better to Michael. He hated to

be left out. Giving him something to do—hide—made the whole thing seem more like a game than, say, being held back because he was the littlest. Michael crawled under his bedspread and tucked into a ball to be as hard to detect as possible. "Shh," he whispered to Nana Bear. "Be quiet."

"All right, girls," Peter said once Lily had joined the huddle. "We're going to herd the shadow under the bed and once the cat catches it, we'll be able to reattach it to me—problem solved! Ready?" The Fairy saluted him— chin up, back straight, right arm at a sharp angle.

"Ready, Peter," Wendy said.

"And then you'll leave?" Lily pressed.

"Of course! Once my shadow and I are reunited, off we'll fly to Neverland."

Now, when Peter said "we'll," Lily assumed that he was speaking only of himself, the shadow, and Belle, which was not the sort of mistake that Lily usually made. However, it was getting quite late and even the skyrocketing adrenaline from being visited by a wayward shadow, preening pixie, and flying boy had its limits.

The shadow ducked, the shadow dodged, the shadow slipped and scurried, but the combined efforts of Peter, Belle, Wendy, and Lily finally herded it beneath the bed where, in a scramble of front limbs and extended claws, Spot proudly pinned it in place.

The cat was enormously pleased with herself.

CHAPTER
6

"I did it!" Peter shouted, throwing up his arms in a V shape. "I've got you now, Shadow! I'm the best shadow hunter of all time! All other hunters bow before me."

"You had a lot of help," Lily reminded him.

Taking that as a cue, Michael and Nana Bear popped out from under the covers, and Wendy scolded her stepsister. "Be nice to the company!"

"They're not 'company.'" With gentle fingers, Lily combed back her little brother's curls and kept her tone light so as not to alarm him. "They're home invaders."

Belle, who had a vindictive streak, was on the floor sneaking up on Spot. She pinched the cat's tail—hard! The tabby yowled, twisting to swipe at the Fairy, forgetting about the shadow.

Taking advantage of the distraction, the shadow slithered away like a snake. But Peter caught sight of it rising near the bay window. He leapt, tearing a long curtain from its hooks, dislodging the brass rod, and trapping the shadow in a jumbled tangle of blue cloth.

"I've got you now!" Peter crowed again.

They tumbled to the floor, wrestling. "Quick, girls! Fetch a needle and thread!"

If he'd suggested they all grow chicken heads, the siblings could not have been more surprised. "Why?" Lily, Wendy, and Michael asked simultaneously.

"To sew my shadow to my foot," Peter replied.

It made as much sense as anything else had that night.

Wendy said, "Um, we don't have a sewing kit."

"Or a sewing machine," Lily added.

"I am a pirate!" Michael announced, bouncing on the bed. "Yo ho ho."

It took every ounce of Peter's self-control, which was always in short supply, not to overreact to that last declaration. Like Belle, Peter had already noticed the pirate décor and, as a result, had firmly decided that Michael himself must be a pirate.

It helped that the four-year-old was too small to matter, though Peter did appreciate the theatrical nature of pirates. He considered them glorious enemies. In any case, Michael would serve as a lure and/or pawn to ensure that Wendy embraced her storytelling destiny, and once that happened, Peter would have no more use for her little brother. So far as Peter was concerned, Michael would be welcome to seek out his pirate brethren on the Neversea.

First things first. "What kind of useless girls are you?" Peter asked. "Don't you have a mother? Mothers are brilliant at sewing. Didn't she teach you how?"

"Mama is brilliant at math," Lily declared. "And managing money."

Though up until that point Wendy had been charmed by Peter, she didn't particularly appreciate him labeling them "useless" or criticizing her stepmother or making sexist assumptions in general. "In case you were wondering, *Dad* didn't teach us how to sew either."

Wendy moved to reposition Michael's craft table, which, after the collision with Peter, was askew on its side. "We could try a glue stick," she suggested, holding one up.

"All right!" Peter stuck out his foot. Belle flew over to supervise. Wendy made a formidable effort, but the shadow refused to remain still long enough for the glue to take hold.

This nonsense had been going on long enough, Lily decided. She wasn't sure what had delayed their parents, but Michael was yawning, and Wendy had a flight to catch first thing in the morning. "If I manage to reattach your shadow, will you leave?" Lily asked again.

"I already said that I would," Peter replied with a hint of desperation as the shadow succeeded in freeing a leg, which it used to repeatedly kick Peter in the rump.

"And you'll take your snotty, sparkly sidekick with you?"

Belle stuck her tongue out at Lily.

"Yes, yes, of course!" Peter gasped, nearly losing his grip. "I promise!"

"Wendy, keep an eye on Mikey. I'll be right back!" Lily left, sprinting down the hall, past the family portraits on the wall, the bedroom she shared with Wendy, and through the country kitchen. If this didn't do the trick, Lily resolved to call her mama for help. Spot darted out from under the bed after her, veering off at the laundry closet for a snack and a trip to the litter box.

Upon arriving in the attached garage, Lily snatched a roll of duct tape from the workbench. "Hey, if it gets the job done . . ."

Across the house, the headlights of Mr. Darling's sedan briefly illuminated Michael's window. Belle whispered to Peter, "Hurry! Their parents are coming."

"Righty-o." Peter genuinely thought the mission was going according to plan, that his flight crew was performing marvelously. That, in no time, Wendy, Lily, and Michael would say goodbye to their monotonous lives in this mundane land ruled by worthless grown-ups. That by morning, the precarious population of Neverland would increase by three. Peter didn't realize that the shadow wasn't play-acting, that its rejection of him was utterly sincere.

"Fine, Shadow, be that way!" Peter exclaimed, pretending to give up the fight. "I have better things to do. If you want your freedom, I no longer care enough to deprive you of it." He sneered at his own dark reflection.

"Farewell, old chap! Without me, you'll be nothing."

The shadow managed to untangle itself from the long curtain and rise to a standing position. It strolled like a fine gentleman across the bedroom, crossed its legs neatly at the ankle, and leaned against the doorframe, pretending to study its nonexistent fingernails.

"I suppose that's that then," Peter said, formally bowing to Wendy and Michael.

"That's that," Belle's tinkling voice echoed as she glided to hover beside Peter.

"Wait, what?" Wendy exclaimed. "You're leaving?" She didn't want them to go. Other than the burst of joy that had been John's graduation, these were difficult days in the Roberts-Darling household, a countdown to even tougher times to come.

Wendy didn't want to think about all that, not the parents' marital crisis, not their family splitting in two— not when she could bask in magic, wonder, and mystery instead.

"I'm afraid we really must go," Peter said. "The Lost will worry if we tarry too long, though I'd very much love to hear more of your stories." As if the idea were only now occurring to him, he offered, "By any chance, would you like to join us in Neverland?"

Peter approached Michael, ruffled his baby-fine curls. "How about you, young man? How would you like to meet some real-life pirates?"

"Pirates!" Michael exclaimed, clapping. "Yo ho ho!"

"And Merfolk," Peter added. "Beautiful Merfolk who are all in love with me."

"Don't forget the Fairies," Belle reminded them, circling Wendy and Michael in midair, shaking her tiny hands to shower them in golden Fairy dust. "Without Fairies, no human child would've ever journeyed to Neverland. And by 'Fairies,' I mean me!"

"Fairies." Michael hugged Nana Bear. "Pirates. Mermaids."

"Neverland," Wendy breathed, charmed by the sound of it.

In that moment, nobody mentioned Indians. Lily was jogging past the laundry closet with the duct tape. In the driveway, seated beside Mr. Darling in her sedan, Ms. Roberts-Darling pushed the button to automatically raise the garage door. And back in Michael's bedroom, Wendy decided to say "yes" to Neverland. "It sounds amazing, Peter. Thank you, I'd be thrilled to meet a mermaid."

"Come along then," Peter urged. "All it takes is a deep breath, a wonderful, lovely thought, and we'll be soaring across the starry sky."

Immediately, Wendy and Michael—their heads already full of wonderful, lovely thoughts—began to rise into the air. They were naturals! Wendy reveled at the sensation, extending her arms like a bird, and Michael whispered to Nana Bear, "Up, up, up we go!"

Peter gestured to the bay window. "This way to fun and adventure!"

If only Ms. Roberts-Darling and Mr. Darling hadn't renewed their conversation, lingering in the sedan parked in the garage so as not to awaken the children. If only Ms. Roberts-Darling and Mr. Darling had come inside immediately, they could've prevented tragedy. But suddenly, the future of the family had seemed more hopeful. The rift had begun to heal, perhaps not toward full reconciliation but a more affirming way forward. While neither could predict for certain the fate of their troubled marriage, they had resolved, at the very least, to remain lifelong friends.

In that intense, heartfelt moment, who could blame them for failing to realize that right then, due to supernatural forces, the safety of their younger offspring was at risk?

Now, it should be noted that there was a moment—three blinks of a moment—when Wendy reached down to tuck her phone into the pocket of her pj's. When it hadn't even occurred to Wendy to go to Neverland without her stepsister. And in that same moment—that three blinks of a moment—the only thought in Lily's mind had been to reunite with Wendy and Michael, reattach Peter's shadow, and send their magical interlopers packing.

The girls had both felt like full-fledged sisters again.

And then they didn't.

Imagine Lily's shock when she arrived to discover her siblings in midair.

"Come on, Lily!" Wendy called. "We're off to visit

Neverland. Take a deep breath, and think a wonderful, lovely—"

"Oh, no you don't!" Lily stormed in. She dropped the duct tape on the floor and rushed to catch hold of Wendy's heel. "You aren't taking Mikey anywhere!" However heartbroken she was over Wendy moving to New York, this was a thousand times worse. Where was Neverland? How would they find their way back home?

What a nagging spoilsport, Wendy thought. Why did Lily always have to have her way? She wasn't in charge of the family. In fact, Wendy was older by nearly a full three months. She considered herself the mature one. After all, Wendy was only two days from becoming a teenager. "You *keep* forgetting—he's my brother, too!" Wendy kicked to free herself and accidentally grazed Lily's forehead. "Oops, sorry!"

"Ow! I don't need your lousy 'sorry'! Wendy, get down here or I'm telling!"

Clinging to Nana Bear, Michael bounced lightly against the vaulted ceiling. He laughed. "Look at me, Sissy!" he called to Lily.

"Come along now, Wendy," Peter urged. "Let's fly!"

Trailing a golden glow, Belle circled around to yank Lily's hair once more—extra hard this time, which was mostly a cover to generously sprinkle Fairy dust on her, too.

"Ow!" Lily exclaimed again, swatting at the Fairy.

Belle let go and twirled beyond her reach, shaking and

shimmering, doubling over with tinkling laughter—with each passing second coming closer to Michael.

Lily's throat tightened. "Mikey, sweetie, fly to me! Please, please fly to me."

Michael wavered, dipped, and stuck out his bottom lip. The Fairy tensed, well aware of the limits of her dust. On her own, Belle could enchant and direct an object through the air, but a person with a will of their own had the power to resist, embrace, even steer the magic.

And Lily's distress was literally bringing Michael down. On her tiptoes, jumping, she almost caught his bedroom slipper.

"Get over yourself, Lily!" Wendy scooped Michael in her arms. "Do you want to stay here forever?" Holding their brother, she sailed through the open window into the May night sky. "It's so boring." Wendy breathed in the fresh, cool air. "There's a reason people call Oklahoma 'flyover' country."

"Snob!" Lily shot back, running to the window. "And it's *Indian* Country, not . . . *Wendy!*" Again, Belle had doused Lily in a bountiful amount of Fairy dust, but Lily's thoughts were not wonderful. Her thoughts were not lovely. She didn't have the lift to join them even if she'd wanted to. "*Wendy! Mikey!*"

Her stepsister and little brother were flying away.

CHAPTER

7

"One, two to the right," Peter called, pointing to the stars. "Off we fly till morning!"

The stars gleamed brighter in merry greeting! Whatever faults Peter might have, and over the years they'd counted many, he appreciated them in a way that other humans, with their silly fussing over the moon and Mars, did not.

Wendy and Peter soared with their arms outstretched, their fingertips touching. A wide-eyed Michael trailed his sister, clutching Nana Bear as Belle nudged him along. They flew over housing developments and more housing developments, grocery stores and chain restaurants, fitness centers, churches and big-box retail outlets, past the first of many highways. . . .

So gleeful were the stars at the sight of airborne travelers that only one of them—a small, serious star—remembered Lily, who'd been left behind. Lily, who still clutched the windowsill, her whole body shaking, tears streaming as her siblings faded from view.

Lily, who had no idea that at that very moment, in the garage, Mr. Darling and Ms. Roberts-Darling sat side by side, quietly listening to "Don't It Make My Brown Eyes Blue" on the radio as they struggled to find words to explain their complicated, grown-up feelings.

"Wendy!" Lily called one last time. "Mikey!" But they couldn't hear her from such a distance, and neither did their parents over the country music station.

Lily never would've guessed that Belle was fluttering her toes far more than strictly necessary in order to leave a more vibrant, longer-lasting trail of light.

Up in the sky, Michael found himself lulled by the soft wind and a Fairy lullaby. He was upbeat and laid-back for a four-year-old, far more so than any of his older siblings had been at that same age. Even before Belle's arrival, Michael already had a long day and the sugar from John's celebration cake had mostly worn off.

In leaving home and bringing Michael along, Wendy had made a questionable choice at best. Were you wondering about that? I'd certainly expect so. I'd certainly hope *you* would know better than to gallivant through the abyss of night with supernatural strangers and your little sibling in tow. Yes, Wendy was more fanciful, less logic-inclined than her budding scientist stepsister, but I swear to you that Wendy knew better than that, too.

Before judging her too harshly, you should know that

Fairy dust tends to magnify the human personality— making the prideful arrogant, the easily irked spiteful, and the adventurous foolhardy. Michael, for example, had gone from generally good-natured to fairly blissful.

Left to her own devices, Wendy was an imaginative, independent thinker, not a selfish or reckless one. Through no fault of her own, she simply wasn't thinking clearly.

Because of the Fairy dust, Wendy Darling was not quite herself.

CHAPTER

8

Tap, tap. Because of the Fairy dust, Lily was not quite herself either.

Tap, tap. She could still clearly see Belle's trail of light in the Tulsa night sky.

So loving and protective were Lily's thoughts that, at first, she barely registered the polite but persistent two-fingered prompt on her shoulder.

Tap, tap. Lily glimpsed the shadow out of the corner of her eye and jerked to one side. "Gah!" Whirling to face it, she demanded, "Why are you still here?"

The shadow drew back, hand to its heart, as if offended. Then it leapt onto the windowsill, pausing to blow Lily a goodbye kiss, presumably eager to begin its life of freedom.

Good riddance, she thought at first, scanning her brother's bedroom. Where were their parents? Didn't Wendy have the phone last? Lily rushed to search through Michael's bedcovers, checked the top of his nightstand, peered under the bed—no luck. Quickly, she reconsidered her options. "Shadow, wait! You can't leave now. Not before you help me bring Wendy and Mikey home again."

The shadow wagged a no-no finger at her.

Lily had never been a huge fan of charades, but its meaning was clear enough. What's more, she couldn't *force* a shadow to do anything. Could she reason with it? Charm it?

Wiping her eyes, Lily said, "Hello, I think we got off to a bad start. I'm Lily, and this is my house. Are you sure this, uh, rift between you and Peter is permanent?"

The shadow reared its head as if insulted by the question. It had standards, after all. It had enjoyed its status as the shadow of a human child. Perhaps not so impressive at first glance as the shadow of a polar bear or pyramid, but human children possessed infinite potential in all sorts of ways that had nothing to do with size. Indeed, their early days together were glorious! Yet more and more of late, the shadow had found Peter's behavior questionable, even appalling. And finally, the troublesome boy's choosing to endanger one so young—darling Michael—that did it! For the shadow, that was the final murky stretch too far. It had had enough of Peter Pan.

"I'm just saying," Lily began again. "Sometimes people who really care about each other get caught up in a bad situation and the whole thing spins out of control."

Perhaps you're wondering . . . Was she talking about the shadow and Peter, about herself and Wendy, about

Mr. Darling and Ms. Roberts-Darling? The shadow wasn't certain either.

Nevertheless, the shadow recognized her desperation and how it felt to be estranged from those who'd once been so close. Sliding down from the windowsill, the shadow recognized love. So, despite being quite finished with Peter, the shadow did sympathize with Lily's aching need to be reunited with Wendy and Michael, to protect them from a grisly fate on the island, even though that would put Lily herself in jeopardy, too.

"Right, none of my business," Lily added, coming back around the bed. "But could you please help me bring back my family?"

The shadow wagged a no-no finger at her again.

"Why not?" Lily asked, exasperated. "You know how to get to this Neverland, right?"

The shadow offered two thumbs-up.

"So, give me one good reason why you won't take me to Mikey and Wendy?"

With a theatrical shrug, the shadow raised a finger.

Charades? Lily thought again. "One word?"

The shadow nodded enthusiastically and cocked its hand to its ear.

"Sounds like?" Lily recited, mindful that with every passing second, her siblings were flying farther away.

The shadow made a snapping motion with its fingers that produced no sound.

"Sounds like 'snap'?" Lily declared. "Clap, map, rap?"

The shadow held its hands, palms facing one another, parallel and vertical.

"Strap?" Lily guessed, pacing on the compass-rose throw rug. "Straps?"

The shadow moved its hands, again palms facing and parallel, but this time horizontal. Then it quickly repeated both motions twice. Lines? Lily thought. Box?

"Trap!" she exclaimed, nearly tripping over the Spider-Man action figure. "You won't take me to Neverland . . . because it's a trap?" She frowned, realizing out loud, "Peter *wants* me to come with you, and Wendy and Mikey are the bait."

The shadow pointed at her to say "yes!" It was impressed with Lily's skill at charades, with her cleverness, but the full truth of the predicament was a bit more complicated than that.

You see, if the reluctant sibling of the family had been a boy, then of course Peter would've expected the shadow to bring that boy to Neverland. But the shadow wasn't exactly sure how Peter might feel about the possibility of a Native *girl* on the island. So far as the shadow knew (not that it knew everything), in over a century, a Native girl had never before set foot on Neverland.

Lily swallowed hard. "It doesn't matter what Peter wants. It matters what Wendy and Mikey need. They're my family, and they need me to rescue them."

How refreshing it was to hear someone dare to say out loud that Peter's whims were irrelevant! The shadow respected Lily more with each passing moment.

Lily straightened her pj top. "Whatever it takes, I'll outsmart Peter Pan."

As was so often true, she sounded more confident than she felt. That said, Lily did possess a formidable intelligence and commitment to her family. It occurred to the shadow that Peter almost always underestimated others, especially those he dismissed as mere girls.

Perhaps the shadow had failed Peter, or Peter had failed it—there was plenty of blame to share. Nevertheless, the shadow did have the power to help Lily try to rescue her siblings. She was in fact trying to persuade it to take her, knowing full well that risk lay ahead.

Wasn't that different from all the times before, when the shadow had helped trick kids into making the journey? Maybe not in result, but certainly in intention. Both it and Lily would be making a choice of their own free will. At the very least, Lily had been forewarned. Which begged the question: Was the shadow really done with Peter or had it simply switched sides?

In a burst of optimism, the shadow gingerly cradled the ember of possibility that this loving girl might somehow save not only her siblings, but all of Neverland.

The shadow nodded. It heartily shook Lily's hand to seal the deal.

"Mvto," Lily said. "Thank . . ." She trailed off, distracted by the sensation. For a second, its touch felt to Lily like smoke, then foam, then Play-Doh.

That's when Spot sashayed back in, licking her chops. Lily felt a burst of appreciation for the cat, who—unlike the events of the night—was consistent, predictable, and made sense. No matter what might be happening, Spot was Spot. She prioritized her stomach.

Fueled by that happy thought, Lily—having been previously drenched in Fairy dust—began to rise into the air. "I'm flying," she whispered. Or rather floating. She'd witnessed Wendy and Michael, Peter and Belle flying, but it was quite something else to experience it herself. Lily felt a flash of panic. *Thud!* Down she landed on the floor.

The shadow cocked its head, wondering if its faith may have been misplaced after all.

Yet Lily was undeterred. Flying might be scary but losing Wendy and Michael would be so much worse. If only there was another way! Yes, of course Lily would have fetched her parents in the garage, if only she'd known that they had already returned home. Lily had just missed them in there herself earlier, remember? She'd been grabbing the duct tape as the sedan headlights had illuminated Michael's bedroom window. Likewise, Lily had no way of knowing that they had decided to stay put for a while so they could talk beyond the earshot of their children. One last time, Lily scanned the room for the phone, not realizing that Wendy had slipped it into her pj's pocket. No use. "What should I do?" she asked the shadow.

It pointed to its head, and Lily whispered, "Think."

It drew a smile across its blank face, and she guessed, "Happy?" Lily remembered Wendy beckoning her, instructing her to think a wonderful, lovely thought. Could that really do the trick?

Lily closed her eyes and focused on joyful family memories. On the rainy Chicago day when Mr. Darling and Ms. Roberts-Darling exchanged wedding vows at city hall. On the way John proudly held up his diploma. Suddenly, Lily Roberts was rising, floating. Flying?

Lily felt the shadow grip her hand. She felt herself drawn forward. On fearful reflex, she gripped the window frame. She took a breath, focused again. She recalled the bright Tulsa morning when Michael was born. She remembered Wendy's voice, reading *Ella Enchanted*. Wendy needed her. Michael, too. Lily flew through the open window, and up, up, up, up. Lily opened her eyes, took a trembling breath of the night, looked to the right.

"Hello, stars," she said.

CHAPTER

9

"Girls!" Mr. Darling rushed out of the stepsisters' room. Lily's bed was messed, Wendy's still made. They hadn't been in the kitchen or the family room. The bathroom was empty.

"Lily!" Ms. Roberts-Darling sprinted ahead of her husband, down the hall to her youngest's room. "Wendy, Michael!"

In those brief, not-yet-but-almost frantic moments, both parents tried to tell themselves that they were over-reacting. After all, the children had been left home alone for short spurts before, at least in the past year, though never so late at night.

"No!" Ms. Roberts-Darling exclaimed. "This can't be happening."

Side by side, the parents gaped at the open window, the fluttering blue curtain and the one on the floor in disarray. At Michael's messy bed, his toys and art supplies strewn across the rug and hardwood. At Spot curled in the denim beanbag, licking her front paw.

If only cats could talk.

CHAPTER

10

"Lean toward me," Peter coached. "That's it! Point your toes. Now, lift your chin."

Wendy felt like a glorious bird—like a Wendybird—soaring, gliding among the wispy clouds . . . her outstretched fingertips never more than a breath from Peter's. She glanced back at Michael, who blinked at the blur of sights, and at Belle, who gently guided him.

Wendy wasn't one who could readily recognize city skylines. Were those the lights of Little Rock, Arkansas? No, no, they couldn't possibly have traveled so far so fast.

Then again, what did it matter on an extraordinary night like this? She wasn't Lily. She didn't have to fret about everything.

"Hurry up, Wendy!" Peter called. "Belle will mind your brother!"

Never once did Wendy wonder whether Belle and Peter knew exactly where they were going. Michael seemed perfectly content. He waved Nana Bear at passing stars like a red-carpet celebrity, chatting as though they could understand him. And, as it happens, they could.

"Do you have any pets?" Michael wanted to know. "Spot is my cat."

Amused by his antics, Belle waved at the stars, too. Michael blew her a kiss, and she pretended to catch it. Her peal of laughter mingled with his, creating a new song.

Belle couldn't have cared less about most children, beyond their usefulness in entertaining Peter. The more energy he expended on them, the less he provoked the island and its original inhabitants. However, she adored babies and really little kids, and not counting Peter himself, Michael was the youngest human child ever to journey to Neverland.

"How did you get all the way up there?" Michael asked the stars. "Are you stuck?" Even the grumpiest of stars chuckled at that, though Michael was the only one who could hear them.

Imagine if Lily could see him now, Wendy thought, having the time of his young life! What a scaredy-cat worrywart her stepsister could be! "Watch this," Wendy called to Peter, executing a front flip she'd learned in gym class.

"I'll do you one better!" Peter crowed, fumbling through an imitation of the same move. "Did you see that, Wendy? How agile I am? I am agility personified!"

Since he was her host, it seemed only polite to agree. "Well done, Peter!"

Inside, Wendy couldn't help fuming a bit. It was just like Lily to sit this out. Yes, Wendy supposed, they were quite high up, and Ms. Roberts-Darling had gently explained that fear of heights and fear of flying were common phobias, right up there with public speaking, insects, and snakes. But Lily adored bugs and found snakes weirdly appealing, so there was no making sense of any of that. And Little Miss Know-It-All spoke up in science class frequently.

Suddenly, Wendy realized that the landscape below had gone dark.

What had happened to the sparkling clusters of city lights, the streaks of roadways?

Was that a lake beneath them? Could it be an ocean?

Yes, yes, those were dolphins frolicking in the waxing moonlight.

How far from home were they? Oklahoma was in the *middle-ish* of the United States.

Fumbling a bit, Wendy managed to extract her phone from the pocket of her star-print pj's, nearly dropping it in the process. No signal, but at least it was fully charged.

How much time had passed? She couldn't be sure. Michael had fallen asleep.

Wind tossed Wendy's curly hair and chilled her freckled skin.

Peter bragged about vicious hunts and epic duels. He

claimed, "The island itself fears me."

Belle dutifully circled Michael, who was softly snoring in a basket-shaped cloud. He had been fading in and out of wakefulness, bone weary from the excitement of John's graduation day, meeting Belle and Peter, and the long, long, long journey to Neverland.

"You're not watching, Wendy!" Peter executed a cart-wheel in the air.

"Well done!" Wendy repeated, realizing there was no limit to his appetite for praise.

For all the wonder of soaring, of every sashay through the Milky Way, Wendy had had a long night, too. Her eyelids felt heavy. Her limbs began to droop.

Peter swept her into his arms. "Shall I carry you the rest of the way?"

Wendy yawned. "I suppose."

"Rest now," Peter said. "That way you'll arrive refreshed and ready to tell stories."

With a jolt, Wendy realized she had forgotten to bring her copy of *Ella Enchanted*, though she'd read the novel so many times, she practically had it memorized. She could retell the story to Peter and his Neverland friends, return Michael home to Tulsa, and still make her morning flight for New York. "Is 'Cinderella' your favorite story?"

"My favorite story?" Peter threw out his arms, spinning like a cyclone. "My favorite story is the story of me!" With that, he released Wendy, almost as if he'd forgotten she was there. Then again, perhaps it wasn't forgetfulness.

Perhaps he simply didn't care all that much. As much as he'd longed for a storyteller, Peter was overwhelmingly enamored with himself.

"Peter!" Wendy plummeted toward the vast ocean far, far below.

CHAPTER

11

If only Lily had known that the stars were watching over her.

If only she'd known that they were cheering her on.

The shadow didn't offer any reassurances. It had slicked into darkness, disappeared. Lily could still sense it, though. She flinched at the inky feel of its fingertips. The farther they soared from her suburban home, the more eerie the shadow seemed.

Was it the chill or the fear that made her shudder? Was it the shock that magic is real?

Lily peeked between her fingers. Pulling her anxiety into a ball at the pit of her stomach, she used it to power through a wall of gray clouds. Were those contrails behind her? How fast was she flying anyway?

She tried, failed, couldn't shut down her overtaxed mind—if anything, it had kicked into highest gear. What if she fell? Drowned? Was stung by a jellyfish? Bitten by a sea snake? Devoured by a great white shark? How high was she? Was that lightning in the distance? Would birds avoid flying kids? What if an albatross crashed into her? Was she at risk from cosmic rays? What if she and the shadow became separated in the night?

What was happening was terrifying in so many ways. Yet buoyed by the Fairy dust, Lily managed not to spiral into despair. Yes, she struggled with panic, but hope blazed inside her.

To stay afloat, to stay alive, she had to embrace wonderful, lovely thoughts.

Jingles, Michael, moccasins, Mama, buttered popcorn. Wendy, blue dumplings, John, science books, Daddy, fishing. Auntie Lillian, Christmas, Spot, Papa George, ribbon skirts . . .

Lily herself! Wasn't she being heroic? Who would've guessed she could be so—

Wait, what was that enormous, loud *noise*? Oh, not to worry. It was a jet plane, only a jet plane. Lily felt the briny wind lift her again. Imagine a *plane* being the least scary thing she had to worry about. At least, her stomach was behaving. Her sweat had dried. She held strong to who she was. Her thoughts returned to Wendy, to Michael. He was only four, four, four, four.

Wonderful, lovely Michael. His messy mop of brown hair, the way he'd bounce when he was excited.

Wonderful, lovely Wendy. Her dimpled smile. Not just stepsister, friend.

Lily trembled, her teeth chattering. She breathed. In and out, slow and deep.

CHAPTER

12

"Peter!" Wendy tumbled through salty air. The ocean rushed up to meet her.

In a burst of glittery gold light, Belle whooshed over, and with a wiggle of her fingers, refreshed Wendy's dose of Fairy dust. "Fly, Wendy! Think of rainbows, think of sunrise."

Wendy felt a burst of gratitude. Soaring again, she said, "Thank you, Belle!"

Peter, who'd been caught up in his own glory, spun to a stop. Floating three clouds and two dollops of starry sky away, he peered at Wendy, Belle, the drowsy Michael, and then Wendy again. "What are you all doing clear over there?"

Imagine how disconcerting it must have been for Wendy, a spirited girl with a keen appreciation of the magical, to realize her guide was so oblivious.

As he flew close again, she asked, "Peter, how did you learn to fly?"

"I'm a Fairy," he declared. "I've always known how to fly!" Though Peter didn't have wings, his ears were vaguely pointy, and his fashion sense skewed toward the forest fey. "A giant among Fairies," he added, puffing out his slim chest.

"Not a Fairy," Belle declared in a weary voice. "A human boy, as I already said."

"Righty-o." Peter clasped his hands behind his neck, elbows out, and took his time swaying in Wendy's general direction. "As I was saying, I am a human boy, the most special human boy who ever lived, definitely the one with the most experience being boyish. Too robust to be welcomed into the Fairy court, too extraordinary to live with dull, everyday humans."

"I am not dull," Wendy countered. "Neither is Mikey."

At the sound of his name, the four-year-old stirred to full wakefulness. "Mama?"

"You're special, too," Peter magnanimously agreed, flipping over. "Not like I am. But you're a storyteller, Wendy. That's something. That's why I'm bringing you to live in Neverland."

"Mama?" Michael was confused. Typically, it was his mother who roused him from bed and pointed him to the new day. But Wendy was there, and morning hadn't come yet. What's more, he was up in the sky. That was by no means unpleasant, but it was certainly unusual.

Had Peter said, "live in Neverland"? Wendy wondered. That couldn't be right. She used her firmest, most grown-up voice. "Peter, we'll have to excuse ourselves after story time. My father is expecting me to join him at Tulsa International Airport, first thing tomorrow, and I need to get Mikey home to his mama. He has Sunday school in the morning." Wendy cringed at a flash of guilt. "Everyone's probably worried sick about him, about both of us." She sighed. "I'm sure Lily gave our parents an earful when they got home."

"Mama?" Michael said a third time. It wasn't that he minded being up in the air. In fact, that was still rather delightful, but it was rapidly losing its initial dreamlike quality.

"Don't worry, Wendy! I know what to do!" Peter drew his sword and waved it high. "We'll cut Matthew in half! One part for you and one part for that Injun girl."

"What?" Wendy launched herself toward her little brother, drawing him close. "You will *not* be touching Mikey with that thing. Stay away from him. I'm warning you!"

"I'm warning *you*." Michael held up an imaginary sword, playing a game of pretend.

Had Peter really called her stepsister Lily "that Injun girl" like there was something wrong with who she was? What was Wendy doing, propelling through midair, above an unknown ocean—basically in the middle of nowhere?

How could she have let this happen? Why had she trusted Peter Pan?

Poor Wendy. Her horror and confusion were only to be expected. She didn't fully understand how Fairy-dust magic worked yet.

If only Wendy could've navigated the stars or hadn't outgrown her ability to understand their language. If only she'd been paying more attention so she could retrace their path to return safely home with Michael. With each "if only," Wendy was slowly losing buoyancy, but Michael was still enjoying the trip. His attitude was like a life preserver, keeping them both aloft.

"You should know better, Peter!" Belle exclaimed. "That is no way to treat your guests. The poor girl thinks you're serious." Belle's choice of reprimand was light and airy, wasn't it? Like she was a bit put out, but nothing that would stop you in your boots.

Peter assumed that the Fairy was merely playacting, according to plan. But perhaps you caught a thorn of warning in her tone. Belle's frustration with Peter had been building for decades.

Curling his lip, Peter returned his sword to the scabbard, took Belle's lead, and reveled in a favorite deception of those with dastardly minds. He acted like Wendy was foolish for recognizing the truth. "Silly girl! Can't you tell when someone is kidding?" He doubled over in pretend laughter. "Haven't you ever been teased before?"

Wendy had three siblings, dozens of cousins (mostly

step-cousins), and had attended three summer church camps—not to mention the recent gauntlet that was sixth grade. Of course, she'd been teased before! But usually in an affectionate way. She cautiously chalked up the exchange to misfired signals, which didn't mean all was forgiven. "That *wasn't* funny."

Perhaps you've noticed that it's occasionally challenging for Wendy—and everyone else—to follow Peter's train of thought. It tends to zigzag, taking others off guard, much as it had her. Perhaps you've also noticed a few hints that this story might take an even more troubling turn. But let's move on, shall we?

Peter, who was in the lead, had already forgotten why he'd begun pretend-laughing, for in that moment, the rising sun illuminated the glorious green sea and enticing island below.

Wendy and Michael felt a cool breath of resistance in the misty air, how it eased as the Fairy dust afforded them welcome passage and smoothed away their doubts and fears. The wind grew warmer, the stars shined brighter. The clouds became more playful, yet substantial somehow. They mimicked the shape of Fairies, Merfolk, animals of the sea and land.

It was dawn, Wendy realized. She'd missed her flight. Her father would be upset. She would have a *lot* to explain when she got home.

Maybe Wendy Darling wasn't in such a hurry to return to Tulsa after all.

She gasped. "Mikey, look there! That must be Neverland!"

Human children tended to arrive at sunrise because the island was already awake and out looking for them. In turn, Wendy recognized the island somehow, perhaps from a dream.

Since the very beginning, each new arrival saw it a bit differently.

To Wendy, the shape of Neverland reminded her vaguely of Scotland, where Mr. Darling and Ms. Roberts-Darling had gone on their honeymoon.

As Wendy circled in descent, she caught sight of the glamorous Merfolk sunbathing on Shipwreck Rock in Merfolk Lagoon. They splashed their proud, iridescent tails and tossed giant, translucent bubbles like colorful beach balls. "Aren't they gorgeous?"

"Like a scorpion or snake or black widow spider," Peter replied with a laugh. "You can't see their fangs from here, but this is the best way to watch them—from a safe distance." My, how differently he spoke of Merfolk above the island than he had in Michael's bedroom!

"You mean they're . . . poisonous?" Wendy couldn't recall reading anything to that effect in any of her storybooks. She'd been under the impression that Merfolk resided in underwater kingdoms of colorful coral, traveled on giant seahorses, and reveled in song and romance.

"Venomous and violent," Peter exclaimed, leading them over the gleaming lagoon, the rolling dense forest, a few decaying huts, and an abandoned house of dewy sewn leaves. Billowing smoke rose from a sleepy volcano. A humpback whale breached the water below.

"No fangs," Belle muttered. "No poison. Really, Peter!"

"Savage sirens!" Peter added, undaunted by facts. "Can't stand anyone with a lick of humanity in them. They used to try to drown me on a regular basis."

"Pirates!" Michael exclaimed. "Look, Sissy, pirates!" Indeed, the four-year-old had already spotted a flamboyance of flamingos, an upside-down paddle boat, and, most thrillingly, an old-fashioned pirate ship sailing off the coast, complete with two square-rigged masts and the trademark skull-and-crossbones black flag.

"That's the *Jolly Roger,*" Belle announced. The ship was a reminder that, along with her fellow Fairies, she and Peter had a diabolical enemy in common. "The crew used to hunt my kind for our dust, so they could wage war with us from the air as well as from the sea and land."

"Not anymore!" Peter crowed. "I protected you. I am the Sworn Protector of Fairies." Bragging again, as usual, and jumping to conclusions.

With such a young child at stake, Belle was having none of that. "Don't get cocky, Peter!" To Wendy, she added, "Best to assume they're still quite formidable."

Michael, distracted by the high-flying antics of another pod of dolphins, failed to absorb Belle's warning. All he heard was "pirates," and to Nana Bear, he softly sang, "Yo ho ho."

Wendy's embrace of Michael remained firm. She was soaring above a strange, albeit enchanting place with her very young brother, and her most glittering companion had just used the words "war" and "formidable." Like all magic, the mood-boosting power of Fairy dust had its limits. "The pirates hunt . . . ? Oh, Belle, I'm so sorry. That sounds awful."

Peter frowned. This wasn't the celebratory arrival he had in mind.

Peter wasn't a sensitive soul, but even he could recognize when a fish was about to slip off his hook. "Never mind those lousy pirates, Wendy!" He winked at Belle. "We're far too clever for the likes of them. They've searched and searched and never once managed to find our hideout. Never have and never will. That's why we call it 'Neverland'!"

"No, it's not! The Fairy queen and Merfolk queen settled on the name *centuries* before humans first arrived on the island. Peter, our history did not begin with you!" Belle willed her pearlescent wings into a faster motion and said to the children, "Fairies live here." She gestured toward the Fairy Wood below. "In the branches and hollows of the trees, in abandoned bird nests, and in a bejeweled hidden castle that no human will ever see." Belle believed in managing expectations. Resigned, she added, "All the Fairies of Neverland, except me."

It wasn't long before another rocky shoreline appeared on the horizon. Michael piped up, "Down we go?"

"Almost home," Peter cooed. "Isn't it perfect, Wendy?"

Cradling Michael, she was circling slowly in descent when—*arrooo!*—a howl rose up from the island, followed by a spray of incoming arrows. "Oh no!"

CHAPTER

13

Unseen, the shadow waved farewell as Lily crossed through the Fairy veil all by herself.

Yet not alone. The stars blew Lily a good-morning kiss. The sun sharpened her senses. She felt disoriented, fearful, yet ever more determined as she reflected on memories from the previous night of Belle, Pan, and her high-flying siblings. Impossible, Lily thought. But Wendy needed her. Michael needed her. So, there she was.

Lily could make out a V formation of—were they geese? No, bigger, more colorful. Flamingos! "Shadow?" she called. "*Shadow?*"

No response. Now, what was she supposed to do? How could it leave her all alone?

By the rising daylight, the ocean below was even more daunting—emerald green, undulating water, unending in every direction until . . . there!

Can you imagine what Lily saw? Land! Glorious land!

Not home, not huge, but substantial enough. Hopefully inhabited.

Could it be Neverland? Lily was sure of it. Drawing closer, she almost recognized the island, not from her own dreams, but from those of someone she dearly loved.

Hope as she might, Lily detected no immediate signs of Wendy or Michael. Belle's sparkling trail of Fairy dust had vanished into the sunlight. How would Lily ever find them?

From the sky, Neverland vaguely reminded her of online wildlife videos from the Big Island of Hawaii, complete with its off-center volcano.

As she neared, Lily heard the distant roar of a lion— was it a lion? They were magnificent, highly social big cats, best left at a respectful distance.

Lily veered in midair to follow the shoreline. In some places, the violet sand reached to touch the forest; in others, a rugged cliff created a rocky border in between. Would she crash into the cliff? No, no, she seemed able to direct her slightly wobbly flight.

"Shadow?" Lily tried one last time to no avail.

Fisting her trembling hands, she focused on the terrain. Humans tended to build homes with views of the water, and given the presence of large, carnivorous animals, it made sense that Peter and the Lost would be wary of the lush tropical forest . . . or was it a jungle? A rain forest? A fairy-tale forest, her mind supplied. That sounded ridiculous but felt right.

Lily's breath caught. The waterfall in the distance was frothy, lacy white, and shot through with rainbows. And beyond that, another one. And another.

Do you recall how Wendy and Michael soared northwest across the island, over Shipwreck Rock in Merfolk Lagoon, guided by Belle and Peter? Not Lily. She let the warm wind carry her to the southwest instead, toward a thin, rising spiral of smoke that she hoped indicated a campground.

Lily took heart at the herd of sunbathing seals, the cacophony of birdsongs, the turtles nesting in the sand. Though bursting with wildlife, the island looked, well, like an island. An alluring island, no doubt teeming with insects and animals and sea life she'd never encountered before. But nothing magical or otherworldly. She didn't even happen to catch a glimpse of the *Jolly Roger*. Yet peril lurked unseen. The shadow had used the word "trap."

Knowledge had always comforted Lily. That's one of the reasons she read so much nonfiction. If only the shadow had told her more!

ROAWWAR! Maybe it wasn't a lion. Maybe it was a tiger. Yes, Lily's second guess was correct. Not so long ago, lions had ruled the Neverland forest and feasted on feral hogs and goats and cattle and sheep. Lions had bared their fangs and claws to defend themselves against swords and daggers. They'd battled Pan for their crown, for their very existence.

And lost.

Lily searched for a safe place to land. Keep breathing, she thought, fighting rising panic. Slow, steady breaths. The surreal nature of the situation was in itself a helpful distraction.

At the edge of the forest—do you see that sleek, reddish bear, foraging for breakfast? Yes, that's the one. Not quite as tall as Lily. About her weight. It looked adorable from a safe distance, not unlike Nana Bear, the thought of which renewed Lily's determination.

It couldn't be a sun bear, she thought absently. They lived in Southeast Asia. No way could she have traveled that far overnight. Then Lily considered the possibility that the island was some sort of off-the-grid nature preserve. Or, worse, a private hunting ground for the wealthy. Sun bears—if that's what it was—could be aggressive, unpredictable.

Lily racked her brain for survival tips. Bears didn't like loud noises. Big cats could climb trees. Lions and tigers were faster than humans. Running or making herself taller would work for some predators, not others. Speed and height didn't always save zebras or giraffes.

In any case, Lily couldn't stay airborne forever. The power of the Fairy dust had almost worn off. She was slowly losing altitude. She could hear the gentle, white-crested waves crashing into the beach, the ever more distinct birdsongs, the wind blowing through the trees.

Peachy-blue clouds blanketed the hills. The apparent lack of human development—no roads or tall buildings—was good news and bad. She felt cautiously optimistic that she'd find Wendy and Michael somewhere in the vicinity of that campfire. Where else could they be?

Were those cottages (more like cabins?) coming up on her right? The roofs were missing, the walls pitted. Who-ever had lived there moved on long ago.

Lily was annoyed at herself. If only she'd had the time, the presence of mind, to pack supplies. At the very least she could've brought the duct tape.

Down, down she went. Quickly circling her out-stretched arms like propellers to slow her descent, Lily landed—"Oooph!"—knees first, and rolled over. She was splayed flat on her back on the violet sand. Her expres-sion brightened. At least she was on the ground. At least she hadn't flown into a hurricane . . . or typhoon? How far could she have possibly traveled in one night and in what direction? She had been so disoriented in the sky last night.

Tick tock. Lily took a moment to collect her courage, dragged herself to her feet, and brushed the sand off her heart-print pj's. Where had that shadow slipped off to? Would it guide her family home? Was it coming back for them at all?

From what she'd gathered, Belle wasn't the only Fairy on the island. Surely a more reasonable one—who was not so fond of pinching or pulling hair—could help them out.

Tick tock. In the morning light, the situation seemed slightly less dire. If Lily hadn't been so worried about Wendy, she would've been furious with her for getting them all into this mess. Lily had always been the responsible one in the family. With John soon off to college, it made sense that she'd assume the role of leader. Lily breathed in the fresh ocean air. She exhaled. Lily might be alone and frightened, but she had survived this far. Good for her!

Tick tock. What *was* that? It sounded like an old mechanical clock.

Out of the corner of her eye, Lily spied an enormous saltwater crocodile lumbering across the coastline in her direction. It appeared eager, hungry, and extremely interested in her.

CHAPTER

14

"Isn't this a fun game?" Peter laughed playfully as he dodged arrows, plucking a few from the air and tossing them down. "Come on, Wendy. Get in the spirit!"

Zing! An arrow glanced off the toe of her house slipper, and another sliced through the armpit of Michael's over-sized outer-space-print pj's. "Whoa," he shouted. "Look out!"

Who was shooting at them? Wendy wondered. Who was hidden in the crowded treetops below? Could it be the pirates that Belle had warned her about?

"Ditch the brat, Wendy!" Peter suggested. "You'll be faster that way." Now that they were on his turf, Peter's pretense of charm was waning fast.

Wendy pulled Michael closer so that they would make a smaller target. "Don't talk that way about *my brother*." She willed herself to fly higher, to no avail.

Belle swooped behind Wendy, tugging her up by the

waist of her pj pants, so her bottom was above her head and feet. Most of the arrows arched far astray or fell short.

Suddenly fearful, Wendy and Michael were quickly losing altitude. He teared up, clinging to his sister. "Sissy?" Dust or no dust, at that moment, there wasn't a lovely or wonderful thought to be had between them. Belle was mighty for her size, her wings strong, a blur of motion, but lifting two children was too much for her.

"Let's get out of here," Wendy called. "Find somewhere else to land."

Zing! That arrow nearly skewered Peter through the forehead. "Ha! You missed!"

Zing! Zing! The archers intensified their attack. *Zing, twack!* Tragedy! An arrow struck the big button on Nana Bear's dress. The impact tore the toy from Michael's grasp. "Nana!"

Too, too close, the Fairy thought, deciding to take matters into her own tiny hands.

"Focus, Wendy," Belle urged. "Think wonderful, lovely thoughts. You can do it!" With that, the Fairy let go, positioned herself like a missile, and hurled herself toward the archers.

Zing! Wendy's stomach clenched at the thought of the Fairy being shot down. Surely, she'd never survive a direct strike, and yet Belle seemed so courageous.

Wendy seized on her admiration for the Fairy's bravery— that was a wonderful, lovely thought. Or at least it was good enough.

Zing! Zing! Using the back of her hand, Wendy successfully batted aside an arrow. She turned her mind to kittens, puppies, and Renaissance fairs. Shrimp tempura and sushi rolls.

Michael's arms tightened around her neck. "Sissy Superhero!" That happy thought did wonders for their buoyancy. Now Wendy was fully in the game.

"Good show, Wendy!" Peter flew in evasive loops. "You're getting the hang of it."

Wendy twisted to successfully dodge another arrow. It was tough, keeping herself and her brother unpunctured while thinking wonderful, lovely thoughts. But for Michael's sake and her own, Wendy did her best. Cotton candy, more kittens, great-auntie hugs.

Another arrow—*zing*—shot toward Peter, who twisted at the waist.

Whoosh, another near miss.

Sunflowers, ice cream, ponies, picnics.

Magic rippled across Wendy's skin.

Ferris wheels.

Zing, zing! As the onslaught intensified, Peter drew his sword to defend himself.

Wendy rose higher, out of range, with Michael tucked on her hip. Storybooks. Pop-up books. Visits to London! Her confidence rose and so did her toes. She couldn't fly with Peter's playfulness or Belle's elegance, but Wendy had found a way with the winds.

Yet the moment she felt safer again, Peter called,

"Game over, Wendy! Time to land."

"What? Did you not notice that someone's trying to shoot us?"

"Not just any someone," Peter replied with a broad grin. "The Lost."

Wendy swallowed hard. His friends, his *family* was behind the attack? Good heavens! If *they* were out to get him, how deadly were his *enemies*?

Yet what else was she to do? Belle hadn't returned, the arrows had ceased coming, and Peter was descending in a series of acrobatic loops. He called, "Come on, Wendy! Everybody is going to love you!"

"Love you, Sissy," Michael said.

"Love you, too, Mikey." Wendy considered fleeing, but how far could they get on their own? How would they ever find their way home? "Hang on. We're landing."

CHAPTER

15

Tick tock, tick tock. Nearly twenty feet long, over two thousand pounds. Jaws that could tear apart a buffalo, boar, or bull shark. Possibly a century old, a goliath among reptiles.

Tick tock, tick tock. Was the ticking coming *from* the crocodile? Yes, it was. Originally the property of a Parisian boy, the alarm clock should've run down ages ago, but it hadn't. A good thing, too, for all the juicy humans who'd escaped after they heard the warning *tick tock*s.

Lily raised her arms up like Supergirl. She tried to fly away from the beach. She thought lovely thoughts, wonderful thoughts. Puppies, penguins, hedgehogs, bunnies, birthday cakes, wild-onion scrambled eggs—the heavy hitters!

No use. The Fairy dust had completely worn off. Lily could outrun the reptile—run, run, in a straight line. No looking back. But uh-oh, there were smaller crocodiles on the sand, spread out in both directions. Several of them longer than ten feet. Where had they come from? Lily hadn't noticed them when she was landing, but the seals had apparently waddled back into the water. She considered the cliffs ahead. Crocodiles were shockingly agile climbers. Maybe not fast climbers, though. Lily searched her memory for any useful information. Crocodiles were dutiful, protective mothers. Territorial. Opportunistic hunters. They played an important role in balancing the ecosystem, not that Lily was particularly concerned with the ecosystem right then.

Are you surprised that she had been reading about saltwater crocodiles only the night before and now one was steadily gaining on her? Surely, you're not so foolish as to think that's a coincidence. The island often plucked images from children's minds for inspiration. That said, the giant crocodile pursuing Lily had an infamous history in Neverland.

Tick tock, tick tock. Lily's instincts begged her to flee, but to where? Her mind reeled. The beach wasn't an option. The fairy-tale forest tempted, but what might she encounter there?

ROAWWAR! What was that, how far away? A big cat? Another bear? Would Lily escape one set of jaws only to be devoured by another? The fear, the indecision, was immobilizing.

Tick tock, tick tock, tick tock, tick tock.

Lily had hesitated, scanning the tropical foliage, trying

to gauge its hidden threats. Her gaze took in the banana and banyan trees, the mangroves farther up the shore, how they rose from the salty water. No more bears, not that she could see, but the plant life was thick and shadowy.

Tick tock, tick tock, tick tock, tick tock.

The crocodile bellowed.

"Run!" someone shouted, and glancing over her shoulder, Lily realized the crocodile had closed more than a third of the distance between them. It was advancing on her—fast. This was no belly crawl. It was trotting at her high up on all fours.

Lily ran. A coconut sailed by her head . . . *clunk*, striking the crocodile in the snout. More sailed after it, striking the surrounding sand. *Clunk, clunk, clunk, clunk.*

The crocodile hissed, snapping at the onslaught.

"This way!" At the edge of the forest, a kid waved his arms to catch her attention. Then he reached down to retrieve and heave more coconuts. *Clunk, clunk.* "Hurry!"

Lily hurried. She was an athlete, but by no means the fastest runner in her middle school—until that morning. Lily ran against the pull of the sand, pushing her muscles.

Tick tock. The beleaguered crocodile gave up the chase, making a wide turn and retreating into the foamy sea. *Tick tock. Tick tock.*

Lily slowed to a stop, watching until the reptile disappeared beneath the surface. Her heart thudding, she bent over, hands braced against her knees, and struggled to catch her breath. "Uh, hi."

"Hi." Her rescuer was a kid near her age, maybe a little older, tall and round with a reassuring smile. He sported a twenty-one-inch, heavily serrated knife, tucked between his two broad leather belts worn in a crisscross around his thick waist. Lily could only hope he carried the knife as a tool rather than a weapon. She wondered if he needed it for self-defense.

"Welcome to Neverland," he said in a soothing voice. "I'm Daniel Headbird—Leech Lake Ojibwe, by way of St. Paul. I'm really sorry this happened to you, but you're not alone. We're not the only Native people on the island." It sounded like he'd said that a few times before because he had. He'd even practiced saying it.

Lily hadn't forgotten that the night before Peter had mentioned Indians living in Neverland. It hadn't made any sense to her then, and it didn't make much more to her now.

She yanked off her right bedroom slipper and shook out the sand.

Daniel looked strong, healthy. He had a broad chest and muscular brown legs. He'd tied back his dark hair in a ponytail. "Where are your people from?" he added, still speaking in the kind of gentle voice you might use with a small child who'd been startled awake from a nightmare.

Lily wasn't quick to reply. She noted his faded black leather jacket, the *Save Our Wild Rice* T-shirt with torn sneakers and cutoff blue jeans. Shaking out her left slipper, Lily watched Daniel pick up a large, empty basket with handles on either side. Anyone with their hands full wasn't planning on drawing a knife.

"Lily Roberts," she replied, all business. "I'm Muscogee Creek from the Tulsa 'burbs. I came for my brother and stepsister. Have you seen them? He's four, and she's annoying."

"Welcome to Neverland, Lily Roberts," Daniel said with a wan smile. "Not yet, but we'll figure out what happened to them. Hang on, okay? I'm going to load the basket back up." With that, he jogged down the beach to retrieve the coconuts. The remaining crocodiles were basking at a comfortable distance away, and it wouldn't take long. Daniel wanted to give her a little space to process, to make the choice to stay with him. Anyone, especially a Native kid who'd had a run-in with Peter the night before, was likely to be overstressed and on guard.

Lily didn't automatically trust everyone she met, Native or not, but rescuing her from the crocodile had certainly made a positive first impression. Putting her slippers back on, she went to help. "How long have you been here?" she asked, tossing a coconut to him.

"I'm honestly not sure." Daniel caught and dropped it in the basket. "The days are short here. Except when they're long. We tried counting from sunrise to sunset— taking turns, seconds to minutes to hours—and we ended up with only three hours of daylight. We tried again only two sunrises later and came in at nineteen hours and forty-two minutes."

Didn't that sound like tedious days of counting? And now you understand about the *tick, tick*, ticking clock inside the crocodile. On Neverland, time itself was out of synch.

That both did and didn't make sense to Lily in a bigger, more profound way than Fairies or Merfolk or flying kids. Earth was enormous. Only the Creator knew who and what all called the planet home. The news media occasionally highlighted "newly discovered" animal species that of course had existed all along. Cryptid hunters searched for creatures widely dismissed by most as myth or fantasy. Though Lily had an inquiring mind, she believed some mysteries were best left alone or dealt with only rarely and not discussed at all. At least not in mixed company. But even taking all that into account, Daniel was talking about the impossible.

And yet, as a stunning pair of white egrets landed on the sand nearby, she believed him.

Daniel was relieved by how well Lily appeared to be coping. Unlike a couple of the previous newcomers, she wasn't shaking or babbling. She hadn't thrown up. In fact, Lily was using coherent sentences and acting with purpose. He assumed it was because she was so focused on finding her family. Daniel didn't realize how practiced Lily was at hiding her fears, especially from those who didn't know her well. Sometimes even from herself.

Lily skipped ahead, then hesitated at the sight of the last remaining coconut, kissing the frothy surf. She was

closer to it than Daniel was. But what if the huge crocodile was waiting right beneath the surface, ready to lunge?
The species was known for surprise attacks.

"Leave it," Daniel called, lifting the basket to one
broad shoulder. "We've got plenty."

Lily exhaled, backpedaling. When she'd first taken
flight with the shadow, she'd been terrified. Terrified for
Wendy and Michael, terrified of heights, of the possibility
of falling, of drowning, of orcas and sharks and barracudas
and the strangeness of it all. Then, even as Lily trembled
high above land and water, she'd held tight to the hope of
quickly rescuing her siblings.

Now Lily had successfully made the journey and found
an ally, maybe even a friend. She'd already surprised herself with her daring and had made some real progress.

"This way, Lily Roberts." Resting the basket on his
shoulder, Daniel led her toward the forest. "We'll figure
out what happened to your brother and sister."

"Stepsister." She paused. "Her name is Wendy. His is
Michael."

Daniel nodded. "At sunrise, I do my best to watch for
new arrivals—I spotted you in the sky, but maybe I was
asleep when they first touched down. Or maybe they
flew in from a different angle across the island, out of my
range of vision."

It went without saying how daunting the task was,
given that the sun didn't seem to rise on a regular sched-
ule. However, Lily correctly surmised that her preexisting

understanding of the rotation of the Earth around the sun still held true, but Fairy magic had shifted how the passage of time was perceived on the island. "So far as I know, they're with a boy named Peter." Lily caught sight of a small, ruddy brown rat scurrying between the lava rocks. "Peter . . ."

"Pan," Daniel said, his free hand falling to the handle of his knife. "Yeah, we've met."

"Wendy and Mikey flew out of his bedroom window with Peter and . . . a Fairy." It still felt odd to say that last word out loud. "She called herself 'Belle.'" Lily paused, suddenly self-conscious. "I know how that sounds."

Daniel didn't seem the least bit fazed by the idea of Fairies. "Huh. Your brother is only four years old. And you three were separated. That's unusual. New kids usually fall between seven and twelve years old, and Pan usually brings siblings together."

Lily hesitated at the edge of the forest. She gazed at the length of the black stone and violet beach, speckled with seashells. Obviously, it wasn't safe from crocodiles, though all but one had slipped back into the water, having been dismissed by the island. Despite the larger lava rocks, the view was mostly clear. The mysterious forest, in contrast, was thick, chittering with life.

"Lily?" Daniel waited for her. "It's okay. I'm bringing you to my friends."

Comforted by the promise of community, she took a deep breath and plunged in after him. The ground was soft and moist. Lily tripped over an exposed root. "Oomph!"

Daniel rushed to help steady her. "I'm sorry, I should've warned—"

"I'm fine," she said, her knee smarting. "I don't need you to keep rescuing me. Or to keep apologizing for the fact that I'm here. It's not your fault."

Daniel recognized pride talking. "Trust me, Lily Roberts. If we both manage to survive much longer, you'll probably be rescuing me in no time."

Moving on, Lily considered his use of the word "if." She flinched at a whisper in the mossy air, but it was only a bird, red with a black bill and black-tipped wings, taking flight. The path had been freshly cleared of thorny branches, and she realized that Daniel was retracing the way he'd come. And then she realized that he probably used the big knife for cutting through the forest.

"Once we're closer to camp, we'll have to rough it," Daniel said. "Push through the woods. We don't want to alert Pan or the pirates to our location."

Pirates? Lily thought. Another menace to worry about. But given her concern for Wendy and Michael, she put a mental pin in that. "About my family," Lily began, watching her step. "I lifted off a few minutes after them with . . . uh, Peter's shadow. I'm not exactly sure when it bailed on me, but—"

"You got played." Their path widened enough to walk side by side. "Don't feel badly. It's not like you're the only one. The shadow is his partner, and the Fairy is their wing-woman. Team Pan has a couple of well-oiled, go-to tricks. He either lures kids with promises of magical adventures. Or he takes something or someone to use as bait."

Like he'd kidnapped Wendy and Michael. "Something like—?"

"This jacket belonged to nimishoomis, and . . ." With his free hand, Daniel smoothed the leather lapels. "It's a nice jacket, you know, and he wanted me to have it."

Lily could hear grief in his voice. Her grandparents and step-grandparents were all living, but she remembered when Auntie Lillian's husband, Uncle Tim, had died only two years before and understood how the sorrow lingered. "You managed to get it back."

"Yeah, but I lost pretty much everything short of my life to do it. Fairy dust messes with your head. It's a quick mood booster. It can make you more likely to say yes to suggestions."

"Really?" Learning that made Lily a little less irked at Wendy for going along with Peter.

Daniel added, "I was the first of the new group of Native kids to come to the island, the latest after a long time between. From Pan's point of view, the jacket never really mattered. Or didn't matter for long. I'm here—he's won."

Lily caught sight of a herd of striped, short-eared rabbits scattering as she and Daniel drew closer. She searched her mind for something sympathetic to say, but then she felt a surge of pain in her right foot. "Ow, ow, ow!"

Daniel set down the basket of coconuts, remembering what she'd told him about not having to keep rescuing her. Tentatively, he asked, "Can I help?"

Lily grimaced, trying to put weight on the sore foot. "*Ouch*. Yes, please."

Daniel thought it was sweet that she was so polite. His elders had drilled manners into him, too. He knelt, bracing her in place with a wide hand on her upper arm, while turning her raised foot with the other. "If we take off the shoe, the thorn might come out with it."

"They're bedroom slippers," she replied, regretting the thin rubber soles. Suddenly, Lily felt a flash of self-consciousness over her pj's. "I don't normally leave the house like this."

"No big deal," Daniel said. "Unless you're a Fairy or Merfolk, the island's not a fashion show." He glanced up at her. "This might hurt worse for a minute. Grab my shoulders."

Lily did as he suggested, squeezing her eyes shut. "Ouch!"

"Got it." Daniel showed her the bloody thorn, then tossed it aside. "You'll feel better before you know it. It's only another five or twenty minutes to camp. I'd wanted to make a little detour along the way but—"

"I can walk. What do you mean: Five *or* twenty? You do know the way?"

"Remember what I said about time?" Daniel was

now carrying the basket of coconuts in front of him. "It's like the land can fold in on itself so that the next major event—a crocodile attack, a high-seas battle, a new arrival like you—happens faster. I don't think the terrain literally changes . . . but rapid healing is often a bonus."

That was good news at least. Good, though disconcerting. Not even twenty-four hours had passed (or had it?) since Belle and Peter had inserted themselves in Lily's life, and she had been confronted with one impossible thing after another. But perhaps the island would hurry up her reunion with Wendy and Michael. She dearly hoped so.

Lily spotted a thin red line rippling in the wind. Limping, she untied the silk ribbon from a leafy fern. It was a bit dew-stained, but not wrinkled or frayed. "Found something!"

"We've come across a few of those lately." Daniel tightened his grip on the basket handles. "Stay alert and keep your voice low. That's how pirates mark their paths."

CHAPTER

16

Though Wendy and Michael had left home before Lily did, they'd spent longer airborne, partly because Peter, as usual, took the scenic route and partly because their arrival had been delayed by the arrow attack. When Wendy finally touched down on Neverland, she dropped quickly into a kneeling position to better support Michael's landing. Then she took his hand and stood in front of him, protective and defiant. "Who do you think you are, shooting at us like that?"

The Lost, who were positioned shoulder to shoulder in a military line, didn't answer. This windblown, indignant girl wasn't their captain. Not that Wendy was impressed with them either. They appeared to range between the ages of nine and twelve, looked unkempt, and smelled unwashed. They carried bows in makeshift slings, their arrows in quivers on their backs. Only Peter wore a proper sword.

"Nana Bear?" Michael called in a small, sad voice.

Wendy quickly noted the birds, the butterflies, the breathing trees. The forest was buzzing with life. Belle was conversing earnestly with a blue-green hummingbird. The fairy exclaimed to the bird, "You spotted pirates where?"

"Hello again, Wendy." Peter twirled his weapon, strutting to inspect the Lost. "I was just telling them about you, our new storyteller, about how you fell in love with me and begged me to bring you to Neverland."

Wendy didn't appreciate his fibbing or his total disregard for her little brother. "Funny, Peter, that's not how I remember it."

"Never mind those arrows," Peter added as if she hadn't spoken at all. "The Lost were only playing, right, men?" The boys remained silent, backs straight and chins high.

As Michael leaned against her legs, Wendy asked, "Why were you shooting at us?"

Peter pointed his sword at the Lost. "Speak up! She asked you a question."

"We thought you were a Neverbird," replied a thin white boy wearing a beat-up, black top hat and a tiger hide. "I'm Frank, by the way. Frank Something-Or-Other from . . . somewhere."

Belle still seemed preoccupied with the hummingbird. Fairies couldn't speak fluently with birds, but they came far closer to it than any human ever had, and they preferred hummingbirds to any other species. Still,

Neverbirds were a sensitive subject, especially for Belle.

"I *told* you there were no more Neverbirds," countered a red-haired kid who closely resembled Frank—minus the hat. He wore a tiger hide, too. "Peter killed the very last one."

"Shut up, Ethan. I spotted a Neverbird yesterday!"

"You shut up, Frank. That was last week, and it wasn't a Neverbird. It was an albatross. Full-grown Neverbirds were much bigger—bigger than me or you."

Frank and Ethan were the exact same height, in case you were wondering. Although both identical twins and redheads were quite rare, Wendy, who was quite proud of her own coppery curls, wasn't surprised to meet them that morning. She was an avid reader, a lover of Story, and stories were absolutely bursting with twins and redheads.

"I killed the last lion on the island, too," Peter bragged, puffing himself up. "Wendy, that's Frank and Ethan," Peter added, as though they hadn't already made that clear. "But you can simply call them 'Lost.' You can simply call any or all of them 'Lost' and leave it at that."

"The last lion was only a cub," clarified a sunburned boy with plump cheeks and stringy blond hair, dressed in bear skin. "It couldn't defend itself like a full-grown lion."

As Belle and the hummingbird took off for the treetops, Michael's small hand tightened in Wendy's. He adored animals, especially young ones. All this talk of killing didn't sit well. Meanwhile, Peter was fuming. Had the Lost boy in bear skin dared to minimize his deed?

"I'm Oliver, by the way." He waved, then realizing his error, stood ramrod straight again. "Welcome to Neverland."

"Welcome to Neverland," Frank and Ethan echoed in unison.

"Thank you," Wendy said. "We won't be staying long." Don't be fooled. Though she spoke as casually as anyone on holiday on a tropical island, Wendy was on high alert.

The boys' Neverbird excuse for shooting arrows at them certainly hadn't—forgive the expression—*panned* out, and Michael was looking up at her for reassurance.

"All clear, Peter!" Belle descended to tug playfully on his ear and twirled up to lounge in a bright yellow hibiscus bloom. "Not a pirate in sight!"

"Nana Bear?" Michael called again. At that, Belle snapped her fingers and zipped off.

Peter thrust his sword toward the sky. "I am Pan the Lion Killer. Let every pirate, Injun, and wild beast tremble at my name." He returned his blade to its scabbard. "At ease, men."

The Lost finally relaxed their postures.

Wendy was aghast that anyone would kill a lion cub for any reason, let alone bragging rights. She was horrified that Peter was threatening human beings, especially since his definition of "Injun" might very well include her little brother. Fortunately, Michael had tuned out the conversation altogether in favor of studying a bluish-pink chameleon on a nearby fern.

"Here you go," Belle said, suddenly reappearing with his favorite toy.

"Nana Bear!" Michael shouted as it dropped into his hands. "I missed you so much."

"Thank you, Belle," Wendy said with a genuine smile.

The Fairy curtsied. It was so nice to be thanked for a change.

Wendy's and Michael's feelings, their personalities, were still slightly magnified by the Fairy dust. (They'd been covered in a lot more than Lily had.) However, they'd also flown a great distance, dodged arrows, glimpsed Merfolk, and sighted the *Jolly Roger*. As far as Wendy was concerned, that was enough adventure for anyone. She erred on the side of graciousness. "This has been quite a trip. Peter and Belle, thank you for bringing us here and introducing us to your family. My, how time has flown!"

Michael turned to peer at her, baffled. That had *not* sounded like his sister talking. She seemed to be channeling their grandmother, who called weekly from London for video chats.

"Our parents must be frantic about us by now." Wendy shook her head at Michael's windblown hair. Her own was probably a mess of tangles. "I was supposed to be on my way to New York this morning—my mistake not mentioning that sooner. And I'll be in big trouble for leaving with Mikey without even asking first. So, I am afraid this will have to be a short visit. If you'll just take us home now, I'd appreciate it. We really must be going."

It wasn't a bad speech, but it didn't do Wendy and Michael a lick of good.

Peter made a show of yawning. Stretching his arms and arching his back. "It's naptime, Wendy. I'm too tired to travel, aren't you?"

Because Peter yawned, the Lost yawned. Belle yawned. Wendy and Michael yawned, too. Yawning is contagious that way. Wendy and Michael were weary. Though he had napped overnight, it wasn't a deep sleep. Wendy had managed to stay awake the whole way.

"Aren't you hungry?" Peter tried again.

Should Wendy insist on leaving then? No, she decided that she needed more information. She needed a plan. Cautiously, Wendy acknowledged, "I am."

Michael tucked Nana Bear under his chin, swaying slightly. "Pancakes?"

"Pancakes? Why not!" Peter clasped his hands. "That settles that. Let's march, men! We're off for breakfast and a nap."

Never mind that the Lost had awakened within the hour after a long night's sleep. They fell into single file and tromped behind Peter, who gloried in leading. Or rather, leading all except Belle, who'd gracefully glided ahead. It was a lovely forest, glistening with dew. A rustling in the branches above caught Wendy's attention. She paused to watch the flying squirrels, and then a kaleidoscope of red-and-black butterflies filled the air. If only Lily had been there to share it.

Michael tugged on her hand. "Sissy?"

Wendy had been distracted, and Peter had momentarily forgotten all about them. What with the undergrowth, it was tough going for both her and Michael, especially wearing bedroom slippers.

As the siblings hurried to catch up, an arm shot out of the surrounding brush to block their path, stopping them short. On reflex, Wendy kicked the newcomer in the shin.

"Ow, did you have to do that?" The boy rubbed the sore spot. "Wendy is it?"

"Yes, and this is Mikey." Wendy noticed the recent buzz haircut and blue soccer uniform.

"I'm K. D.," he announced. "After my granddads, Kyle and David." His lips curled in a wistful grin. "My mom says I'm her little katydid!" There was a time when that last bit had embarrassed him, but now he pined for his mother's voice. "I'm one of the Lost."

"The Lost?" Wendy shuddered. "It's creepy how you call yourselves that."

"Creepier than that?" K. D. asked. A gorgeous brown snake with a darker brown striped pattern slithered across their path in a sliding S formation. Nearly seven feet in length.

Lily would've loved it. Michael did love it. He exclaimed, "Wow!"

Wendy lifted him up on her hip, though he'd become too heavy to carry around that way for long. She wished she'd paid more attention when Lily prattled on about reptiles. "Is it poisonous?" she wanted to know. "Will it try to . . . ?" Boa constrictor, that's what she was trying to think of. "Try to squeeze us to death and eat us?"

"I don't know," K. D. replied. "I don't think so. But if it is poisonous, it'll be more potent for little kids. Lower body weight." He was sensible about things like that.

They waited out the slithering snake. Wendy wondered what it might mean that K. D. hadn't been with the others earlier. Wendy thought K. D. was probably a white boy, along with the rest of the Lost, though she knew you couldn't always tell by appearances. She added, "Do you, uh, have a phone I could use? I'm not able—"

"Sorry, no signal on the island. Phones don't work here."

That was disappointing. "You haven't been here long," Wendy guessed correctly, based on his sporty outfit and haircut. "In Neverland, I mean."

He was oddly flattered by that. "That's right, and I haven't forgotten myself either. My name is K. D. Anders, after my granddads, Kyle and David." He repeated himself like it was important to do so. "My parents are Alex and Cory Anders and my baby sister is Jewel and my best friends are Isaiah and Hailey and my soccer coach is Mr. Ryan and I'm from . . . I'm from . . ." K. D. fisted his hands at his sides. "It'll come back to me. Any minute. It'll come back."

The tip of the snake's tail had disappeared into the tall, swaying grass, and Wendy set her brother down. She appreciated K. D.'s warning about the snake, but she didn't trust him. She didn't trust any of them. "When we were flying in, your friends shot arrows at us."

"Toronto!" K. D. ran a hand through his short, spiky hair. "I'm from Toronto!"

"Uh, congrats," Wendy replied as they began hiking again. "I bet you're looking forward to getting back to Toronto, too. I bet Oliver and the twins—"

"They don't like to be called that, 'the twins,'" K. D. said. "They're separate people."

"But calling all of you 'Lost' because . . . What? You're interchangeable. That's okay?"

"*I* didn't say it was," K. D. replied. "Anyway, I'm not sure Oliver is in such a hurry to get home. His stepdad has a temper when he's drinking, but Oliver's mom can't afford to leave."

Wendy knew that not all kids had safe, loving homes like hers, whether it was in Tulsa or New York City or anywhere else. If it was money in the way, her stepmother might be able to help. For now, there was nothing Wendy could do except hope that Oliver's mom was safe.

"About the arrows, what was that?" Wendy nudged along Michael, who'd positioned Nana Bear on his hip like she'd held him. "Did they forget that Neverbirds are extinct?"

Maybe it was K. D.'s distress over his slipping memory. Maybe it was the novelty of Peter bringing a girl to the island or the way the breeze played with her curls. In any case, K. D. decided to tell her the truth. He slowed his pace and lowered his voice. "It's partly a game, a chance for Peter to show off. The Lost always pretend like they're trying to shoot down whoever he brings to the island, but they're supposed to lay off once the new kids are in range." K. D. shrugged. "Peter gets to play the hero and he usually blames the attack on the Indians."

"Creek Indians?" Michael was young and tired, but he knew who he was.

You'll recall that this time the Lost had taken responsibility for the onslaught of arrows. Consequently, you may be wondering why Peter had deviated a bit from his standard nefariousness. Well, he wasn't always so observant, but even he had realized it wouldn't be so easy, turning kids from the Roberts-Darling family against Native people. As distressed as Wendy was to learn of Peter's attempts to do so with other children, she sensed there was even more to his foul agenda. Wendy prodded K. D., "It's dangerous! Why take such a big risk?"

"Let me ask you this: How did you feel when you left home and flew here?"

Wendy brightened a bit. "Excited, curious, like I was special somehow."

"And how did you feel once the arrows started flying?"

Sensing an ally, she answered honestly. "Confused, overwhelmed, scared . . ."

"Weaker," K. D. supplied. He gave her a hand over a large fallen branch and then lifted Michael over it, too. "That's how Peter wants you, now that he's got you here.

At least until you forget who you really are and do whatever he wants without asking any questions."

Wendy wasn't pleased to hear it. She wanted to dig deeper into the ill will between Peter and the Native people on the island, but given little Michael's presence, Wendy decided to put a pin in that. "So, you're saying you all shot arrows at us so Peter could show off and I wouldn't . . . what? Call him out for being a bully?" She paused to poke K. D. in the chest. "I have news for you, one of those arrows hit my shoe—slipper. It nearly took off a toe." She raised Michael's arm to show the hole in his pajamas. "Look!"

"And Nana Bear's button!" Michael held up his toy. "It's broke."

Wendy bent to inspect it. "Not broken, Mikey, just chipped."

"I'm glad you're both . . ." In a gesture of goodwill, K. D. patted Nana Bear's head. "I'm glad you're all okay. I didn't mean to . . ." He glanced up. "That's why I was in a tree, so I could shoot higher." Raising his hands as if in surrender, K. D. said, "I'm sorry. I've got lousy aim."

"Lousy aim?" Wendy echoed, furious. "Were you trying to hurt us?"

"No, no," K. D. assured her. "Not you. I was aiming at Peter Pan."

CHAPTER

17

Daniel's guesstimate of a five-to-twenty-minute hike from the beach to the Native kids' camp normally would've been spot-on, give or take a minute or two. But it wasn't only that the island seemed to fold in on itself, impatient for what might happen next. Sometimes the land seemed to unfold, to s-t-r-e-t-c-h time while it considered its options.

The breeze smelled of nectar. Lily retrieved another red silk pirate ribbon from a branch.

"I doubt the pirates even know we're on the island," Daniel said. "They've got Pan and the Merfolk to deal with. It's a lot of work just to keep a ship like that afloat."

Another ribbon. Since Daniel didn't seem overly concerned, Lily tried not to obsess over her growing collection. "Here, I'll take the other basket handle," she said, moving alongside him. Lily paused to examine the bottom of her foot. The ache had faded. The bleeding had stopped.

"I had it," Daniel said as she eased his burden, but he was breathing easier.

She suspected that he was warm in the leather jacket. "To recap: We're stranded on a magical island, populated by Fairies . . . There's more than one Fairy, yes?"

"Yes," Daniel replied. "Countless Fairies. A whole queendom of Fairies. So far as I know, Peter's Fairy friend is the only one who associates with humans."

Lily blinked at that. "Magical island, unfriendly Fairies, large carnivorous animals. No tech to communicate with the outside world. Our enemies are Peter Pan and the Lost, plus a ship full of pirates." She cocked her head. "*Seriously?* Pirates?"

"Yep, pirates as in 'yo ho ho and a bottle of rum.' Old-timey storybook pirates on an old-timey pirate ship called the *Jolly Roger*. We've managed to steer clear of any direct contact, but a couple of us have spied on the crew when they've come ashore. To be honest, they're fun to watch—lots of 'Ahoy! Arrrg!' Big talk and big swagger—"

"Like Peter? He's all big talk and big swagger."

"He's worse than that," Daniel replied. "Here, let's put down the basket for now."

Daniel set it between flowery bushes and used his knife to whack at a tangle of leafy vines covering a rocky hillside. "Last time, this wasn't so hard to find."

"What wasn't?" Lily was becoming impatient. "Daniel, we have to rescue Wendy and Mikey and . . ." Her mind raced. "We could build a signal fire or write 'HELP' and 'SOS' in huge letters using rocks on the beach. Or we could try to talk some reason into Belle, although she's—"

"There's something I need to show you." Daniel put away his blade and ripped the rest of the greenery free, revealing the entrance to a lava rock cave. "How's the foot?"

Lily flexed it. "Not bad." She peered into the jagged opening and the deep, midnight darkness beyond. How cold was it inside? Was the cave stable? Did they need to worry about falling rocks? "Should we come back later with flashlights or . . . torches?"

"We don't have flashlights, and we won't need torches for long enough to bother making them." He ducked inside and waited for her. "You ask a lot of questions," he added. It was an observation, not a complaint. "Understanding Neverland isn't easy. Be patient with yourself. Try to take it one step at a time."

Didn't Daniel realize that anything could happen to her siblings? Lily wondered. She wanted nothing more than to leave this strange place with Wendy and Michael right now. Of course, she was asking a lot of questions! Of course, she was on guard! Lily considered it wise to be vigilant in her normal day-to-day life, let alone in Neverland. Crossing her arms, she said, "I'm trying to work the problem. To do that, I need all of the available information."

"Some of the answers are in here," Daniel replied. "If you'll follow me, you'll see."

Why couldn't he simply *tell* her? Lily wondered.

"How is the air quality?" she asked instead, stalling. It was a dark cave. Lily didn't want to go inside, but she didn't want to be left outside alone either. "What if there's a bear?"

"The air is cooler than outside, but not cold." Daniel offered a reassuring grin. "No bear."

Daniel did seem trustworthy, Lily thought. After all, he had saved her life back on the beach. Lily felt torn between fear and curiosity as she wondered what was so important that Daniel needed to *show* it to her. Lily took a breath and slowly released it. Maybe, for Wendy and Michael's sake, it was something she needed to see for herself. Lily took another breath, held it, blew it out slowly, and stepped in. "Is this cave where the Native people are holed up?"

"Used to be, a really long time ago." Daniel advanced into the darkness, as if she were right behind him. "Stay close, along the wall, as far from the stream as possible." His voice grew more distant. "Small steps around this curve. The floor is uneven."

"Wait up." Lily was careful as she followed. "Are there any other ways in?"

"At least one, probably more. There's a whole under-

ground network of crisscrossing tunnels. Previous generations of Native kids used them more than we do."

"Previous generations?" Lily bumped into him.
"Sorry!" Resting her fingertips on Daniel's shoulder
blades, she could hear the chatter of birds and insects
from outside, the shuffling of small stones as they inched
forward. "I can't see a thing. How are you—"

"Ow!" Daniel stopped abruptly.

"What?" Lily exclaimed.

"Scraped the top of my head on the same stalactite
I ran into last time. It's not serious, but we should slow
down."

Inching forward, Lily was impressed that he knew the
word "stalactite," though she thought "lavacicles" might be
more accurate. She kept a hand flat against his back and
raised the other one right above and in front of her head.

Moments later, he said, "Hang on. Stopping for a
minute." Daniel grunted softly, and Lily flinched at the
loud, gritty noise of rock sliding against rock.

An uneven oblong of light appeared in front of them,
and suddenly, she could make out Daniel's profile again.
The backlit hole was about four feet above the ground,
big enough for him to crawl through. "There's an opening
in the ceiling of this cavern. I cleared it of overgrowth
when I spotted you flying in, so that we could see better."
Daniel bent, threaded his fingers. "Need a boost?"

Lily stepped from his cupped, interlocked hands to
crawl through the hole in the rock, slightly tearing the

cuffs of her pj's, and into a magnificent green grotto with a stream ending in a glittering pool. Diffused light poured through narrow openings in the rock ceiling, which was riddled with spikes and spirals, thin and blobby. She marveled while Daniel scanned their surroundings. Finally, Lily asked, "What are you looking for?"

"There." He pointed to a hand-painted chart on the rock wall titled *Neverland: Population & Sightings* in red writing. "You deserve the truth. Pan lures and leads kids to Neverland. They live here, and they die here. Most survive to adulthood, but none of us ever go home."

Horizontally, Lily read: *Indians, Boats, Planes.* Vertically, she read *1900s, 1910s, 1920s, 1930s, 1940s, 1950s, 1960s+, 2020s.* According to the chart, up until the 1950s, there'd been between twenty-one and thirty-seven Native kids on the island over the course of any given decade. And after that, only one . . . or at least only one recorded until the 2020s.

In all that time, there had apparently been zero sightings of boats or planes. Not that Daniel or Lily had any way of knowing it, but that was because the veil protected the island from visual and electronic detection. In fact, countless air travelers had flown over Neverland, and to this day, none were the wiser.

"The night I first met Pan, I'd strolled out on the dock near my uncle's place." Daniel's voice was momentarily wistful. "I used to love to do that. Go out by myself to look at the stars. Listen to the water and the bugs and birds. It was pretty quiet. I could think." He straightened his shoulders. "Anyway, the Fairy caught my eye over the lake, and . . . next thing you know, Pan called me 'Lost,' and I told him he was wrong. I wasn't lost. I was on the rez. I was home."

Lily was still staring at the chart. She normally loved quantifiable data. Not this time.

"Then Pan turned on his song and dance, pitching Neverland, and I said I had everything I needed right where I was. I said I was Ojibwe, and he didn't know what that meant. When I tried to explain, he kept interrupting, so I told him to buzz off."

"Good for you." Lily's fingertips hovered over the zeroes on the chart. She believed in her heart that Daniel was being truthful, but who had created the chart? Could the source be trusted? So far, she hadn't seen any sign of advanced electronic technology, of sophisticated radar equipment. No one could've monitored the sky and seas all day and all night for decades on end. Best-case scenario, the chart represented anecdotal evidence, not scientific evidence.

"Pan didn't know what I meant by 'Native.'" Daniel took a tentative seat on a nearby rock. The texture felt like Velcro. "But he recognized the word 'Indian' in this big aha! moment kind of way. Like he'd completely forgotten we exist—and maybe he did—until I reminded him . . . or like he'd suddenly found us after a really long game of hide-and-seek."

"That sounds disturbing," Lily said, refusing to give up hope of returning to Tulsa. Just like she refused to consider that Wendy and Michael weren't still alive, and like she'd refused for so long before that to believe their parents would go ahead with the trial separation. When an idea was too huge, too scary, Lily shut it out as much as she could for as long as she could.

"When I saw the Fairy up close, I ran. I ran home." Daniel was gently touching the sore spot on his head. No swelling, though it would bruise. "The whole thing had been so weird. The next day, I could've sworn I'd dreamed it. But then the following night, I woke up around midnight on the sofa, and Pan was in the family room, trying on my leather jacket. The shadow distracted me. I failed to catch Pan before he flew off. Then the Fairy told me my only chance of getting the jacket back was to come with her."

Was that a faint splash in the pool? Lily glanced over her shoulder. Could a crocodile reach this grotto? Maybe. Some fish could jump—salmon, catfish, sharks. It had been such a small noise, perhaps nothing more than the lapping of water against rock.

"At first I thought I was the only Native person on the island. But then an elder found me, warned me against traveling farther north. Said that's where Pan and the Fairies lived. He was a Seminole man, Clifford, from Florida. He died days later."

Lily felt a surge of grief for this elder she'd never met.

"That's how you know so much about the island. Clifford told you."

Daniel nodded. "Pan had brought him when he was ten. Clifford had thrown in with the pirates for a few years in his teens and then lived in secret on the island. He warned me to steer clear of the *Jolly Roger*. He showed me the canoe he'd tucked away in these tunnels, and"— Daniel gestured to the chart on the wall—"that."

Lily's heart clenched at the realization that the source of the numbers had been Clifford, a Native elder, some-one Daniel had trusted. Still, her logical side argued that Daniel's story clearly didn't add up. Something was way off about the timeline. How could a boy Peter's age have brought Clifford as a child to Neverland? Was Pan a family name? Maybe the boy she'd met was Pan the Fifth? Lily was about to lean into the question when Daniel rubbed his eyes, and she realized how upset he was.

"It's my fault," Daniel said. "I never should have reminded Pan of Native people. You—none of you would be here if it weren't for me."

Lily frowned. She still had a lot to learn about the island, but one truth was already clear. "Put that out of your mind right this minute," she insisted. "Peter is the one to blame, not you."

Daniel nodded slowly, equal parts grateful and impressed by the steel in Lily's voice. He was patient as she pored over the dates, the numbers, committing them to memory. Every time a new Native kid arrived, Daniel experienced a surge of remorse, an urge to apologize, and a renewed, grim realization that nothing could be done to make things right.

Perhaps you're wondering, did Peter really forget about Native people in the first place? Not exactly, though he is forgetful, that being a consequence of Fairy dust and him having been exposed to so much of it for so long. Rather, it was that Peter had become fully consumed by a compelling conflict with a pirate captain of old, Captain Jameson, whose diabolical reign was fueled by his—and his crew's—frustration at being trapped forever within the veil. Jameson had led the pirates in a rage against the island's inhabitants. Over time, Peter began to emulate his merciless enemy and brushed aside his preoccupation with Native people, dismissing them as relics of the past.

After finally vanquishing his seafaring archfoe, Peter fell into an unexpected mourning. He began lashing out against the wild beasts of the island and, alas, had yet to give that up. He also returned to his yellowed storybooks for comfort, a reminder of times gone by.

A few days or months or years later (who could say for sure?), upon encountering Daniel at the lake, Peter experienced a flash of nostalgia, of inspiration. He seized at the chance to reignite his so-called game of kidnapping and waging war against Native kids.

Not that Daniel had any way of knowing all that, and being the responsible sort, he was sometimes a bit too hard on himself. Possibly you're like that, too, or know someone who is.

Lily registered another soft splashing noise, but Daniel's guilt was louder. She slowly exhaled, turned away from the hand-painted chart, and moved to lean against the rock where he was sitting. Lily affectionately bumped her shoulder against his. "You told Peter who you are. You're proud to be Ojibwe. There's nothing wrong with that."

"Nothing wrong?!" a lyrical voice exclaimed. "You humans shouldn't be here at all." The unexpected speaker had propped herself on her elbows. Though she was still mostly submerged, her fishlike tail was rhythmically slapping the water. "Beware, pirates! I am Meredith of the Merfolk." Two more of her people surfaced, one on each side, at the jagged edge of the pool. "These are my cousins, Ripley and Cordelia."

The exquisite aquatic trio appeared to be about the same age as Lily and Daniel.

"You are trespassing," Meredith went on. "Leave our waters be. Humans do not belong in the Neversea or on our island."

When it came to Merfolk, this was a first-time encounter for both Lily and Daniel. They tended to cluster on the other side of the island. Lily noted their voluminous hair, their varying shades of lovely brown skin, their turquoise-green scales, which rose up from their tails much like bodices, and the horizontal tail flukes common in marine mammals like whales or dolphins.

"What if they're dangerous?" Lily whispered.

"They think *we're* dangerous." He tilted his head, considering. "From what Clifford told me, the Merfolk are no friends of Pan." At the very least, they all had a common enemy.

Lily and Daniel rose from the rock to come closer, pausing only steps from the pool.

"We're not pirates." Daniel crouched so as not to tower over Meredith. "My people—"

"Humans, pirates," Cordelia pointed out. "Same difference."

"Pirates plunder," Ripley added. "Pollute the water." If they viewed all humans as pirates, it was impossible to argue with that. Humans had made a tragic mess of the seas.

"Maybe you're not yet pirates when you first arrive," Meredith acknowledged. "But all—save one—who've survived past childhood have pledged their lifelong allegiance to the *Jolly Roger*. Pirates who contaminate, pirates whose hooks and nets take Merfolk lives."

Lily was appalled. "That's horrible." She knelt beside Daniel, feeling a surge of sympathy for their losses. "Listen, we're . . . we're not here by choice. We won't stay any longer than necessary. Believe me, I much prefer Tulsa to Neverland."

"Leave now, then," Meredith demanded. "Fly away, sail away, swim away, go."

"I wish we could," Daniel said. "We can't fly or sail through the veil without Fairy dust. We are prisoners here. Clifford told me that Native kids before us—"

"You didn't know Clifford." Ripley smacked the water with her tail.

Daniel was offended. "I did so—"

"Enough!" Meredith shouted. "Dive deep beneath the veil. It can't extend beyond the surface of the ocean. We Merfolk may come and go as we please."

"Swim away," her companions chanted in unison. "Swim away, swim away."

"We can't swim away," Lily said. "Even if we managed not to get captured by pirates or eaten by, well, anything that could eat us, we're humans. We don't have enough endurance to make it to the nearest body of land."

"You'll never know until you try," Cordelia said with a grim smile. Without further warning, she grabbed Daniel by an ankle and Meredith grabbed Lily by a wrist, tugging them into the temperate water—swimming deep, deep, deep in the underground pool.

CHAPTER

18

"Should we build you a home of your own, Wendy?" Peter asked. "Or would you prefer to live here with the Lost?"

"Where is 'here'?" Wendy couldn't begin to fathom what he was talking about. To her, this clump of tropical trees and meandering vines seemed no different from any of the others they'd hiked by already. "Peter, I thought you were too tired to fly us back to Oklahoma. Where would you get the energy to build me a house?"

"Second wind, Wendy! Get it?" He laughed. "Wind, Wend-y. Besides . . ." With a sweeping gesture, he indicated the Lost. "They're not tired. My talents are better suited to supervision anyway. That's why I'm the captain. Just you wait. It'll be the prettiest, littlest house you've ever seen with funny walls of rosy red and a mossy roof of blue and green."

Oliver pretended to cough into his hand to cover up

muttering, "Jackass."

Peter's expression grew somber. He strode to Oliver. "You sound like a teenager."

The rest of the Lost kept quiet. From what Wendy had observed so far, Frank and Ethan, the redheaded twin brothers in tiger skins, appeared to be wholly committed to Peter. K. D., the new kid, was clearly struggling to hang on to the boy he'd been. He'd also tried to shoot down Peter without the other boys finding out. Oliver was less cautious with his rebellious streak.

"A teenager?" Oliver echoed. "Want to talk *years*, Pete, or *maturity*?"

Peter was gripping the handle of his sword so tightly his knuckles were turning white.

"What about Mikey?" Wendy asked, partly because she needed to know and partly as a distraction to diffuse the tension. "Where do you expect my brother to live?"

"He's Lost," Peter said, as though that were blatantly obvious. He studied the four-year-old, whose bedroom had been dripping with pirate décor, apparently forgetting the standoff with Oliver. "Your brother will live with the Lost." At least for the time being, Peter thought.

"Then so will I," Wendy replied, realizing it was no use arguing that she and Michael should stay together, separately from the rest.

Over the past few weeks, Michael had overheard one too many conversations about moving, visiting, who would live where. "Sissy, stay with me and Nana Bear," he implored.

She almost said "always," but that wasn't a promise she could keep. When they got back to Oklahoma, Wendy would be leaving Michael behind. Lily and John and Ms. Roberts-Darling, too. "I'm right here," Wendy replied instead, giving him a quick hug and kissing the top of his head. When Michael held up his toy, she kissed the top of Nana Bear's head as well.

Frank twirled his hat. "What is Wendy exactly? You know, if she's not Lost."

"If you don't mind him asking," a cheeky Oliver added, stealing the hat.

"Wendy is a storyteller," Peter declared as Oliver and K. D. began playing keep-away with Frank's hat. "I have brought her here to tell bedtime stories so we can be a proper family."

"Tonight?" Wendy pressed. "You brought me here to tell a story tonight?"

"Tonight, certainly," Peter said with a bright grin, though what he meant was that night and ever after. "Now, Belle, it's time for a Fairy dusting, so we can give Wendy a first-class tour of her new home." But the Fairy was nowhere to be seen. Of late, she wasn't constantly hovering about Peter the way she used to. He added, "Wendy and Matthew's new home."

"I'm *Michael*. Not *Matthew*." The four-year-old was

famously easygoing, but he knew his name. In his very young life, Michael hadn't met anyone he truly disliked, but he was already developing mixed feelings toward Peter.

"Belle!" Peter shouted. "Belle, where did you fly off to?"

The Fairy reappeared then, in a gorgeous swan dive through the air. Spinning, she sprinkled a dash of glistening golden Fairy dust on each of them. A far, far less generous dosage than the one Wendy and Michael had received in Tulsa and on their journey to Neverland. It might reasonably be assumed that Belle was stingier with the dust *only* because the very quick trip awaiting them would be over in a moment or three. That assumption would be wrong.

Meanwhile, Ethan intercepted the black top hat and returned it to his brother Frank.

Wendy felt trapped, tempted to make a run—or rather, a flight—for it with Michael. But again, where would they go? Where in the world was Neverland anyway?

She reached for the phone in her pj's pant pocket—still no signal. K. D. had been telling the truth. The whole island was a dead zone.

They needed, if not Peter's help, then at least Belle's to return home safely. So, with some trepidation, Wendy gathered up her brother. A couple of wonderful, lovely thoughts later, she (spring tulips!) and Michael (orange Popsicles!) floated with the Lost to the top of an uneven ring of hollow tree trunks. One for Frank, one for Ethan, one for Oliver, one for K. D., one for Peter—which Belle gracefully descended, and one for Wendy . . . and Michael. Each functioned as a slide.

It was time for a less wonderful, less lovely thought. One that would allow them to whoosh downward, but not so fast that they would plummet. By nature, Wendy was a high-spirited, optimistic girl. She wasn't used to managing her emotions so carefully or having to navigate such disastrous ramifications if she didn't. She briefly thought of how Lily wouldn't travel with her to New York City, even though Wendy's birthday was only days away—sooner now. Tomorrow? But it was too much, that feeling of rejection, and only Michael's thought of Popsicles slowed their bumpy descent. "Oh, oh, oh!" Michael exclaimed.

"Oomph!" Wendy landed hard on her bottom, breaking his fall.

"That was awesome!" Michael and Nana Bear scrambled up to investigate their surroundings.

The tree-trunk slide had funneled them into a large underground room, punctuated by colorful, stool-sized mushrooms, which—it became apparent as the Lost settled in—were used for that very purpose. The musty space was about twice the size of their bedrooms back home with its earthen walls, veiny from tree roots, and a glowing, warm fireplace. Thin fibers stretched across its length, functioning as clotheslines. Wendy was relieved. Perhaps Peter and the Lost were spotty in their own bathing habits, but at least they washed their clothes. Eventually.

"You can also use doors hidden in the base of each of the tree trunks," Oliver said in a matter-of-fact voice. "It's less dramatic, but a lot faster and more straightforward."

"The tree-trunk slides are so much more fun," Ethan gushed, hanging his bow and quiver of arrows on a wall beside the other three sets.

"Here's to fun!" Peter said, as if making a toast. "That's what we always say, isn't it?"

"To fun!" echoed Frank, Ethan, Oliver, and K. D.— the twin brothers exhibiting far more enthusiasm than the other two. They all raised their hands as if toasting, too, which was a bit odd, but Wendy still regularly played pretend with Michael, so it didn't set off alarm bells.

Somebody could've mentioned *the doors* earlier, she thought, rubbing her sore bottom. "Yes, that really got the blood flowing!"

"Fun," Michael muttered, studying the scorpion that slipped between rocks in the hearth. He knew not to get too close. There were scorpions back home in Tulsa.

Belle had vanished again. Perhaps out one of those convenient hidden *doors*, Wendy thought. Or back up another tree trunk as she and Michael were descending.

Still, Wendy had to admit there was a certain coziness to the boys' abode.

A series of baskets—well lined with makeshift bedding and large enough to sleep in—were secured in alcoves anywhere from two to three feet off the ground along the perimeter.

A shelf made of branches displayed various treasures from Neverland, swiped from the *Jolly Roger*, and places far beyond—a large conch shell, a metal Big Ben keychain with no keys, a decoder ring, random game pieces (a battleship, a rocking horse, a wheelbarrow, a top hat), a set of dice, a miniature white Ford Mustang coupe, a red-and-blue beaded barrette, a harmonica, a flute, a thumb drive, a pocketknife, a shimmering silver thimble, fish hooks, various loose keys, a Rubik's Cube, a New York City snow globe, and frayed storybooks. A blue electric guitar had been propped, already forgotten, against the same wall, not far from a bow saw.

Wendy was starting to relax when she spotted a tarantula scurrying across the dirt floor. Before she could react, Frank scooped it up and lovingly carried it to a clothesline vine. A pet? Wendy wondered. Was it poisonous? If only Lily had been there. She would know.

Having already inspected Peter's collection of treasures, Michael dashed to the freshly sawed tree trunk at the center of the room and sat down with Nana Bear on one of the stout bright mushrooms surrounding it. "What's for breakfast?"

"We call this the Home Under the Ground," Peter declared, ignoring the question. "Don't worry, Wendy! The pirates and Injuns will never find us here. It's the best, most wonderful, Peter Pan–ish place in the whole world. It's the place where we celebrate all things me!"

What Wendy was thinking was that she hadn't seen any Native people on the island other than her own little brother, who needed to be fed soon. She wondered where exactly they might be located, how to reach or send word to them.

That said, she dearly wished Peter would stop talking about Native people in general and stop using that word in particular. Wendy would've fiercely scolded Peter, too, except that she apparently needed him to get herself and her little brother safely home. So much to consider, but Michael was her number-one priority. "How charming, Peter! You have a delightful home."

"Yes, I do," Peter said, as always, reveling in praise.

Indeed, the Home Under the Ground was charming. Perhaps you're weary of your day-to-day routine and are imagining a life of adventure among the Lost. Be warned: For over a century, Peter had brought a steady stream of kids to live with him. However, not one of the current residents—or any before them—had yet to remain there into their teenage years.

Surely, you don't think that's a coincidence. You wouldn't make the mistake of assuming they were all devoured by crocodiles or drowned by Merfolk or impaled by pirates. Surely, you have noticed the kind of person that Peter is and that he always has a deadly weapon in his hand or at his side. No doubt you've picked up on several clues that not all was well in Neverland.

Belle peeked out from between the black-and-blue butterfly-wing curtains of her private apartment, which was no bigger than a household birdcage and positioned in a recess of the wall across from the shelves. The Fairy was every bit as besotted with her compact quarters as Peter was with the Home Under the Ground. How merry they had been in times gone by!

Still no sign of his shadow, she thought. Certainly, it had threatened to abandon them before and even flitted rebelliously about the island. Yet this was unprecedented. Apparently, what Belle had assumed was its typical play-acting in Michael's bedroom hadn't been that at all. The rift between Peter and his shadow was real. Belle was horrified. For the shadow to give up on its own human— what a catastrophe! The very worst of all terrible signs.

Yet did Peter himself notice its absence in the Home Under the Ground? Did any of these children? Did you? The Fairy wrinkled her tiny nose and retreated again.

Michael's stomach rumbled. "Breakfast?" he tried again.

"Right, I'll pick some mangoes," Frank declared. "Bit of dust, Belle?"

"I'll beat you to them," Ethan countered, echoing, "Bit of dust, Belle?"

Everyone paused to look expectantly at her curtains, but they didn't so much as flutter.

With a shrug, Frank began climbing the wall toward one of the tree-trunk slides, using hand- and footholds that Wendy was only then noticing. Ethan followed suit.

"We don't have enough basket beds for both you and your brother," K. D. pointed out.

"He can bunk with me," Wendy said. "After all, we won't be staying long."

K. D. and Oliver exchanged a measured look. "We'll get some vines to weave another one," Oliver said.

"Just in case," K. D. added. Then they were climbing up, too.

This left Wendy and Michael alone with Peter, who leapt up to the center of the Nevertree stump table and began sharpening his sword with a rock. He towered over them in the flickering firelight, and the sound of stone on steel was ominous. Michael blinked up at him, eyes wide.

"What silliness was that, Wendy?" Peter asked, almost too casually. "What do you mean, saying that you won't be staying long? You're our storyteller now. Like I'm the captain, and the Lost are the Lost. You know how the stories go—happily *ever after.*"

Wendy kept her voice light. "But Peter, I have to take Michael home. The rest of our family must be so worried about him. About both of us."

Peter hurled his sword like a spear across the room, skewering an empty bed basket. "Matthew, Matthew, Matthew! He's all you care about." Peter stomped back and forth across the table. "I'm Peter Pan! I brought you to Neverland. Matthew is a—"

"What's wrong with you now?" Belle asked in her

chime-like voice, swooshing, midair, into the underground room. "After all that fuss about wanting a storyteller, you've finally got one. You're just jealous because she pays more attention to Mikey than she does to you." The Fairy made a sweeping gesture at the siblings. "They come as a set. We *talked* about that, remember? Up in the tree in their backyard? You said, 'Fine, a dandy set they shall be.'"

Peter put his hands over his ears and shouted at Belle, "Shut up! Shut up! Fly away!"

"You shut up!" Belle pinched him fiercely on the tip of his nose and zoomed out of range. She retreated to her apartment before he could swat her like an insect.

Peter looked shocked, stricken at the Fairy's betrayal. His nose was bright red.

The thought blazed across Wendy's mind: What if she and Michael *were* stuck in Neverland forever? Peter was a bully, and bullies were never soothed for long.

That did it. Wendy resolved to escape with Michael the first chance they got. Peter and Belle clearly weren't getting along. She'd ask the Fairy for help. And if Belle refused . . . Supposedly, there were Native people on this island. She and Michael would try to find them.

"Peter, I can do so much more than tell stories." Wendy crossed her fingers behind her back. "I'll take on the same chores that the Lost do. I'll work twice as hard—for myself and Mikey."

At the sound of his name Michael piped up. "Where's

Mama and Dad? Where's Spot?"

"Not now, Mikey," Wendy said, but her tone was gentle.

With a shrug, he wandered over to examine the electric guitar. Using a chubby finger, he drew a heart in the dust covering the glittery blue body of the instrument. Michael could imagine Spot's claws on the strings. He missed his parents, but right then, he missed the cat more.

Meanwhile, Peter pulled himself into a standing position, tilted his chin, and clasped both of his hands behind his back. "You are special, Wendy. You know all the stories."

He hung his head as if much put-upon and trudged across the room to retrieve his sword. "Belle has been persnickety lately." He returned the weapon to its scabbard. "And the Lost, not all of them respect me the way they should. Not yet. How I have searched for a storyteller like you who can make us a true family! That's what stories do. They bring families together."

At least Peter seemed to think he needed Wendy. Did that make her and Michael any safer? She could only hope. "Not to worry," Wendy replied. "I've always helped out with Mikey. I'm twelve, you know. The oldest sister of my family and far more responsible than Lily."

"Twelve?" Peter slapped his knees, laughing. "You're ten, eleven at the most."

Wendy was used to people assuming she was younger. "I'm short for my age. Petite. I was the second shortest girl in sixth grade, but I'm very mature. In fact, I'll turn thirteen in two days." She paused. "One day now, I guess."

For a blink, Peter looked as though he'd swallowed a whole baby turtle. Shock turned to dismay, then frustration and fury. *Thirteen?* He flew up his tree trunk without bothering to say goodbye. No one was irreplaceable. Not even a very special storyteller.

CHAPTER

19

Lily and Daniel kicked, twisted, and squirmed underwater, and that is what put their young lives most at risk. Not that they had the presence of mind to realize it.

Neither would you, under the same circumstances.

Lily caught a glimmer of tiny red fish. Daniel kept his eyes shut tight. In those midnight-blue moments, they knew fear, panic, and the salvation of air bubbles, gifts blown like glass by Merfolk lips. They experienced the stomach-plunging sensation of spiraling downward, out through a curving underwater tunnel, and then up, up, up, up into the open sea.

Tick tock. Did you recognize that sound? So did the Merfolk. Like all their people, they were sworn to protect the island and sea from pirates. Presenting themselves as formidable and unwavering was a proven deterrent. They hadn't been trying to harm Lily and Daniel so much as to teach them to cower. Or, as their queen was fond of saying, "Better to be feared than filleted."

Tick tock. What's more, the Merfolk were charged with protecting sea crocodiles and other marine creatures much like the Fairies took responsibility for the tigers and other wild beasts. However, to be candid, Lily and Daniel didn't seem like much of a threat to anyone, and the relations of these three particular Merfolk to humans was a bit more complicated than you might expect. Besides, none of them could bear the thought of any child suffering a grisly death. In fact, they had rescued children before.

And so Meredith and Cordelia released their captives and assessed the crocodilian threat. For a moment, Lily and Daniel floated free in the water, discombobulated, unsure which way to swim. Which direction was the sunlight coming from?

Tick tock. Ripley seized each human by a muscled forearm, using her tail like a paddle to propel them through the salty sea. Together, they rose up, up, up to break the water's surface.

Lily and Daniel gasped. They experienced the brief, weightless sensation of being tossed like sacks, they felt the breeze and salty spray, until, *thwack*, they hit the violet sand. They landed hard side by side, coughing water in the bright sunlight. For the moment, they were safe.

Tick tock. What a relief! If Merfolk hadn't been among the oceans' fast swimmers, faster even than marlins, Lily and Daniel might've perished. If Meredith and Cordelia hadn't peeled off in opposite directions to lure away a certain *tick, tick, tick,* ticking crocodile or Ripley hadn't guarded that stretch of sandy shoreline until Lily and Daniel had sufficiently recovered to move on, well, you can surmise the rest. Suffice it to say, tragedy averted.

However, Lily and Daniel didn't know any of that, and they weren't feeling at all grateful to the ocean dwellers who'd dragged them under in the first place.

"Huh," Daniel said, dripping. *"Cough*, we're back at the beach."

Lily was soaking wet, shaking, and grimy from the sand. She had lost the bedroom slippers that had been a gift from Great Auntie Lillian. "First . . . first, Peter—*cough*—Pan, his creepy shadow and pinching pixie! Then, *then* it was a giant, huge, enormous crocodile! *Cough*. Now, it's Mean Girls with Tails. Is everybody on this horrible island trying to kill me?"

"I'm not." Daniel decided it was healthy that Lily was spitting mad. He took off the leather jacket and tried to wring out the moisture. All that salt water couldn't be good for the coat, but at least they'd have a story to tell back at camp.

CHAPTER 20

"You may never visit unless invited," Belle began, opening the butterfly-wing curtains to her apartment. "I despise intrusions into my privacy. However, this is a momentous occasion, your first day in the Home Under the Ground. So, I welcome you both as my guests."

"Want Mama," Michael grumbled, still hungry, the adrenaline fading fast. He ambled toward Belle's alcove, and when she blew a sparkling, dusty kiss that cascaded across his curly brown bangs, Michael began floating up so he could peer inside.

Remember Belle's special affection for the very young? Perhaps you're wondering the reason for it. There's a simple explanation. Fairies are irresistibly drawn to babies, like Belle was first drawn to baby Peter, cooing in his carriage more than a century ago in Kensington Gardens. On impulse, Belle snatched him to Neverland. She had come to regret that decision.

"Wow!" Michael exclaimed, reaching with chubby fingers into her apartment.

Swat! The tiny blow startled more than it stung, but Michael took the reprimand to heart. No one had ever raised a hand to him before, not even a tiny Fairy hand. He didn't like it.

Wendy didn't need to rise to peer in. The alcove was positioned level with her head.

"Was that really necessary?" she asked.

"No touching," Belle scolded from within her ornate quarters. "No touching of Fairies or their precious, elegant possessions without express permission. Do you understand?"

Michael nodded solemnly. "Sorry."

Wendy put a hand on his back to comfort him. She would've come down harder on the Fairy for swatting her brother, except that she was angling to ask for a favor.

"It's quite all right," Belle said, feeling magnanimous. "Now you know better."

Behind the black-and-blue butterfly-wing curtains, the residence was a lovely combination of a bedchamber and dressing room—what fancy people used to call a boudoir.

Basking in the siblings' attention, Belle draped herself—the back of her hand flung across her forehead—on the couch with club legs. "In case you didn't know," she began with a sigh, "this is a genuine Queen Mab." Then Belle assumed the same pose on the bed, which was covered with delicate, pink star fruit blossoms that gave the alcove a fresh, fruity scent.

From there, Belle rose to admire herself in the looking glass. "One of the last three unchipped Puss in Boots mirrors that appear on the Fairy dealer register."

Wendy was hopeful that Belle's eagerness to exhibit her abode would translate into a willingness to help. That said, the Darling girl wasn't feigning her enthusiasm. Wendy didn't own a dollhouse herself, but she'd always enjoyed studying the miniature furniture when her grandparents took her shopping at toy stores in London. "I adore the chest of drawers."

Belle proudly patted the top. "Handcrafted, an authentic Charming the Sixth."

"The rugs?" Wendy inquired as Michael floated across the Home Under the Ground to the curio shelf, looking for something to play with.

"Early Margery and Robin." The Fairy tossed her hair. "Quite old. Quite valuable. Excellent condition."

Wendy merely glanced at the Pie-crust washstand, though it too was of the highest quality. "That chandelier. It's lovely. It's—"

"Tiddlywinks," Belle declared. "Good eye! I know what you're thinking—however can she afford it? As you might imagine, I'm well compensated by the Fairy queen for this assignment overseeing Peter and the Lost."

Assignment? Wendy thought. So, for Belle, this was . . . what? A mission? A job? The answer was yes and no. Yes, she was tasked with keeping the boys in line. No, it wasn't strictly a business proposition. She and Peter had been together so much, so long, Belle hardly knew who she might be without him. Oh, the fun they used to have! The salad days of yore.

Belle curtsied to Wendy, not minding Michael's waning interest. She had a fairly short attention span herself. "So nice to have such polite, appreciative guests." Belle leaned in. "You know how Peter is. He'd be lost without me, yet he takes me for granted." With that, she burst into giggles. "Get it? Lost? He'd be *Lost* without me."

Given the affection in Belle's voice, Wendy didn't think it was the right moment to ask the Fairy to defy him. She mustered a polite smile. "Well, your apartment is really pretty."

"It's so kind of you to say so. You're lovely company, for a human."

Poor, proud Belle. Watching over Peter and his ever-changing crew was a lonely lifestyle. It had been decades since she'd been welcomed to sip nectar and sample crumpets on a gilded Fairy veranda. Decades since she'd been invited to don her fanciest gown for a Fairy ball.

The other Fairies didn't exactly fault her for bringing baby Peter to the island. They didn't exactly fault her for bringing more human children to entertain him or for the unpleasant fact that many of those children had grown into pirates who hunted them for their dust. They didn't exactly fault Belle for the fact that Peter had slain so many of the wild beasts either.

Then they'd found out about Peter and the *last* lion. Peter and the *last* Neverbird.

The queen had warned her: No further tragedies would be tolerated.

CHAPTER
21

The rolling landscape rose to the base of the volcano, creating rocky drop-offs, some of which bordered the beach. As Daniel hiked through the forest, Lily—whose bedroom slippers had been lost at sea—rode piggyback. Her knees hugged his belly and her arms hugged his neck.

After their harrowing experience with the Merfolk, Daniel decided to retrieve the basket of coconuts later so Lily could settle in with the rest of the Native kids as soon as possible.

"You're saying Peter's been about eleven years old for at least eighty-some years?" As baffling as that may have been, information was empowering. It helped to soothe Lily's nerves.

"So far as we know, at least. He looked to be the same age when Clifford first met him."

"Robot?" Lily theorized.

"He bleeds, he sweats, he pees."

Strictly speaking, that had been a little more information than she needed. "So, he's not a regular kid or a robot. But he's not a grown-up either. He's something else entirely."

"Understatement," Daniel agreed.

"That's . . . weird." Lily frowned. "Peter lured Native kids away from their homes for decades, then stopped, and now he's doing it again." It was not only weird, but also horrible. She realized she'd been thinking too small. She would rescue Wendy and Michael and find a way home. A way home for *all* of them.

Lily kept asking questions—working the problem, as she called it, and Daniel answered as best he could. They were both grateful to their elder Clifford for having gifted them with knowledge of the island, its mysteries and its inhabitants.

Daniel also told her about the Native kids she was about to meet. "We call ourselves 'the United Native Nations.' It's sort of a joke, sort of not. We might be stuck in Neverland, but we know who we are. We don't belong here. We're just doing our best to take care of each other."

By the time they reached their destination, their hair and clothes were only damp.

"We're here," Daniel said. There wasn't a cabin, lean-to, or any form of shelter in sight.

Lily had managed to collect three more red silk pirate ribbons—but none within the last several minutes, for whatever that was worth. She could hear muted voices from above.

Daniel called to the treetops. "Unroll the ladder! We'll climb up."

Normally, the other Native kids took what Daniel said to heart. But, excited by the arrival of a newcomer, they were already on their way down. Lily was eager to meet them, too.

A wiry, short boy in a basketball jersey and workout pants dropped five feet from a thick knobby branch. "Hey, man. Thought you went to fetch food, not another mouth to feed."

"Nice manners, Mateo." Daniel chuckled. "Meet Lily, a Muscogee Creek girl from Tulsa. Way better than coconuts."

"Way better," Mateo agreed. "Good to meet you, Lily. Even though I've developed a real taste for coconuts." Lily took the affectionate teasing for what it was—a good sign. From Daniel, she knew that Mateo was a Navajo boy who had a schoolteacher mom living on the reservation and a construction-worker dad based in Albuquerque.

Daniel briefly lifted Lily's wrist, showing the row of tied red ribbons. "We found—"

"Did you say 'Creek'?" The next kid descended from an unfurling ladder of cut branches and knotted vines. "I'm Terri." She had a fresh, shiny scar, shaped like a crescent moon on her chin, and wore a Spider-Man tee, torn into a crop top, over a long-sleeve black shirt with faded blue jeans.

"And you're Cherokee from Tahlequah," Lily replied with her first genuine grin since setting foot on the island. Lily had cousins who were Cherokee Nation citizens, and Tahlequah was only a little over an hour's drive from Tulsa.

Then Lily said to the final kid, "And you must be Strings, the legendary guitar player."

"Hey, Lily." Strings busted out an epic air-guitar routine. He was a Black Seneca Indian from the Bronx, which was a borough of New York City. "I like writing songs just as much as performing them. My uncle Jake taught me how to play."

"You look, uh, a little more pirate-y than I expected," she said. "Except the shoes."

Indeed, Strings stood out in his white linen shirt, woolen waistcoat, wide breeches, black leather belt, and high-tops with neon-green shoelaces. "Found this stuff on the beach the same day I got to the island before I met up with Daniel. Near as I can figure, a pirate decided to go skinny-dipping and spaced off where he left it. There was a canteen, too."

Squee, snort, squee. Something big rustled nearby. "Up," Terri said. "Up the ladder."

"Feral pigs," Mateo explained. "Best to get out of their way fast."

Squee, squee. Lily knew they could be deadly. She took her turn hurrying up to safety.

"I don't think Team Pan figured me for Native," Strings called over his shoulder. "I think I got dropped off not far from where the *Jolly Roger* was anchored because he'd decided I'd make a good pirate." Strings's tone didn't let on how annoyed he was by that.

When Peter had shown up, Strings had been visiting his grandparents, waiting up for his cousin, who'd gone out on a late-night paramedic call for their Tribe. He and Lily both knew from experience that some people—like Peter Pan—had the wrongheaded idea that all Native people looked a specific way. That said, she hadn't realized that Pan was populating the pirate ship, too. She'd assumed that all the kids coming to the island were either here or with him. It made her wonder: Had Peter separated Michael from Wendy?

Squee, squee. Lily was talking as much to herself as the other kids when she announced, "My brother and stepsister—Peter has them or maybe *pirates* have them." Her eyes welled. "Mikey's only four years old."

Squee, snort. Squee, squee.

Daniel was worried that his new friend was about to hit a breaking point. From below her on the ladder, he said, "Try not to worry. We'll come up with a plan to find Pan and your family. Meanwhile, you really need to get some rest."

Squee, squee. The ladder was a lot longer than Lily had expected. How high up were they? How much farther did they have to go? She risked a glance at the feral hogs foraging in the forest below. They were furry and fierce, gray and brown, piglets and adults, some with sharp tusks. How long would it be before they moved on? She had come all this way, survived so much already to be stuck in the trees. "But Daniel . . ."

He said, "Listen, maybe those Merfolk only meant to scare us off, but we still could've drowned. You must be—"

"What?" Mateo, Terri, and Strings exclaimed at the same time.

"Did you say 'drowned'?" Terri added.

Squee, squee. "Do you have *any* idea where Peter lives?" Lily asked.

Hooking an arm around the ladder, Daniel spotted her as Strings and Terri helped Lily onto a platform in the treetops. Mateo said, "We think, *think*, he and the Lost bunk up north toward the Fairy Wood, but that's a lot of terrain to cover. Most of the time, we try to avoid them."

Avoid the pirates, Lily thought. Avoid the wild animals, Merfolk, Fairies, Peter, and the Lost. She understood their strategy. She saw the wisdom in it. Lily had spent much of her life dodging potential threats. Despite everything, she yawned. Maybe Daniel was right. Lily was so, so, so tired, but she couldn't sidestep the conflict ahead, not if she wanted Wendy and Michael back.

"Flying gives Peter and the Lost a huge advantage," Mateo added, gesturing to welcome her inside. "They're usually the ones who find us."

"What a treehouse!" Lily breathed, taking in the sight. "Wow, I'm impressed."

Lily snoozed away most of the day—curled in one of four hammocks that slowly swayed in the treehouse while her new friends started weaving three more. The feral hogs moved on. Daniel went to fetch the basket of coconuts and returned again. Lily dreamed of lake fishing, then of the sunny afternoon when her family had adopted Spot from the humane shelter.

She blinked to blurry wakefulness. Lily could still hear the dreamy echo of her cat's mewing. The hammock felt confining. Something screamed—sharp and piercing— from the palm-leaf camouflaged roof, and suddenly she was wide awake! But where? Where was she? Where was Wendy?

It took Lily a long moment to process that the scream had come from a tropical bird, that she was in Neverland. She gulped, overcome by the strangeness of it all.

Then Lily remembered being separated from Wendy and Michael. She remembered the new friends who'd welcomed her. This was their treehouse. Lily focused on her breathing—in and out, in and out. She climbed out of the hammock, nearly stumbling. No need to panic, she told herself. No need at all. No, she'd been doing fine so far. In fact, the Lily of yesterday never would have imagined herself being so brave. Keep breathing, she thought. Work the problem. Where had everyone gone?

Through the window Lily spotted Terri braiding her hair, decorating it with tropical blooms and the red pirate ribbons as she kept watch. Having a quiet moment to herself, Lily took advantage of the opportunity to study the maps covering the walls, all signed *Clifford*. She took note that the treehouse was on the southwest side of the island, toward the southernmost tip. Meanwhile, *The Lost* was marked to their north, bordering the *Fairy Wood*. *Shipwreck Rock* was located just offshore of the other side of the island in *Merfolk Lagoon*. Good to know, Lily thought. She could only hope that Wendy and Michael had been spared any scary underwater encounters. Or worse. "Hang on," Lily whispered. "I'm coming."

Clifford had also managed to map the underground cave tunnel network. With her finger, Lily traced the subterranean path leading from the cave with the grotto to the general area marked *The Lost*. Would that subterranean route allow her and the other Native kids to avoid the Fairies, to avoid the pirates, Pan, and predators? Or would the Merfolk block their way?

"This place is really something," Lily said to herself.

"Wado," Terri replied from the doorway. "My family owns a treehouse-building company. Sometimes I help out." She handed Lily a banana and a coconut bowl filled with cooked fish, dried seaweed, and star-shaped berries.

Terri was glad that the newcomer had managed to get some rest. She was relieved that Lily seemed to have a healthy appetite. As Lily ate, Terri made small talk to put her at ease. Among other things, Terri assured Lily that the blessings of the island included that biting insects, if there were any, tended to leave humans alone. "Daniel thinks it's because we've all had some Fairy dust exposure, but between you and me, he's been using magic to explain a lot lately." Terri added that the boys had gone fishing. "We talked about it because we pretty much talk over everything. But everyone agreed right off. Lily, we'll all help you find your brother and sister. We'll fight Pan or the pirates for them if necessary. Whatever it takes, we're in."

"Mvto," Lily said, her heart full of gratitude. "Then what?"

"Big picture, our plan is to stay together, stay alive— feed and protect ourselves, intercept and train new arrivals. We take turns keeping watch."

"What about going home? *Home* home. Daniel seems to have given up hope, but—"

"We tried approaching a few Fairies for help," Terri said. "Belle's not the only one on the island. Not by a long shot." She touched the scar on her chin. "Didn't go well. I don't think it was personal. It's like they were angry with all humans. Probably something Pan did."

Like the Merfolk, Lily thought. Mad at humans. The berries tasted delicious. "How did Peter lure you to Neverland, if it's okay to ask?"

"He already had Mateo," Terri replied. "Our moms are close friends from way back. They were roomies at

Arizona State. My family was visiting his family when Mateo went missing. Apparently, Pan dosed him with dust in the middle of a dream, and I—"

"You came to rescue Mateo. Like I came to rescue Wendy and Mikey."

"Yeah." Terri began pacing. "Did Daniel mention that I'm two-spirit?" Indeed, on the trek through the forest, he had mentioned that and said, "It's 'Terri' with an I. Terri as in she or her." Terri didn't usually blurt out what was on her mind, but she had been longing for someone to talk to about what had happened, someone who wasn't a boy themselves. Plus, there was the fact that Lily was from home. It made confiding in her feel like the natural choice. At Lily's nod, Terri went on, "I think Pan assumed that I was a boy like he is."

That sounded just like Peter, Lily thought. Making hurtful assumptions.

Lily said, "I'm so sorry that—"

"Thanks, add it to the list." Terri shrugged. "One Hundred and One Horrible Things Pan Has Done. The thing is, he normally *only* takes boys like himself. Because of course the more like him you are, the better he thinks you are." It merits noting that though it had been some years since the last one, Terri was by no means the only kid that Peter had lured to Neverland on the false assumption that they were a boy like him.

"But you're here. I'm here." Lily set aside the bowl. "My stepsister, too."

"Exactly. It's a break in his pattern. Pan can be impulsive, random. But so far as we know, for more than a century, he's made a point of bringing only boys to Neverland."

"So, you think it means something?" Lily asked. "That he's changing somehow?"

Rwowowow. It was high-pitched, somehow cute. "Did you hear that?" Terri hurried outside to lie on her stomach, peering over the treehouse platform at the floor of the forest.

"A cat?" Lily had moved beside her. "Sounds young. Its mother probably isn't far."

Below, the boys approached with fresh-caught seafood, mostly striped clams, and a young tiger cub. "The mother is dead," Daniel called. "Come on down."

Terri unfurled the ladder. Fueled by fresh fruit, fish, and a love of baby mammals, Lily cautiously followed her to the forest floor, gripping tight to each rung on the way down, where Mateo was mostly unsuccessfully leading the cub on a woven-vine leash. Or perhaps "playing tug-of-war" with the cub would be a more accurate way to put it.

Lily estimated that the tiny tiger was about six to eight weeks old and weighed between ten and thirteen pounds. It was also furry and adorable and in a cranky mood. *Rwowowow*.

"Not enough that all the lions are dead." Daniel clenched his fists. "Now Pan has slaughtered the last adult tiger. There are a few adolescents on the other side of the volcano, but—"

"Do we know for sure that it was Pan?" Lily asked.

Mateo replied, "We know it was killed with something pointy."

"We've spied on the pirates when they've come ashore," Strings said. "So far as we can tell, they hunt for food, not sport. Sheep, mule deer, wild cattle . . ."

"Always keep your distance," Daniel reminded them. "We have enough to worry about without taking on the crew of the *Jolly Roger*." He grimaced at the memory of tales Clifford had shared from his teen years aboard the ship, tales of mayhem, of a Captain Jameson who punished the slightest hint of mutiny with a stroll on the plank, ending in a grisly death of blood and water. Captain Jameson, who had first trained a certain overgrown crocodile to crave the taste of human flesh. Terri moved to start a fire as Daniel threaded tuna through a spit. Lily, whose family considered a roadside motel "camping," admired their survival skills.

"The cub caught and, I think, ate a little lizard on the way here," Mateo said. "But that may have been an accident. It needs milk."

"Too bad we can't ask the Fairies for help," Daniel said. "They tend to the animals of the island. Probably the best we can do is goat's milk. There's usually a herd on this side of the island, south of the volcano. We should be able to find it on our way up toward Pan's hideout."

Watching the cub roll over, Lily felt a sharp pang of longing for her cat, Spot.

The cub was too young to fend for itself. As the campfire flared, Lily decided not to mention that they probably couldn't trust the adolescent tigers not to kill it. As Mateo tied its leash to a tree trunk, Lily circled the young animal. She'd watched videos of tiger cubs playing with littermates. A pity that it was alone. Making a happy chuffing noise, the cub scampered after a fluttering black-and-blue butterfly.

"We can't tame it," Lily said. "Tigers are wild animals."

Mateo held up his hand to show thin, bloody claw marks. "Tell me about it."

"You should wash that with boiled water," Terri said, "just to be safe."

"Tigers are an endangered species," Lily went on, thinking out loud. "Not only here in Neverland, everywhere in the world." She wasn't pleased. The cub so vulnerable and yet another responsibility. "We'll have to take care of it until we get home, and then my mama will figure out something—maybe an animal sanctuary or a rescue zoo." Lily wished she'd studied tigers more carefully. She missed the library. She missed the internet.

Rwowowow. Nobody had anything to say to that. The other kids were sensitive to Lily's feelings, but they'd all been on the island longer.

Daniel wasn't the only one who'd lost faith in the possibility of returning home.

CHAPTER
22

With a wet, dead splat, a gleeful Peter thumped the decapitated head of the mama tiger onto the Nevertree stump table in the center of the Home Under the Ground.

"Whoa!" Michael exclaimed as Wendy, with a gasp, covered his eyes. The Roberts-Darlings weren't vegetarians. They fished. They had relatives who hunted for food. But this was something else entirely. It was blood sport for selfish reasons.

Belle burst out of her apartment, buzzing Peter's head, pinching his ear. "How could you? Are you trying to kill off *all* the large, wild beasts?"

"Hey!" he protested. "Stop that!"

"How dare you!" She pinched him again, harder this time, and on the nose again. "The birds and *animals*, the Merfolk and sea creatures, and most of all, the Fairies—we are the beating heart of Neverland." Belle dodged his efforts to swat her away. "You, you—you silly ass!"

"You'll regret calling me a silly ass!" Peter nearly crushed her with a loud *clap* of his hands. "I'm sick of your bossiness, Belle! You're not the captain. I am!" Peter's off-key attempt at a musical voice was a mocking mimicry of Belle's own. "'Don't do this, Peter! Don't kill that, Peter!'" He sprang into the air, drawing his sword with one hand, grasping for her with the other. "I am the boss of the Home Under the Ground, Belle, and you—you're a lowly squatter!"

How vile of him to say such a thing! To her, a Fairy, on her own island . . . and in the home they had made together. Words could hurt like weapons or even worse sometimes.

In a spirited chase, Fairy and boy sped up, down, criss-crossing, and in uneven, hectic circles and zig zags around the room. The chaos reminded Wendy of Peter chasing his shadow in Michael's bedroom, how that had seemed all in fun, how she'd joined in and encouraged Lily to do the same. This time, there was a steelier edge to Peter's pursuit. He wouldn't really harm Belle, would he?

"Sissy?" Michael looked at her quizzically. "Is Peter a silly ass?"

"Yes, stay down." Wendy tucked alongside him for cover against the base of the table.

"Nobody around here needs you anymore, Belle!" Peter shouted, inches from catching her. "All you've ever been good for is Fairy dust, and now I can fly without it."

She gasped, wounded. "You'll . . . you'll . . . you'll

rue this day, Peter Pan!" Belle escaped up a tree-trunk slide. *Whoosh!* She flew away from the Home Under the Ground.

As she wove through the leafy branches, Belle stewed in fury, despair, and resignation. She tried to push aside misty memories of a very and truly young Peter who took joy in assisting her caretaking of the Fairy Wood, how he had painstakingly repaired dragonfly wings and returned fallen Neverbird fledglings to their nests. How he had gathered colorful, sweet-smelling blooms to refresh her apartment, how he had charmed their frequent visitors from the Fairy court.

The first inklings of a troubling turn arose not long after Peter began regularly flipping through one of his storybooks at bedtime. Before long, he began stealing children from beyond the Neversea, pitting them against each other in hopes of bringing the book's pages to life. Then came the vicious clash with Captain Jameson, Peter's spiral of grief, his wild beast hunts, and the dire punishments he inflicted upon those who failed to fulfill his tyrannical whims.

And now, what was left for Belle, the high-spirited Fairy who had brought home a boy who never grew up, but to grovel in apology before her queen?

Meanwhile, in the Home Under the Ground, Wendy thought, Wow. Peter really was a malicious, spoiled brat.

Now that the fray had dissipated, she rose slowly, bringing Michael up alongside her. She would protect her brother, whatever it took, and instinctively Wendy knew it was not wise to cower before Peter.

Thud, thud, thud, thud! The Lost returned—K. D. and Oliver with coiled vines, then Frank and Ethan with sunny mangoes—through the tree trunks, landing on their bottoms.

Peter rubbed his sore nose, shrugging off his spat with Belle. "Wendy, are you and Ma—Michael ready for breakfast?" Peter bowed, suddenly cheerful again. As though it were nothing, he added, "We used to eat shark and dolphins, but the Merfolk put a stop to that."

"We are *not* eating that tiger head," Wendy replied.

"The head is not for eating," Peter informed her, washing off the blood on the striped fur with rags and water from the pot on the fire. "Maybe the brain. We could roast the brain. Then we'll hollow out the head for a hat. K. D. could use a tiger hat and skin to wear. Right now, he looks ridiculous. But for now, the head makes a spectacular centerpiece, don't you think?"

"No, I do not." In fact, Wendy was rather a fan of K. D.'s soccer uniform. It was a reminder of the life they had all left behind. Fighting the urge to vomit, she summoned her courage and, using both hands, carried the dripping tiger head behind one of the large mushrooms alongside the fireplace. With Michael trailing her, Wendy set it on the dirt floor, out of view. "That'll do for now. But Peter, you should be ashamed of yourself."

"First Belle, now you, too?" Peter sulked toward Belle's apartment and punched the underground wall next to the entrance, tilting the black-and-blue butterfly-wing curtains sideways and rattling the Tiddlywinks chandelier. "Take that, silly Fairy!"

The Lost stayed out of it. K. D. and Oliver tied off the thick vines they'd gathered, which they hung on an iron hook. Frank and Ethan used water boiled in the cast-iron pot above the fire and scraps of cloth to clean the stump table. Then they folded a swath of denim into a makeshift mat and placed a small pile of ripe mangoes on it, erasing any reminder of the tiger head.

It was Oliver who dared to speak up. "Breakfast!"

Wendy, her brother, and the Lost gathered round the table on the stool-sized mushrooms.

When Michael reached for a mango, Peter shouted, "No! Those are for dessert."

"Don't yell at him," Wendy scolded. "He's a little kid. You . . ."

Under the table, K. D. knocked his knee against Wendy's. He was whispering, almost like a prayer. "My parents are Alex and Cory Anders and my baby sister is Jewel and my best friends are Isaiah and Hailey and my soccer coach is Mr. Ryan and I'm from . . . I'm from . . ."

Seated across from her, Oliver announced, "I know

what I want for breakfast."

"Muffins!" Ethan exclaimed. "Salmon."

"Yuck, who likes salmon?" Frank put in. "How about sausages and tea?"

"Pancakes," Oliver added. "Juicy blueberry pancakes."

Joining them at the table, Peter laughed heartily. "Apples and gingerbread!"

Now, if the children had been at a restaurant, ordering from a waiter or perusing a banquet buffet or delighting in the bounty of a well-stocked home kitchen, the conversation wouldn't have seemed too remarkable. But nothing of the sort was going on.

Instead, Peter and the Lost appeared in earnest to be eating—raising their cupped hands to their lips, chewing and swallowing—except there was no food (other than the untouched mangoes) on the stump table. It was as though their breakfasts were invisible.

"Yum!" Oliver exclaimed with a big grin. "Maple syrup!"

"Delicious!" Frank put in. "Like Mum used to make." As the last word left his lips, a panic crossed his freckled face. The Lost froze in place.

Wendy was baffled, and Michael, whose stomach overrode his better judgment, grabbed a real fruit. Did the four-year-old enjoy pretend games? Of course. But he hadn't eaten since John's graduation reception the night before . . . or was it a couple of nights before?

Michael bit in deep, and mango juice ran down his chin.

"Mothers," Peter muttered. "Fathers. Parents! Bah! Who needs them anyway? They're so old and demanding. All they're good for is telling bedtime stories, and we have Wendy for that." Or so Peter had hoped, but it was turning out that she was old and demanding, too. He narrowed his eyes at her. "Pray tell, Wendy, what have you chosen for breakfast?"

"Fruit punch." She took a pretend sip from a pretend cup. Wendy hadn't forgotten, even for a moment, that Peter was armed. She had to choose her battles, for her safety and Michael's. "With chocolate-raspberry cake." She used an imaginary fork to take a delicate imaginary bite.

Bang. Peter's fist landed hard on the trunk table, and everyone flinched. His moods were as changeable as the Neverwinds. "An inspired choice!" he declared.

Everyone cheered, except for K. D. He was still struggling to remember where he was from.

CHAPTER 23

Belle knelt, penitent, at the base of the dais beneath the Fairy queen's throne.

"The last full-grown female tiger!" Queen Mab, Protector of Neverland and the Wild Beasts, held her tiny crowned head in her tiny bejeweled hands as if she was in excruciating agony. "It wasn't enough that your pet human had already slaughtered her mate. At this rate, the island will be bereft of wild beasts. We Fairies are the Guardians of Neverland, Belle, or did you forget that?"

"I did not, my queen." It wasn't the first time Peter had gotten her in trouble.

The normally gossipy Fairy nobility had fallen silent, their luminescent wings still, their piqued expressions hidden behind elegant, tiny fans made of twigs and blossoms.

"Why, pray tell, should we continue to tolerate his presence? What little good he does in distracting the pirates is insufficient to justify these tragedies. You must return him to . . ."

Belle swallowed hard. "Kensington Gardens?"

"Yes, wherever, the world of human beings. Your foundling has grown into a monster."

Belle felt the tug of loyalty. Though he could be dangerous, even deadly, Peter couldn't fully fend for himself, especially outside of Neverland. He was a bit like an orphaned tiger cub that way. "Begging your pardon, Your Majesty. It's not Peter's fault. Not entirely."

Not that anyone else could tell, but Queen Mab had a soft spot for Belle, the famously rebellious granddaughter of her most adored handmaiden. "Rise and explain."

Belle drew herself to her full height of four and one-fourth inches. "As you know, Peter has been enchanted with quite a lot of Fairy dust over the years—more than any human in history—making him more playful and imaginative, enabling him to fly." Belle left it unsaid that *she* had been the one who had done the dusty enchanting. "However, the magic has resulted in a few less desirable"— what was that expression humans used—"side effects."

The queen drummed her fingers on the arms of her throne, which was decorated in Neverbird carvings. "Such as?"

"A boost of happiness, a slip-slide into forgetfulness. It also slows aging." Belle gathered her thoughts, daring to articulate what she'd only begun to admit to herself. "Over the past century, Peter—though always unruly—has become . . . cruel. His pirate nemesis—the one called Jameson—was a terrible influence." She swallowed hard. "I'm not certain Peter even has a conscience anymore."

"Whatever makes you say that?" asked the skeptical queen.

"His shadow has abandoned him—permanently."

The Fairy nobility recoiled as if one. Their wings fluttered in dismay.

"I see," the queen said. "For the time being, do as you will, Belle. But know that you will be held responsible for any further crimes committed by your pet . . . what is it called again?"

"Thank you, Your Majesty. I named him 'Peter Pan.'"

Fire crackled in the lava-stone hearth. Tropical birds, tending to their chicks, rustled in the trees connecting the Home Under the Ground to the forest above.

Wendy and Michael had slept much of the day. By the time they'd awakened, refreshed, Belle had quietly returned, and the decapitated head of the freshly slain tiger was gone. She and Peter appeared to have reconciled. He was on his best behavior, skipping around, playing a jaunty tune on his tarnished silver flute. The Lost had gathered around the hearth, poised on large colorful mushrooms, finishing their feral-pork stew.

"I won again!" Belle exclaimed, teaching Michael how to play a Fairy game. She'd employed a sharp twig to draw lines and circles into the earthen floor and piled up translucent peach- and golden-colored jingle shells to use as markers.

"You cheat!" Michael countered.

"I do," Belle agreed. "I really do."

"After dinner, bedtime!" Peter announced, never mind that the two new arrivals had only just awakened. His crew had had a busy day, and "bedtime" could be a several-hours proposition. "Wendy, a story, if you please!"

"All right!" She could think of worse things. Wendy gathered the old books from the display shelf, and the silver thimble poised alongside them glowed.

Leaving Michael to arrange tiny seashells in tiny piles, Belle flitted to Wendy's shoulder. "I brought home that one!" The Fairy pointed to a collection of tales—full of royalty, witches, dragons, and, yes, Fairies—that long, long ago she had come across in baby Peter's carriage, along with another storybook that, only moments ago, he had tucked out of view.

Returning to a hot-pink stool-sized mushroom to the left of the hearth, Wendy flipped through yellowed, illustrated pages of evil crones, helpless princesses, coura-geous princes, spells, curses, and menacing dragons. Not one heroine hinted of the spirit of her beloved Ella.

"And where did that book come from?" Peter pointed to the collection of pirate legends, his tone begging for credit.

"You pinched it!" Belle exclaimed, giggling. "Pinched it from the nursery of one of the earliest Lost." From her merry tone, you might conclude she'd completely brushed aside Peter's crimes against the wild beasts and was unbothered by her own queen's rebuke and warning.

You would be wrong.

"I don't recall that," Peter mumbled. "I don't recall that at all."

"You don't recall a lot of things," Oliver said. "Do you recall the female tiger?"

"Or the last lion?" K. D. asked.

Frank and Ethan shouted together, "The last lion is dead!"

Wendy ignored the boys' respective preening, prodding, and efforts to ingratiate themselves with Peter. The first page of the pirate book depicted a bound and blindfolded captive at sword point, walking the plank above stormy seas. The fourth page was all swords and cutlasses, booming cannons and gunfire, severed limbs and dead bodies. Recalling the babyish pirate décor in her brother's bedroom, she said, "I'm sure you've heard of all these before. I'll make up a story." With that, Wendy returned the books to the shelf, exactly as they'd been before with the Rubik's Cube functioning as a bookend.

An hour or three later—it was hard to say for sure—the large, subterranean room was quiet except for Wendy's voice. "The good-hearted queen gave Lucia a choice. Now that the senator-princess had triumphed in many adventures and rescued her friends from the hungry monster, she could either stay with them in her new home in the woods or return to her family, where—"

"That's *not* how the story goes," Peter interrupted— not for the first time. "The queen is an evil, old witch and the princess is young, meek, and beautiful. So, they hate each other and—"

"Didn't you bring *me* here to tell bedtime stories?" Wendy countered. She wished he would settle down, but Peter, always restless, was hopping from one colorful stool-sized mushroom to another. It was getting on her very last nerve and making it hard to concentrate.

Her brother and the Lost, however, were utterly engrossed by every word she said.

Michael hugged Nana Bear. Frank and Ethan hunkered lower in their hanging bed baskets. K. D. was playing with the snow globe of New York City, and Oliver was cleaning his fingernails with the pocketknife. Belle had retired for the evening, though she was listening.

Wendy tried to explain. "Peter, fairy tales are often different from place to place. They change over time. Think about 'Cinderella,' 'The Goose Girl,' 'The Elves and the Shoemaker,' *Spider-Man* . . ."

"Spider-Man!" her little brother piped up.

Technically, Spider-Man appeared in superhero stories, not fairy tales. But Wendy and Michael adored the character, who had been reinvented a lot. Frank and Ethan traded a bewildered look, as if on the verge of remembering . . . something.

Peter plopped down on a turquoise mushroom. "But young princesses always hate their wicked, old stepmothers. The stepmothers are always horrible to them."

Wendy remembered how Ms. Roberts-Darling brought long-stemmed roses to her ballet recitals, made time for just-the-two-of-them days (usually highlighted by ice cream and matching pedicures), and lovingly nursed her through last winter's flu. "No, that's not right."

Peter stomped his foot on the ground like a toddler. "Yes, it is."

Wendy decided to let it go rather than bicker pointlessly. Peter didn't know anything about any kind of parent, except perhaps Belle. And that certainly wasn't going well.

Arrooo! A rising howl permeated the tree trunks, roots, rock, and soil to reach the Home Under the Ground. "Wolves!" Peter said, brightening. "I'll—"

"You stay put." Belle burst out of her apartment. "Wolves belong to the island." For the space of a breath, the aloft Fairy hesitated before saying, "Listen to Wendy. She's in charge until I get back." With that, Belle took glittering flight up a tree trunk to investigate. *Arrooo!*

Peter reared his head and leaned on his toes. Who was Belle to tell him no? Should he follow her anyway? What if he missed out on a wolfish adventure? And what was that about Wendy? A girl in charge? Impossible! Peter could hardly wait to rid himself of her—and soon!

Wendy had no idea her pending birthday had pushed

his always fickle nature into overdrive. To distract him, she called, "I know! Let's *all* tell Peter a story. Boys, what's your favorite make-believe story from home? Frank, how about you?"

"Am I Frank or are you Frank?" one of the twin brothers asked the other.

Wendy was almost positive that Frank had been wearing the top hat, but it's not like he couldn't have handed it off to Ethan. As she was trying to puzzle that out, the most disturbing thing happened. Oliver said, "I thought I was Ethan."

And K. D. scratched his head. "I thought we were all Ethan."

Peter laughed like it was the funniest thing he'd ever heard. "You're not all Ethan. You're all Lost. You've always been Lost, and that's the most you'll ever be."

Until that moment, Wendy had been almost certain she could count on Oliver and K. D. to support her against Peter, if necessary. She got up and strode over to K. D.'s bed basket, setting a firm hand on his shoulder. "You are K. D. Your parents are Alex and Cory Anders and your baby sister is Jewel and your best friends are Isaiah and Hailey and your soccer coach is Mr. Ryan. You're from Toronto." When he didn't react, she added, "It's in Canada!" Wendy didn't know a whole lot about Canada, but she was a fan of the Winter Olympics. "People play hockey there."

A glimmer of memory rose in K. D.'s eyes, but he

blinked it away. "I don't know what you're talking about."

She was shaken. Hadn't the Lost known their names only hours earlier? She pointed at herself. "I'm Wendy." Then she pointed to her brother. "Who are you?"

"Mikey!" he shouted, and she felt a warm glow inside.

Wendy tried again. "Boys, what's your favorite make-believe story from home?"

As you might imagine, the Lost were unnerved by the mention of their true homes, for Peter fiercely frowned upon that subject. But somehow the fact that Wendy was the one asking, and asking about stories specifically, subtly shifted what happened next.

"Go ahead," Peter encouraged them. "Answer the question." Did that sound as though Peter was being supportive? He wasn't. Rather, Peter considered the question a test of the Lost's allegiance. It couldn't be fully assumed until they'd forgotten their former lives entirely.

"A beautiful princess—" Ethan began. "She ran away from home, into the woods."

"Her evil mother was trying to kill her with a poisoned pear," Frank added.

"No, no," Oliver put in. "It's the stepmother, always the stepmother who's the villain."

"Told you!" Peter crowed.

"Stepmothers aren't like real mothers," K. D. said. "And it wasn't a pear."

As Peter nodded his approval, Wendy muttered, "Not this again."

"A mango!" Peter said. "A poisoned mango and a sleeping curse and no parties for the princess until the brave prince saves the day." Sneering at her, he declared, "Old witches are the worst. Old people are the very worst. That's why we—what, boys?"

"Never grow up! Never grow up! Never grow up!"

They began bouncing in their bed baskets—causing Oliver's to tumble. Then they bounced out around the room, breaking into head-banging, bottom-shaking, shoulder-sliding dance moves and mimicking the light, airy way—spinning in circles and clasping hands—that Fairies danced, too. "Never grow up! Never grow up! Never grow up!" Frank or Ethan bumped into Michael's basket, jostling it loose, and it slid down the wall, tilting him out onto the dirt floor.

"Mikey!" Wendy sprang across the room, kneeling to check on him. "Are you all right?"

No bumps, no bruises. He grinned up at her. "I'm okay, Sissy."

"Never grow up! Never grow up! Never grow up!" the Lost carried on.

Wendy asked, "Mikey, what's your favorite story from home?"

Now, keep in mind that Michael had always been surrounded by Story. Wendy and Lily (and sometimes John or Ms. Roberts-Darling) read to him every night at bedtime. Mr. Darling watched animated stories, often about superheroes, with Michael on TV and at the movie theater. Michael heard stories of generations past and present from Auntie Lillian and other elders around kitchen tables, and sometimes they all went together to community events with storytellers, too.

"Never grow up! Never grow up! Never grow up!"

"Could y'all please hush?" As an Oklahoma twang rose in her voice, Wendy sounded quite a lot like her own stepmother, Ms. Roberts-Darling. "That is so annoying."

Baffled by Michael's hesitation—he often had strong opinions when it came to bedtime stories—Wendy asked again, "Mikey, what's your favorite story from home?"

Across the room, in front of the fire, Peter was whistling and twirling his silver flute, pretending not to be interested. Although he'd already categorized Michael as a pirate, Peter hadn't forgotten the four-year-old's proclamation of Indigenousness.

While Peter seldom to never admitted making a mistake, he had been fretting to what degree the Fairy-dust magic might work on an Indian.

Peter had a lot of wrongheaded ideas about Native people—what a surprise it had been to him that they still existed at all! And Peter had noticed that the Indian boys on Neverland held tight to their original selves. That said, their exposure to Fairy dust was limited to only the dose that transported them to the island, as compared to the Lost, who received more dust, courtesy of Belle, every time they flew off on an adventure. So, there was that to keep in mind.

"Mikey?" Wendy nudged, slightly alarmed. She noticed something in his toppled bed basket—*The Wild & Wily West* storybook, which Peter had slipped in there when she wasn't looking. Michael reached for it. "Home now."

"No, no, Mikey," Wendy insisted. "Tulsa is your home." She lowered her voice so only he could hear. "Muscogee Creek Nation, not Neverland. Think of our dad and your mama and Lily and John and Auntie Lillian and Uncle Hank and Aunt Deidre and Cousin—"

Michael pointed to her. "Mama Wendy." He opened the book. "Read?"

So, this was where Peter had picked up the term "Injun." Wendy leafed through pages of illustrated caricatures of Native people. Garish, monstrous men colored bright red, wielding bloody tomahawks and hollering Hollywood-style "war whoops."

Peter tossed up the flute, caught it one-handed, and curling his fingers round, punched up with his fist. He shouted, "Never grow up! Never grow up!"

The Lost chimed in. "Never grow up!"

"Never grow up!" another voice echoed. "Never grow up!" It was Michael's.

Wendy stared, aghast, at her little brother as Peter concluded, "Never grow up . . . or else."

CHAPTER
24

Hiking north, the Native kids hovered along the edge of the forest bordering the beach. That was the surest way of not getting lost while also staying mostly hidden from threats. The terrain was uneven, rocky, and rolling. It slowed them down.

Daniel, in the lead, kept a loose grip on the handle of the serrated knife at his waist. He gently plucked off a caterpillar that had somehow landed on his wrist and set it on a leaf.

Lily tripped over a thick gnarled root and nearly fell to her knees. Luckily, the Seminole elder Clifford had pointed Daniel to a stash of clothes and other belongings, long stored in a trunk, protected in a cave. Lily had chosen pucker-toe moccasins, a red calico shirt that fell past her knees, and blue jeans. "Could we move out and walk on the lava rocks?"

"We don't want Pan to spot us from the sky," Terri

explained. "Or the pirates at sea to catch sight of us in a spyglass."

"You'll get used to the rain," Strings said as the clouds began to sprinkle. "It comes off and on practically every afternoon. Nothing serious, more like pockets of spring showers."

"Showers that make the air more humid," Mateo added.

Morale could've been higher. The Native kids had only a general idea of their destination and how to find Wendy and Michael once they reached farther north. They knew nothing of the Home Under the Ground. They had no knowledge of Peter's fall from grace from the Fairy queen or Belle's precarious status among her people. So far as they knew, Peter had thousands of tiny, magical, flying allies, any of whom could readily alert him and the Lost to trespassers.

Rwowowow. The cub begrudgingly followed Mateo on a leash. Or rather Mateo patiently followed the cub on the leash and periodically picked it up and set it pointed in the right direction. Along the way, the hikers had no trouble locating a mama goat, who had been blessedly accommodating of Mateo's request to share her milk. The tiger cub was well-fed.

"What are you?" Lily asked Mateo with a smile, slightly envious of his obvious hands-on expertise. "Some kind of zoologist?"

"Hardly," Mateo answered. "But I know a thing or two

about goats, and my big sister fosters kittens. They're a lot easier to handle, but . . ."

A *lot* easier, Lily thought. The cub was cute now—an adorable striped furball with wide eyes and chubby paws, but eventually, its bite and claws would become deadly. The little tiger didn't sleep as much as Lily expected. She theorized that the way time passed on the island had affected tiger development and behavior. She wondered if the animals of Neverland could survive anywhere else.

Daniel pointed out to sea. "There, ahead! The *Jolly Roger*'s on the move."

With its two bold masts and the skull-and-crossbones flag, the ship was an impressive, menacing sight. A shadowy contrast to the vibrant beauty of the sparkling water and puffy gray clouds in the sky. Staying low against the rocks, the Native kids sprinted for the highest point ahead for a better view. Mateo, who'd wrapped his hands in leather, scooped up the tiger cub.

The rain was coming down steadily. "The ship is turning away from the island," Daniel said. The others watched in silence, shoulder to shoulder, peeking over a flat black rock.

"They're moving at a fast clip," Strings said.

"The captain is stubborn," Daniel explained. "Keeps circling the island, trying to ram the ship through the veil. From what Clifford said, they've tried, failed, and repaired the *Jolly Roger* several times over the years. Maybe they're trying to find a weak point, but there isn't one."

"Maybe it's not stubbornness," Terri mused. "Maybe it's optimism. Hope."

"Maybe they finally caught a Fairy," Strings mused out loud.

The Native kids and tiger cub resumed their steady trek north in silence. Lily remained alert for any sign of bears or boa constrictors in the nearby forest, of a *tick-tock*ing crocodile along the sandy shore. She'd correctly deduced that the wildlife of the island was a mash-up of creatures naturally occurring—or perhaps supernaturally occurring—and those long ago brought by sailors.

"What's worse?" Lily wondered out loud. "Life with the pirates or with the Lost?"

Strings kept his gaze to the sky, watching for Pan. "It's got to take a lot of hands to sail that ship," he mused. "And a lot of work to maintain it."

"Mikey's not big enough to help," Lily said. "They wouldn't consider him useful."

Terri tensed at a glimpse of something large overhead, relaxing when she realized it was only a flamingo. "Life with the Lost has got to be all Pan, all the time."

Rwowowow. Mateo couldn't help smiling at the baby growl. Fortunately, tigers liked water more than other big cats. Finally, the rain slacked off.

The hardest thing for Daniel about having been the earliest arrival of the new group of Native kids in Neverland was passing on the most terrifying truths he'd learned from Clifford. The first was that there was no way home.

And the second? From what Lily had said, her stepsister Wendy was about her same age, and that worried him. The Lost they had encountered so far all had appeared younger than the Roberts-Darling girls. Clifford's most disturbing warning was more urgent now. Daniel began, "Back in the olden days, a few runaway Lost managed to escape to the Native kids living in the caves, who took them in. But most of the Lost runaways joined the pirate crew."

"Running to us makes sense," Terri said. "But why the pirates?"

"Desperation," Daniel explained. "Ignorance, prejudice—a lot of the Lost were afraid of so-called wild Indians. Who knows, maybe they still are." He rolled his eyes. "Anyway, about the Lost . . . I guess you could say they have an expiration date. Once they turn thirteen, it's like Pan decides they've betrayed him somehow by growing up. So, he punishes them."

Wendy's thirteenth birthday! Was it today? Tomorrow? Lily wasn't sure. She forced out the question. "Punishes them how?"

There was no gentle way to say it. "He feeds them to that big crocodile, the one with the loud mechanical clock inside."

CHAPTER

25

Wendy awakened to find three long, inch-thick, sky-blue ribbons and a pair of navy tennis shoes, only a size too big, waiting at the foot of her bed basket. They were much better suited to traipsing around the forest than her flimsy bedroom slippers. Pleased, Wendy rolled two of the ribbons to tuck into the toes of the shoes and tied the third in her curly hair.

She was even more delighted to find sneakers in Michael's bed, too—a perfect fit!

Peter watched, perplexed. How strange of Belle to have procured such thoughtful gifts! She must've slipped through the veil and returned while everyone else was sleeping. Why hadn't she brought him something instead?

What a pointless endeavor! The little one hardly mattered, and Wendy wouldn't be needing shoes of any kind much longer. Alas, through no fault of Peter's, the girl's usefulness was running out. She had clearly announced that her thirteenth birthday was on the horizon, and thirteen was a clear gateway to becoming an oldster. What a shame it was to have to rid himself of her so soon, but what else could he do? "Happy birthday, Wendy! How do you want to celebrate?"

The Lost, Wendy, Michael, and Nana Bear were stunned. Well, Nana Bear was as stunned as a plush toy could be. It was not Peter's way to think of anyone else before himself, let alone to *ask* them what they wanted. Belle knew better, though. She was already on guard.

"Thank you, Peter." Wendy dearly longed to celebrate with her family in Tulsa, in New York City, in London—anywhere except Neverland. "Hm, let me think a moment."

Normally, Peter didn't associate birthdays with a calendar and countdown to a candle-lit cake. It wasn't about that for him, so much as about a feeling.

You know how adults sometimes exclaim, "Why, you're growing up so fast!"?

That had never happened to Peter, who'd transformed from baby to toddler to child slower than any human ever before. Now that he could fly on his own and his shadow wasn't holding him back, Peter might well remain the boy he was forever.

But he could recognize "growing up" in other kids and sought to smite them for it.

Wendy tried out her new shoes. "Peter, would you please take Oli—I mean, would you please take the Lost out to collect mussels and papaya for breakfast?"

"Would you like a bear to roast instead? I can go hunting and kill a bear."

Wendy pursed her lips. "No bear. Papaya and seafood." She glanced at her little brother, who was clutching Nana Bear like it was in danger of becoming breakfast. "You're okay, Mikey. Nobody is going to hurt Nana. I promise."

Bringing their bows and arrows, the Lost climbed up the walls to leave by the hidden doorways in the tree trunks. They held on tight at the top and waited for Peter to take the lead.

"Off we go, men!" Peter crouched slightly, as if to spring into flight and . . . hopped instead. Tried again. Hopped again, landing off-balance. "What in blazes?"

Frank asked, "Should we come down?"

"No, no," Peter said with a puzzled expression. "I'm . . . I'm gathering my energy."

He crouched, arms extended, and leapt! Landing— *thud*—in a heap on the earthen floor. "Ow!"

"Peter," Ethan whined. "Our arms are getting tired." As the walls were slightly curved in, the Lost were forced to hold tightly to knobby roots. Their muscles were beginning to shake.

Peter backed against the far wall, took a sprinting start and . . . *jumped*, failing to launch for a third time. The weary Lost landed, *thud, thud, thud, thud* on the dirt floor. They barely managed to maneuver their bows and quivers to prevent them from breaking.

"Belle, Belle!" Peter called. "Wake up! I need a fresh dose of dust."

Parting her newly repaired, butterfly-wing entrance, the Fairy—who'd been peeking with great interest at the unfolding situation—leaned out of her apartment. "*You* need dust? You've had enough dust for a lifetime. Many lifetimes!" She sniffed. "In fact, I recall you saying that you don't need me or my dust to fly anymore." And hadn't we all taken Peter at his word?

"A fresh dose gives me zing!" Peter refused to admit, even to himself, that he'd been wrong about being able to fly without her help. Not quite yet apparently. "Come on, Belle!"

"You have zing enough." She covered her tiny, pointed ears. "Listen to Wendy. Go. Fetch food. It's too early for you all to make so much noise. I require my beauty rest."

Belle was pleased with her declaration. Without the power of flight, Peter would lose his advantage of ambush from the skies. The wild beasts would be more likely to hear him coming and could more quickly flee or defend themselves. A stubborn, loving part of her even hoped that, if Peter wasn't looking down on the island so often, it might diminish his superior view of himself, his sense of entitlement to destroy at whim. Yet Belle knew—especially given the absence of his shadow—any chance of Peter changing for the better seemed slight at best.

Meanwhile, Wendy could sense an opportunity. She

took down the newly dry clothes from the vines strung across the room. Michael and Nana Bear did their best to help fold them.

"But Belle, you need me!" Peter implored—big smile, oozing charm. "And not only for breakfast!" He drew his sword. "I'm the one who protects the Fairies from pirates, remember?"

This declaration riled up the Lost, who began stomping around the room. "Death to pirates!" Frank and Ethan shouted. "Death to pirates!" the other two Lost boys chimed in.

"The *Jolly Roger* is having a go at the veil again," Peter added. "It's only a matter of time before they try to snatch a winged magical passkey. Or should I say, until they try again?"

"Shiver me timbers!" Ethan exclaimed. "Arrrg!" Frank added.

Michael bounced up and down. "Pirates!"

"Don't you start," Wendy scolded.

Michael protested, "But Mama!"

"I am *not* Mama," Wendy enunciated clearly. "I am your sister, Wendy."

"Sister Wendy," he grumbled. Michael could pout with the best of them.

"Belle!" Peter shouted. "I am your captain. I order you to dust me and my crew."

The quite comfortable temperature of Neverland was

one of the least changeable, most pleasant things about the place, but suddenly, there was a distinct chill in the air.

As an alarmed Michael cowered against Wendy, Belle flew outside her apartment, hovering. "I bow only to the Fairy queen. You are not my captain. *I* am responsible for *you*."

Wendy was pleased to have that spelled out.

"Children need playmates to be happy, healthy, and whole," Belle acknowledged with a sweeping gesture. "Well, here they are. You are supposed to be Captain of the Lost and Sworn Protector of Fairies! I've done my job, Peter Pan. You figure out how to do yours."

He'd survived her temper, unscathed, many times before. Peter oozed across the dirt floor. "How about a kiss? Blow me a kiss of dust, Belle! Just a kiss, that's all I'm asking."

"A thousand times, no!"

"Belle, so help me!" Peter raged. He pined for the dust—for the vicious glee it sparked in him, the magnification of his Peter-ness. He depended on the dust to fly. But most of all, Peter needed it to stay young, to stay a boy forever. And apparently, he hadn't absorbed enough to do without more. Almost—*almost*—but not quite, shifting the balance of power back to Belle.

Wendy was fascinated and inspired. She caught the Fairy's eye and made a subtle shooing gesture, indicating that Belle should clear the room so they could talk privately.

The Fairy brightened and rubbed her hands together. "Very well!"

"You changed your mind?" Peter asked. "Lost boys, atten-*tion*!"

"Not entirely." Belle curtsied, winked at Wendy, and zipped above the military line of the Lost, zigging in front of Frank's top hat, zagging in back of K. D.'s noticeably longer hair, zigging around Ethan, tugging a lock of his red curls, and finally zagging in back of Oliver, pinching his full cheek. But she left Wendy, Michael, and, to his chagrin, Peter untouched.

As the Lost, fueled by wonderful, lovely thoughts of romanticized pirate battles, began to rise from the earthen floor, Peter opened his mouth to protest. Then he abruptly closed it again, and in an impulsive, defiant moment, rushed to the curio shelf.

Grinning maniacally, Peter shook the shimmery silver thimble over his head, showering himself in the pinch of Fairy dust he'd painstakingly gathered and stored just in case he needed more when Belle was off at the Fairy court. "A thimble is as good as a kiss any day." Floating, he exclaimed, "Ha-ha, Belle! I've shown you. Nobody says no to Peter Pan!"

Blasted begonias! Belle thought. "That won't last long, and it's all you'll get—you have my word on it." She stuck out her tongue, and pivoting on one heel, turned her back on him.

Peter squared his shoulders, smoothing his locks into a

less unruly state. Belle could be so stubborn, he fumed. Surely, she couldn't be serious. Or, even if she was, he was certain that the Fairy would soon forget about their quarrel. Peter relied a lot on forgetting.

"Buzz off on your errands," Belle said. "And while you're at it, *leave the bears alone*!"

Whoosh, whoosh, whoosh, whoosh, whoosh! Peter and the Lost flew away.

CHAPTER
26

Belle rubbed her pointy chin. She'd experienced a moment of relief when Peter had struggled to fly. But that pinch of dust in the thimble! Could it have tipped the scales?

Could Peter truly fly completely on his own now?

Pacing in midair in front of her apartment, Belle realized it was too soon to say. She should've been more careful with her dust. She'd never expected Peter to do anything as meticulous and conniving as to gather and store it. She wouldn't underestimate him again.

Wendy folded the last of the clean laundry, a pair of faded jeans with a hole at the knee. Now that the Home Under the Ground was empty except for Belle and Michael—who was still comfy in his outer-space pj's—Wendy changed into an *I ♥ NY* T-shirt and those same jeans, making sure to switch her phone to the back pocket. She was normally more of a ruffles and lace girl, but it would do.

"Thank you for the sneakers and ribbons," Wendy ventured.

Belle was too preoccupied to respond. She had little interest in housework or drab human apparel, so dreary compared to Fairy fashions. Yet it was clear, even to someone with wings, that the siblings' bedroom slippers were insufficient for forest trekking. Besides, Michael was her favorite, and today was his sister's birthday—poor thing. The blue ribbon in her hair did complement her eyes, Belle thought. Wendy didn't *fully* appreciate how much she might need the shoes, that she could soon be running for her life. The Fairy had been in her apartment, paying the children no attention, when Wendy had mentioned turning thirteen to Peter.

What had inspired Belle? Once upon a time, she had gloried in fetching delightful presents from beyond the veil for her Fairy friends . . . back when she had Fairy friends.

What a lonely thought! Belle refused to dwell on it. She wasn't a mopey worrywart. She was a free and festive spirit, the most well-traveled Fairy of the Neverland royal court.

"Hey, Belle!" Michael called, as if first catching sight of her.

"How are you?" she replied, charmed by his random enthusiasm.

"A turnip can't be a fire engine," he said, which is the kind of answer that makes perfect sense if you are a four-year-old or a Fairy.

Heartened, Belle glided to the curio shelf, snatched the white Mustang coupe toy, set it on the tree-stump table, and, using it like a skateboard, began performing tricks to entertain him.

Wendy was impressed that Belle had drawn a firm line with Peter. She'd initially figured the Fairy for a sort of magical sidekick, like she'd seen in many stories featuring a hero from home and a strange being from a fantastical world. But that wasn't the case at all.

"And how are you today, Belle?" Wendy asked, reaching to turn on her phone.

"Me?" Belle paused with one foot on the table. She smoothed her glistening leafy skirt. Had Peter ever inquired after her well-being? Not in recent memory. Perhaps never. "I'm . . ." She thought about it. "Not entirely satisfied with my circumstances. Thank you for asking."

"I'm sorry to hear that." Still no cell service. Wendy took a seat on an aquamarine-colored mushroom near the stump table. "It's something we have in common, though. I'm not . . . entirely satisfied with my circumstances either. I need to take Mikey and go home to our family."

How boring, Belle thought, disappointed in the human girl. Most children new to Neverland whined about the lives they'd left behind, though Peter didn't tolerate that for long.

"Belle, you flew us here. You could fly us back. Would you, please?"

Meanwhile, Michael and Nana Bear were carrying on their own conversation. Wendy could've sworn she'd heard him mention Spot's name, but she wasn't 100 percent sure.

As you'll recall, Belle adored babies and toddlers but only tolerated children, even intriguing ones. Humans might start out as squishy, leaky, and endearing, but then they degraded to occasionally useful, and finally, in adulthood, became a threat. Then again, Wendy had shown grand courage in the face of Peter's temper. Belle recognized something of herself in the girl.

Wendy changed tactics. "Neverland is lovely, by far the most, um, exquisite place I've ever visited. I'd like to learn more about it and those who live here." Hopefully, that sufficiently buttered up the Fairy, and she'd be more forthcoming, Wendy thought. "I've noticed that you don't have a shadow. Neither does Peter." She took a breath. "Why not?"

"Fairies don't *need* shadows. Fairies emit a magical glow, which is far more elegant. Our relationship with light and darkness is entirely different from yours." It was refreshing to have children paying attention to *her* for a change. Clearly, these two were of far better character than the other Lost children that Peter had brought there.

Belle pushed off, and Wendy took a photo of her surfing on the roof of the toy car, leaning with her arms extended to try to turn it before the wheels soared off the table.

"Woo-hoo!" Michael cheered, waving Nana Bear.

The little Ford Mustang banked a hard right, and Belle hopped off a second before the toy careened to the dirt floor. She curtsied to the four-year-old before returning her attention to his sister. "Humans have shadows. The Lost have shadows. So do the Indian children on the southern tip of the island."

Michael was still focused on the tiny sedan. "I'll save it!" He rushed to pick up the toy.

Meanwhile, Wendy wondered, which way was south?

Belle explained, "Grown-up humans are disappointing, monotonous people. So, I enchanted Peter with Fairy dust again and again and again and again so that he wouldn't grow up."

"Wouldn't grow up?" As the truth slowly dawned on her, Wendy remembered the boys' chant—never grow up, never grow up, never grow up.

Michael returned the toy car to the tabletop. "Again?"

Wendy asked, "Peter has lived on the island for a very, very long time, hasn't he?"

At Belle's nod, Wendy swallowed hard, putting her phone away. There was something a bit vampiric about Peter Pan. "But you didn't dose him before he left. You refused."

Belle favored Michael with a smile and waved her hands to sprinkle dust on the tiny car. She did a handstand on the hood as it glided through the room. Belle's dust had imbued the toy with magic. Still, she felt weighed down by her queen's disapproval, by Peter's misdeeds, by her own role in the matter. "Peter wasn't entirely wrong earlier. He's been enchanted so often over the years that soon he really may not need more Fairy dust to fly. Maybe he's reached that point already because of that thimbleful. How I wish I'd known it was there!"

Wendy didn't fully appreciate the gravity of the situation. "You're upset that Peter won't need you for more dust? That he'll be able to fly off whenever he pleases?"

"Worse." Belle swung her body forward, feet first, through her arms to rest on the hood of the car, eye level with Wendy. "Peter *shouldn't* be able to fly on his own. That magic is too big for a human being. It may well cost him his humanity. He's becoming something else, something monstrous, something well beyond my control."

CHAPTER 27

Wendy had heard enough. "That's it. We're leaving now!" Bracing her legs, she tore a mushroom from the ground and placed it alongside the dirt wall. "Mikey, come over here."

Alas, Belle thought, there go the only two humans she could more than tolerate. The Fairy watched Wendy and Michael climb up on the formidable fungus. She didn't offer any assistance, but she didn't try to stop them either. Belle was still preoccupied with Peter.

After all, the Fairy thought, his own *shadow* had abandoned him. For worse and better, humans were defined by the actions they took, reflected by the shadows they cast. Peter's shadow had been so repulsed by him that it had split off entirely. It refused to have anything more to do with the way he lived his life.

Of course, Belle and Peter's shadow were old friends. She had faith in its judgment. Upon reflection, she admired it for breaking ties, forging its own path.

Talking mostly to herself, the Fairy said, "I'm finished with Peter, with all of this nonsense. I have no further interest in humankind."

Wendy wasn't sure how to answer. She settled for "Okay, then." With that, Wendy boosted her brother up. "Climb, Mikey, climb!"

"I am climbing!" he insisted. "Don't forget Nana Bear!"

"I would never forget Nana Bear." Wendy wasn't sure what to say in farewell to the obviously disgruntled Fairy. "Um, nice meeting you, Belle."

The Fairy, feeling dejected, didn't deign to reply.

Holding Nana Bear by the ear with her teeth, Wendy used the knobby hand- and footholds to climb up and out of the trunk into the forest. Once she'd crawled out the hidden door of the tree, Wendy helped her brother up, stood, reached for the phone in her back jeans pocket and checked the compass app. "That's south." She took Michael's hand. "Come on. Let's find the Native people."

"Here we go, Sissy!" The island quickly realized that they were hiking steadily in the direction of Lily and her Native friends, who were, in turn, advancing toward them. Perhaps the kids would've all met up rather quickly in a heartfelt and celebratory reunion, except that the island had other things in mind.

Caw, caw! A tropical bird perched on a high branch— bright blue and green, shaped like a crow. *Caw, caw!*

"Pretty bird, Mama!" Michael exclaimed.

"Yes, pretty. But I'm your *sister Wendy*, remember? Sometimes you call me Sissy. Sometimes you call Lily Sissy, too."

When Michael failed to react to Lily's name, Wendy recalled the striped brown snake that had crossed their paths shortly after their arrival on the island. K. D. had warned that venom could be more deadly to a small child like Michael because of his lower body weight. What if Fairy dust worked the same way? What if it was eroding Michael's memory more quickly than it would have a bigger, heavier kid's?

Out of habit, Wendy raised her phone to take a picture of the bird and realized her photo app was a treasure trove of memories. She checked the image she'd taken of Belle. It was a blurry glow. Apparently, Fairies were far too brilliant to be captured in photography.

"Here, look." Wendy crouched beside Michael. "That's a picture of your mama playing minigolf. Remember how she putted the ball into the mouth of the make-believe gator and got a hole in one?" Wendy scrolled. "That's our dad washing her minivan. He's all wet!" She swiped at the screen to advance to the next image. "There's John in his cap and gown for graduation. Do you see the eagle feather? Oh, and here's Lily reading on her bed with Spot."

"Spot!" Michael laughed. "Spot and Lily!"

Wendy laughed, too. "That's right, Spot and Lily! And here are your great aunties Lillian and Zella and Betty and Bea. They stopped by last week on their way home from antiquing."

"Mama?" Michael breathed. "Where did Mama go?"

"Hang on . . ." Wendy found a happy picture, taken on Mother's Day at a local barbecue restaurant, of Ms. Roberts-Darling with Michael seated on her lap. He'd been planting a messy kiss on her cheek, and she'd been all lit up with love.

In the vast, mysterious forest, Michael said, "There she is. That's my mama."

"Yes, there she is." As her heart echoed Michael's words, Wendy choked up. Her stepmom had become, in every way that truly mattered, a mother to her. Should Wendy have said yes to the offer of adoption? Surely, her mum in heaven would've approved. Blinking back tears, Wendy added, "Enough pictures for now. We'll look at them again later, okay?"

Wendy's mood swung between overwhelmed and cautiously optimistic. On one hand, she and Michael were alone on a magical island, fraught with enemies and danger at every turn. On the other hand, at least her beloved little brother had regained a grasp on who he was. Plus, with every step, they were getting closer to the Native people. With any luck, together, they would all find a way home.

"What's that?" Michael asked, pointing toward a fluttering wisp of something dark red, hanging from the base of a tropical leaf that was bigger than his head.

Wendy examined it. "A ribbon." Maybe an eighth the width of the sky-blue ones she'd received from Belle. Wendy caressed its length with her fingertips. "I wonder how it got there." Wendy studied the complex knot attaching it to a branch. A sailor's knot, though she didn't recognize it as such, having only been on motorboats. She hoped it was a good sign.

"This way," Wendy said, more confident. "Don't drag Nana Bear on the ground." They'd have to travel through the woods, almost the full length of the island, past the smoldering volcano to the east, and . . . then what?

With any luck, the Native people would find them. Double-checking the compass app, she adjusted her phone to low-battery mode and kept moving forward.

Squee, snort-short. Wendy stiffened as the grunting grew louder.

Squee, snort-short! Feral hogs could be violent, cannibalistic. Lily had mentioned that last bit in the children's area at the Tulsa Zoo over spring break, and Wendy had scolded her that not every factoid needed sharing. But that day in Neverland, Wendy was grateful for the warning. Enough with the blooming forest, she thought. The wild animals, hairy spiders, darting lizards, and thorny plants. "Mikey." Wendy checked her compass. "Let's turn toward the beach."

Squee, snort-short. The hogs sounded farther away that time.

"Happy birthday," Michael exclaimed, suddenly wondering if there might be cake in his immediate future. "Happy birthday—"

"Shhh . . ." Wendy briefly revisited her despair over Lily's refusal to come to New York City and found that her hurt feelings had mellowed. Wendy's birthday seemed so trivial to her now. What difference did it make if she was thirteen, finally a teenager? The bigger question in Wendy's mind was whether she would live to turn fourteen. And an apt question it was. If only you could warn her how truly unlikely her survival might be. *Tick tock.*

Michael tugged her arm. He'd spied a small herd of mule deer. Touched by the look of wonder on her little brother's face, Wendy felt the full weight of how much he needed her.

A rustling in the undergrowth made them flinch. A mongoose slinked by. At least Wendy thought it was a mongoose. If Lily had been with them, she would know for sure.

The forest was humming, rustling with life. Though Wendy wasn't there by choice, she felt like an intruder. Her brother's voice rose up again. "Happy—"

"Hush, Mikey. We'll celebrate later, okay?"

Parting two enormous palm leaves, Wendy stepped onto the black stone and violet sand beach. The cawing, buzzing sounds of the forest faded in favor of the soft roar of incoming waves. She spotted an abandoned rowboat, large enough to carry a half dozen people, upside down on the shore. Wendy and Michael hurried over to investigate. Unfortunately, the vessel was long aged, falling apart. A hole in the bottom had rendered it useless.

"I'm tired," Michael complained.

"Me, too." The clouds started to sprinkle. Maybe they could drag the boat farther inland, take shelter beneath it. Wendy could keep watch through the hole while they rested. At his age, Michael could only be pushed so far. She said, "Let's stop here a while—"

"Miss me?" Peter's voice rang out from behind them. He scooped Wendy up by the arms and lifted her into the air, toward the tumultuous green sea. "Hello, Wendy. Goodbye, Matthew."

"Mikey!" Wendy screamed, kicking, as the Lost surrounded her brother. She saw Nana Bear fall from his hands, tumble down the lava rocks. "Mikey!"

CHAPTER 28

"How much farther?" Lily asked from atop a twenty-foot cliff. She could've sworn the *Jolly Roger* had turned around but lost sight of it beyond the curve of the shoreline.

If only Lily had known what a triumph of seafaring it had been for the vessel to execute those maneuvers in the absence of so many crew members. If only she'd known that the captain's showy display of defiance against the veil had been an act of misdirection.

The Native kids had passed the smoldering volcano in the distance. The Fairy Wood and home of the Lost couldn't lie too far ahead.

The fact that they'd hiked uneventfully for so long might've suggested that Neverland had turned its attention elsewhere. On the contrary, it was plotting mischief.

Arroo, arrooo!

"Can't tell where that's coming from," Strings said. "But there are wolves on the island."

"Maybe they smell the tiger cub," Mateo put in.

"Maybe they smell us," Daniel replied. "I expect that they'll keep to themselves. So will we." He paused, somber. "Peter is a danger to them, too."

Arroo, arrooo! Lily knew Daniel was right, but the mournful quality of the howls sharpened her longing for home, her concern for her siblings. "Could we pick up the pace?"

"Sorry," Mateo said, carrying the yawning tiger at the rear of the group. "My fault. I can take the cub back to the treehouse if the rest of you want to go ahead."

Drinking from a coconut, Terri said, "It's not safe to hike that far by yourself."

"We stay together." Daniel's hand rested on the hilt of his long knife. Clifford had emphasized that the Lost were kids, too—kidnap victims, too, but that in Neverland, they tended to forget who they were. With each flight of fancy, they fell more deeply under Peter's spell.

Lily caught sight of a familiar fuzzy brown lump on the sand. "Nana Bear!" she shouted. She surprised her friends by briefly rushing back in the direction they'd come—then circling around to a more gradual slope where she sprinted, stumbling once, toward the beach. Baffled, most of her companions hurried after her.

"You go ahead," Mateo said, setting the cub down. "We'll wait here." He had mixed feelings about staying behind, but it was important to be careful with the little tiger, too.

Below, on the beach, Lily fell to her knees, hugging Nana Bear. "Mikey!" she yelled, scanning the shoreline, the skies. "Mikey! Wendy!"

Strings reached Lily first, covered her mouth. "Shh! Stealthy, remember? Are you trying to get us all killed?"

Lily nodded, and he let go. "I'm sorry."

Meanwhile, at the sound of Lily's voice, the Lost had paused in the forest. They couldn't quite make out what the voice had been saying, but . . .

"Pirates?" Frank whispered.

"Injuns?" Ethan wondered aloud.

For a flash, both K. D. and Oliver wondered hopefully if someone had managed to pierce the veil and come to their rescue, but then their memories became fuzzy again.

"A girl?" K. D. asked. "Didn't sound like Wendy."

"A pirate then?" Frank theorized. "Peter says there're no girls among the Injuns."

"Is one of us missing?" Oliver mused aloud, counting heads—one, two, three, four.

"Peter," Frank said, and Ethan added, "Peter flew away with a Wendybird."

Not far away, Terri helped Lily to her feet. "We must be close. Don't panic. Little kids lose their toys all the time." At Lily's distraught expression, Terri added, "Even their favorite toys."

"Off the beach!" Daniel called, thinking they'd be safer hidden by the forest's edge.

Daniel couldn't have known the island was counting on him to make that decision.

Lily stood, holding Nana Bear. Holding all she had of her family.

Moments later, Terri held up a leafy branch for Lily to duck under. "You okay?"

"I am." She wasn't, but Lily had to keep her wits about her. Michael and Wendy might be close by. They might be in trouble. They might need her help.

Then—*thwunk, thwunk, thwunk, thwunk*—the Lost dropped from the treetops, their bows drawn, circling Lily and her friends. "We've got you now, Injuns!" Frank shouted.

"Tell me he did not just say that," Strings said.

"Okay," Mateo replied. "I won't tell you."

Arrows flew! "Look out!" Daniel shouted. Terri grabbed Lily, pulling her behind a fallen tree trunk. An arrowhead glanced off the side of Daniel's leather belt, leaving a bloody mark.

"They've got a tiger!" K. D. exclaimed. "A pet tiger!"

"We should kill it!" Ethan added, clearly under Peter's influence.

Fortunately, the Lost were all lousy shots, and their hearts weren't in the battle.

"You'd think we'd have the bows and arrows," Daniel muttered with a grim smile.

Had any of Peter's crews and Native kids ever crossed swords in the past? Yes, at Peter's urging, too often with injuries on both sides. On several occasions, like Daniel had explained, a Lost boy had taken advantage of the chaos to request sanctuary at the Native camp and successfully changed sides for good.

But those Lost were not these Lost, and those Native kids were not these Native kids. Their predecessors had lived and died long before. Besides, Peter was absent, preoccupied with Wendy wherever they'd flown off to. And while Peter and *The Wild & Wily West* storybook had told Frank and Ethan, K. D. and Oliver that "Injuns" were "wild and bloodthirsty," this was their first direct encounter with real-life Native kids on the island, not counting Michael of course. Had they sufficiently forgotten themselves, been so thoroughly won over by Peter that they would battle in fierce earnest? No, not quite. What's more, they weren't particularly skilled at it.

One of Oliver's arrows accidentally knocked off Frank's top hat.

As Mateo crouched over the squealing cub, Terri seized Ethan's bow. "I'll take that."

Strings tripped on the undergrowth, accidentally tackling Oliver as they fell into a flowering bush, crushing Oliver's bow between them, sending grasshoppers flying.

Daniel dodged an arrow, knocked K. D.'s weapon aside with his long, serrated knife, and, pointing it, backed him against a Nevertree. "Nobody move. We don't want trouble."

The Lost were stunned. Why was he so serious? They'd only been playing, right?

"Pan could be anywhere," Terri reminded her friends.

Warily eyeing Frank's and Ethan's tiger skins, Mateo set the cub in the crook of a nearby tree. "Nobody touches the cat."

Lily stormed directly in front of Frank's cocked bow, holding Nana Bear between them as a shield. "Where are Wendy and Mikey?"

Strings and Oliver pushed away from each other, and everyone else stopped whatever they were doing. Then Oliver asked, "Who's 'Mikey'?" Remarkably, they had no trouble remembering Wendy, perhaps because she was a storyteller, perhaps because of the novelty of a human girl having lived—however briefly—in the Home Under the Ground.

"The little one," K. D. said. "I think. He's the little one, right?"

"He's *four*," Lily practically shouted. She gestured. "He's this tall."

"Well, uh," Ethan began. "You can't have Mikey. He's Lost, and Wendy is—"

"Uh, where did Mikey go?" Frank interrupted, lowering his bow.

"I thought *you* had him," Oliver called to K. D.,

struggling to remember names.

"I thought *you* did," K. D. answered, still wary of Daniel's blade.

Lily was furious. "What have you done with my brother?"

"He's not your brother," Ethan said. "He's Wendy's brother."

Lily whirled on him. "What happened to Mikey?"

"That's what I'd like to know!" Oliver explained. "Seriously, where did the kid go?"

Frank put his hat back on. "I don't know."

"What do you mean, *you don't know?*" Daniel asked, bracing for bad news. "Where's Wendy? Where's Pan?"

"Peter and Wendy are together." Ethan raised his hands in surrender. "Or at least they were. Today is Wendy's birthday, her thirteenth birthday, and for some reason, she ran off with Mikey. So, Peter found her and flew off with her over the Neversea."

Oh no! Had Peter already fed Wendy to the giant crocodile? What a dreadful thought!

"We were too late," Lily whispered. It was almost too much to fathom. Michael was missing in the vast forest, and Wendy was gone forever.

CHAPTER

29

Wind swirled, sea churned, and a clock ticked in the belly of the crocodile. *Tick tock.*

"You turned thirteen!" Peter exclaimed in midair, still gripping her by the arms. "And you ran away—after only one night, only one story! How could you?" It was just like him to be furious with her for trying to escape, even though he had decided to rid the world of her anyway.

Tick tock. "How could *I*?" Wendy countered. Unaware of the saltwater reptile tracking them from the waves, she considered twisting free, swimming for shore. Wendy was a capable swimmer—in pools, in the lakes of Oklahoma. She wasn't desperate enough to risk the deadly pull of sea currents, not quite yet. Wendy tried reason. "If you don't enjoy my company, fly me back to Mikey and let us go. I don't belong to you. Neither does he."

Tick tock. Peter called out, "Hello, old friend. Hungry? I've brought a tasty treat."

Wendy dared to glance down, and that's when she spotted the enormous sea creature. It moved like lightning through the rippling, white-crested water, its binocular-like eyes fixed on her dangling feet. "Peter, no! How could you? Why are you doing this?"

Tick tock. Tick tock.

Swirling its scaly tail for propulsion, the crocodile leapt for her, breaking free of the water—and narrowly missed. *Ka-splash!* Down it went. *Tick tock.* The reptile submerged, but Wendy could still see it below the surface of the water. If only she could buy herself more time. "How do you *know* I'm thirteen, Peter? Seriously, I don't even know what day it is." How true that was, for in Neverland, time was baffling. How clever of Wendy to remind him of that! She added, "How long has it been since we left Tulsa? I could still be twelve, right?"

Was she thirteen? Peter had been so certain. And yet he felt torn. He had searched and searched for the perfect storyteller. Maybe he shouldn't feed her to the crocodile so soon. It wasn't clear, even to Peter, whether he might *really* drop her or whether it was all a game, like so many of his battles and escapades. Though you could say the same for his high seas duels with pirates of yore, including a ferocious captain or two who had met their demise.

"Take me back!" Wendy reached up, grabbed his neck with her hands, squeezed tight. "Take me to my brother, Peter, or so help me, we're both going down!"

He choked out, "B-bad form! Bad form, Wendy!"

"If I'm crocodile stew, so are you!"

Tick tock. The gigantic reptile resurfaced.

"Stop that!" Peter shouted. "I'll put you down. I'll put you down!"

"On land!" That point was nonnegotiable.

Tick tock. The crocodile leapt high, jaws wide, dripping salt water.

Wendy screamed, tucking her knees tight under her chin.

Sharp, jagged teeth crashed together inches shy of her toes.

Ka-splash! Down went the crocodile again—foiled—only to be distracted by the distant smell of the Merfolk approaching from farther below it, threatening to intervene.

"Peter!" Wendy tightened her grip. Anyone who knew her as an effervescent, friendly girl from middle school might've been surprised by her grit. But her ballet dancing required discipline, determination, and, up to a point, the willpower to push through pain.

And sometimes, being a good big sister required even more.

"Peter, now!" Wendy insisted. "I'm not kidding!"

Was she thirteen or not? Wendy was petite, Peter had noted. Shorter than all the Lost except baby Michael. She didn't look especially grown-up to him. And, now that he thought about it, did her age matter so much, given that she was a *girl*? Were the rules of growing up somehow different for girls? Should they be? Peter wasn't sure. After all, she was nothing like the girls in his storybook of fairy tales, so how was he supposed to know?

As you may have noticed, Peter seldom arrived at the right answers, in part because he tended to ask the wrong questions of the worst sources.

When it came to gender, his attitude swung somewhere between confused and awful. Usually that was a bad thing. This time, though, it was lucky for Wendy.

"Very well, here we go," Peter said agreeably, powering toward the violet sand beach. "About your birthday . . . How about we give it a couple more passes of the sun and moon?" Then Peter, being Peter, added, "Or another couple of hundred."

CHAPTER

30

Rain fell again, heavier. Peter's crew had been baffled by Michael's disappearance.

What didn't they know? All of them—Frank and Ethan, Oliver and K. D.—had been so distracted on the beach, watching Peter fly above the Neversea with Wendy swaying in his grip, that they'd failed to notice the four-year-old make a break into the fairy-tale forest, only to be seized by the eager hands of pirates lying in wait. Didn't you miss Michael only moments ago when Oliver was counting heads? If not, I'm afraid you're in no position to judge the Lost.

"Mikey!" Had Lily yelled her brother's name before? This time, in her grief and fear, her voice rang out farther. "*Mikey!*" This time, no one warned her to keep her voice down.

"Lily?" Michael called, wide eyed. The generous Neverwinds carried his thin voice from a distance, through the storm. He hadn't known she was on the island. *"Sissy, Sis—!"* A pirate's hand clamped over his mouth.

"I'm coming, Mikey!" Lily plunged into the soggy depths of the forest, carrying Nana Bear under one arm like a football. "Hang on, I'm coming!"

The Native kids were tempted to chase after Lily, but they had the upper hand against the Lost and they were unaware of the immediate threat of pirates. Turning Peter's crew loose might kick off the clumsy battle all over again.

K. D. muttered, "Mikey was with us, but . . ."

"He probably went chasing after . . . after . . ." Oliver trailed off, blinking. "Rabbits, we saw rabbits earlier. Mikey loves ani—" A kaleidoscope of memories flashed through his mind, but Oliver couldn't seize on any of them. He staggered backward as if he might pass out.

"Hey, man," Strings said. "You all right?"

"My . . . my . . ." K. D. was struggling to remember himself, his family. Do you recall his grandfathers' names?

Mateo said, "I think the guy in the bear skin and the soccer dude are sick or something." It struck Mateo, who was sporting his basketball jersey, that perhaps the two groups of kids had more in common than anyone realized. One of the Lost was an athlete, too.

"Daniel," Terri put in. "We can't stand around like this all day. We should go after Lily. She might need our help."

"Everyone, calm down," Daniel replied. "You, Lost boys! Besides being Pan groupies and lousy babysitters, what's your deal? Explain yourselves."

As you are no doubt aware, the Lost, overcome by the Fairy-dust magic, had seemed as if they'd wholly embraced Peter's fantasy life as their own. Were they too far gone? They had felt a lingering responsibility for Michael, being that he was so little. Striving to make sense of what had become of him had triggered other paths of memory as well.

K. D. stepped firmly away from the Nevertree, closer to the point of Daniel's knife. "Peter's a bully. He's . . . I almost forgot but . . . My, my parents are Alex and Cory Anders and my baby sister is Jewel and my best friends are Isaiah and Hailey and my soccer coach is Mr. Ryan and I'm from Toronto." With a furrowed brow, he added, "Pan is no friend of mine. My name is K. D. Anders— after my granddads, Kyle and David. And I'm with you, if you'll accept me."

"That makes two of us," Oliver chimed in, his eyes clear again. "I don't remember my family or my home, but I have a dog, Charlie—he's a Saint Bernard."

But it wasn't a unanimous turnaround for the Lost. "Never grow up, never grow up," Frank and Ethan chanted, bouncing in place. "Never grow up, never grow up."

A flash of lightning lit the sky. Silent gray-and-orange monkeys watched the kids from the trees. Colorful birds, startled to the air by the kids' conflict, began returning to nearby branches.

Strings gestured at the twins. "Somebody had too much sugar for breakfast."

"It's not their fault," K. D. insisted. "They've been here longer than the rest of us."

"Never grow up, never grow up," the brothers continued to chant.

And Peter Pan had been there longer than all of them put together, Daniel thought. He briefly considered filling them in on the fate that awaited them if they stayed too long under Pan's thumb, but he doubted they would believe him or listen to reason.

"Never grow up, never grow up."

Terri dropped Ethan's bow and grabbed him and Frank by the wrists. "Stop!"

They stopped, surprised and deflated.

Terri let go and tried the best thing she could think of to jog their memories. She pointed at the superhero logo on her T-shirt. "Spider-Man."

Frank and Ethan focused on the symbol. Raindrops clung to their lashes, slipped down their necks and beneath the tiger skins. Neurons caught fire in their brains.

It was like a movie montage was playing backward in their minds.

Images of . . . the last lion . . . Belle's Fairy glow . . . the Home Under the Ground . . . Peter's fits of ego . . . and from *before* all that . . . of wide, green seas and a sparkling night sky . . . the lure of magic . . . bunk beds . . . fish and chips . . . an otherwise ordinary rainy afternoon, in front of the television, watching a Spider-Man movie.

"I'm Ethan," Ethan said. "I'm Frank," Frank said.

"Ethan and Frank Taylor," they said together. "221B Baker Street," Ethan added.

In the subsiding rain, Strings chuckled. "That's not their address."

K. D. frowned. "How do you know?"

"That's where Sherlock Holmes lives," Oliver said with a grin.

Strings nodded at him, recognizing a fellow fan.

Rwowowow! The cub had heard the monkeys chattering overhead. Mateo had no idea if monkeys would hunt a cub but hurried to retrieve the young tiger just in case.

"K. D. and Oliver are with us," Daniel declared. "How about you two?"

Frank said, "We're in." Ethan added, "If you'll have us."

From the Native kids' point of view, the alliance nearly doubled their number, though—so far as they knew—Peter still had the Fairies on his side. Daniel lowered the knife and winked at Terri in her Spider-Man T-shirt. "Good job."

In a burst of self-esteem, Terri was reminded that the world was far better off with a certain two-spirit Cherokee geek. Then she called out for her absent friend. "Lily!"

"Lily!" Daniel echoed. She'd been gone too long, and one could never tell when peril might arise in Neverland. "This way, everybody!"

United, off they ran. Daniel in the lead, using his knife to clear the way, Terri trailing him, Strings and Oliver steps behind, slipping in the mud, K. D. with Frank and Ethan—carrying their bows—slightly to their left, and Mateo with the cub, bringing up the rear.

Surprise! *Whoosh, whoosh, whoosh*, up, up, up they went in elevated large snares, the force knocking Daniel's knife from his hand and Frank's top hat from his head. The bows broke in two. Arrows rained down from their quivers into the mud.

Swinging and spinning from the trees, in rope nets, the jumbled kids shouted. "Whoa!" "Yowza!" "Ethan, is that you?" "Let us go!" "Frank, I'm over here!" "I'm upside down!" "Ouch, that's my face!" "Get me out of this thing!"

Rwowowow! The panicked cub's claws narrowly missed Mateo's eyes.

"Silence, sprogs!" called up a husky voice. "You're captives of the *Jolly Roger.*"

Over the next green hill, sunshine split the clouds, and a frothy, multitiered waterfall seemingly burst from the rock, birthing foggy mist and drowning out their voices.

Lily called, "Mikey? Mikey!"

She caught sight of a red ribbon, drooping from a fern. Then another.

Light glinted off a round stone. No, a gold button. Lily plucked it from the black rocks, held it to the breaking sunlight. A skull above crossed cutlasses had been engraved into the round metal. Pirates! she realized. Pirates had kidnapped her little brother.

CHAPTER

31

Almost safe! *Almost.* Swaying in the ocean air above the crocodile, Wendy tried not to squirm, praying it might lose interest. She didn't entirely trust Peter's offer of a reprieve and kept her hands loosely around his neck, but he was flying directly, if a bit wobbly, toward the beach.

Was Peter losing altitude? Again, the reptile leapt, and again, Wendy screamed, tucking her legs under her chin. The crocodile's jaws barely missed her bottom. Peter nearly dropped her.

"Fly higher!" she shouted. "Higher!"

"Stop yelling at me!" He faltered. "Be still!"

"I'm trying to stay alive." Wendy scanned the choppy sea. What was that? Not the crocodile . . . A dolphin? No, not with that long, dark hair and iridescent tail. Could it be? Too bad she had more pressing matters to worry about. "Peter, what's wrong with you?"

"Low on magic. Carrying a passenger takes more power, uses up the magic faster."

She loosened her hold. "A little higher! Try, Peter! Please."

Are you worried? You should be. If the crocodile leapt again, they'd both become a tasty snack. But hold on, look there! Remember the Merfolk? The reptile was swerving, chasing one.

Yes, that was Ripley from the cavern. She routinely patrolled the western shore.

Peter, struggling to remain aloft, hadn't noticed. He descended in an uneven semicircle.

Violet sand appeared beneath Wendy's sneakers. She let go of his neck. "Drop me here."

But Peter's timing was off. Together, they crashed onto the beach. Wendy tumbled into a recovery roll. Peter landed hard on his knees. He squinted at the water. "Is it coming?"

"The mermaid?" Wendy asked, breathless.

"The *croc*! There was a Merfolk?" Peter winced as he checked himself for broken bones—there weren't any, but he'd be bruised, his knees and neck both, come morning. "Of course, a Merfolk would come to my rescue! They're all in love with me. You, Merfolk, Belle, the other Fairies. All the girls love me. Everyone does. I'm irresistible."

Wendy ignored him. "Mikey, Mikey! K. D., Oliver? Frank, Ethan? Where did they go?"

Peter laughed. "I keep telling you, Wendy! The Lost don't remember their silly old names. You can simply call them 'Lost' now. You can call all of them 'Lost.'"

Wendy ached to hug her little brother. "Mikey!"

"Up there!" Peter pointed. "I told the Lost to wait for me on that cliff." He trudged to the base of the incline, his knees still smarting. A far cry from his aerial spins and jaunty marches. He brightened. "Thank you for running off, Wendy! That was the most fun I've had in ages!"

"Fun? You call that fun? I could've been eaten." She whirled on him. "You too, Peter."

He laughed. "That old croc will have to settle for mahi-mahi and pirates." Rubbing his hands together, Peter added, "How I long for a duel with the *Jolly Roger*'s captain, but the ship is out to sea." Brushing violet sand and broken seashells from his leggings, he added, "The Injuns are so boring. Ordinary. They're afraid to go on the warpath against me."

"Stop using mean words and saying ignorant things about Native people," Wendy scolded, hiking uphill. "You don't know what you're talking about, and it's hurtful and mean."

True, Peter had no idea what he was talking about and didn't care enough to find out. "Why is everyone telling me what to do?" He kicked a small rock. "First, Belle. Now, you."

Aroooooo! A now-familiar howling rose from the forest.

Wendy ran ahead to the top of the cliff. "Mikey!

Somebody! They're gone." She wasn't too alarmed about her little brother's safety, not yet. It seemed most likely the boys had all simply returned to the Home Under the Ground or wandered off just beyond earshot.

Peter was too sore to keep up, and for him, it was slow going. By the time he finally arrived to find Wendy alone, he was livid. "I told the Lost . . . I *ordered* them to wait for me here. I will not stand for mutiny!" He turned on her, drew his sword, advancing. Wendy was what was new and different about Neverland. She had to be the one to blame. "Your fault!" Peter exclaimed. "Before you arrived, everyone on the island listened to me."

Suffice it to say this was yet another untruth, but moving on . . .

Wendy took one uncertain step back, then another, mindful of the jagged, forty-foot drop closing in behind her. "Take it easy, Peter."

Aroooooo! "Those howls." Peter frowned. "Maybe the Lost went to investigate."

Inches from the edge, Wendy said, "We should find them, make sure they're—"

He waved the sword. "You silly, silly girl! You're not the one who gives orders. I—"

Twack! A coconut struck Peter's hip, cutting off his thought, rattling his scabbard.

Twack! Another one knocked his sword clean out of his hand.

Wendy lunged for it with a dancer's speed and agility.

Twack! At that same moment, a third coconut collided with Peter's ankle. Wendy dodged past him, gripping the hilt of the weapon. Safely away from the edge, having snatched the sword, she should have felt more secure, but who was throwing coconuts?

"Listen . . ." Wendy waved the blade back and forth between Peter and the woodsy area from which the coconuts had originated. "All I care about is my little brother. The wolves—"

"Not wolves, Wendy." Lily emerged from behind a large boulder, wielding Daniel's knife. "Pirates are howling. Actual pirates! They took Mikey! I think it was an ambush."

"Lily!" Wendy was shocked. "Lily, you're *here*! How did you . . . *pirates* have Mikey?"

"They do. The pirates kidnapped Mikey, the Native kids, and the Lost, too." Lily's voice betrayed no hint of her flooding relief that her stepsister was alive and apparently unharmed. Lily knew that bullies like Peter tended to take advantage of tender emotions. Her radiant joy at finding Wendy alive was none of his business anyway.

Wincing, Peter tested his weight on the sore ankle. He didn't pause to wonder, given Lily's presence, why his shadow hadn't reappeared, too. Though Belle had taken its absence to heart, Peter hadn't given his shadow a second thought since returning to Neverland.

"No, no," Peter protested. "The *Jolly Roger* isn't anchored offshore. It's out at sea."

"Enough of the crew must've stayed on board to keep it sailing. The rest are here on the island." Alas, Lily had tried to intercept the kidnappers, but to no avail. She hadn't so much as caught sight of them. But she had stumbled upon the remnants of the Native kids and Lost. Daniel's knife. Frank's top hat. Fallen arrows. It wasn't hard to deduce that they had been captured, too. She had been wise to bring the knife with her. "Why am I talking to you?" she asked Peter. "You've caused enough trouble. Fly away! Shoo!"

"He can't fly," Wendy explained. "Belle cut off his Fairy dust. He's out of magic."

"You're sure? It could be a trick."

"I'm sure. He does lie, all the time, even to himself. But not about this."

The girls exchanged a weighted gaze. Lily could tell this Wendy was savvier than she'd been before Neverland, that now she had a better grasp on reality. Wendy could tell that this Lily was more courageous and open to possibilities, that she could recognize magic in her midst.

"Go back down to the beach," Lily ordered Peter. "Walk north toward the Fairy Wood." From their vantage point, the stepsisters could watch him depart for a good, long while.

Ignoring her, Peter said, "Now, girls, let's be reasonable. Wendy, we're a family. You, me, Belle, the Lost, and . . . Matthew. Together, we'll—"

"His name is Michael," Wendy scolded. "You heard her. Go."

"At least return my sword. It belongs to me."

"I don't think so," Wendy said.

Lily allowed a half grin. "We'll make you a deal, Peter. Talk to your snotty, glowing sidekick. *If* you can convince her to fly every human kid home and *if* you promise never to bring anyone to Neverland ever again—"

"And never to harm another endangered animal," Wendy added.

Lily nodded. "Then we'll *think* about returning your sword."

"Bad form, bad form!" Peter stomped his foot, forgetting his ankle injury. "Ow!" Hopping on one foot, he reluctantly surrendered. "Very well, I promise."

Wendy Darling and Lily Roberts sat silently, side by side on the cliff, watching Peter limp into the distance as the sun set over the turquoise-green ocean. Nana Bear—who Lily had briefly stashed behind the boulder during the standoff with Peter—sat between them.

"Nice shirt, by the way," Lily said, gesturing to the *I ♥ NY* logo.

"Thanks, nice job with the coconuts," Wendy replied. "Good hand-eye coordination."

"Volleyball," Lily replied. "One of the Native kids, Daniel—he's kind of our leader—he saved me from a crocodile using that strategy when I first arrived. So he gets partial credit." Lily was considerate about things like that.

A crocodile, Wendy thought. She had met a crocodile, too.

For a long moment, the girls gazed at the vile, selfish shell of a boy as he faded from view in the distance. Somehow, they knew they'd never see *that* Peter ever again.

Wendy sighed. "I was wrong to bring Mikey here. You must really hate me."

"Hate you?" Lily teared up. "Wendy, I thought you'd been *eaten* by a giant crocodile." The words tumbled out. "Back home, I was upset. I didn't want you to move away, and I was afraid to get on an airplane, and I took it out on you. When Peter offered a magical—"

"You tried to stop me. I should've listened. None of us belong here, Lily. The Fairies and Merfolk, the land animals and sea creatures—Neverland and the Neversea belong to them. But now, what can we do? I honestly don't know if we'll ever get home."

Perhaps you're wondering if it was Lily who first reached to hug Wendy or Wendy who first reached to hug Lily. Of course, the answer is that it didn't matter, though Nana Bear was temporarily smushed.

CHAPTER

32

Did you forget about the stars? Because they never forgot you, and they never forgot Peter's shadow either. All this time, the shadow had been pacing beyond the misty veil, second-guessing itself. Should it press on to Neverland, return to the human world, or float free in the heavens?

For many years (a generation or two), the shadow had been slowly distancing itself from Peter, ever more repelled by his braggart, bullying, barbaric ways.

Four-year-old Michael had been its breaking point. Targeting a child so young, simply as an afterthought because Wendy was attached to him and Peter longed for a storyteller.

Yet, upon reflection, wasn't *Story* how humans defined themselves, how they connected, how they learned to care? Had Peter's longing for Story indicated an inkling of humanity? Had Peter's longing for Story indicated that perhaps there was hope for him after all?

With every limping step up the black stone and violet beach, pain flashed up his leg and Peter cursed his enemies. "Ow! Blasted Injun girl, injuring my ankle!"

The white-crested waves dismissed him as a sore loser.

"Ow!" Peter's knees and neck hurt, too. "Blasted Wendy, taking my sword. *Stealing* it, really—bad form! I never needed a storyteller. Who cares about silly stories anyway?"

Peter did. He always had. The teeming life of the forest, the pelican overhead paid him no mind.

"Ow! Blasted Lost, abandoning their post, leaving me outmanned . . ." Peter paused on that last word, but he refused to admit, even to himself, that he'd been out*woman*ned.

The albatross soaring across the twilight sky had no patience for his self-pity.

"Ow! Blasted Belle, cutting off my Fairy dust, and after all I've done for her!" His lower lip began to tremble. "Blasted Belle, for taking me away from, from . . . my mother in Kensington Gardens in the first place." He kicked a large, horned helmet shell. "Ow, ow, ow!"

The island was unimpressed. Peter had fallen out of its favor, and as a result, Neverland greatly lengthened his painful, petulant, limping retreat to the Home Under the Ground. From Peter's perspective, the hike felt endless. Then he finally arrived, sore and weary, only to be greeted by gaping emptiness. No Belle, no Lost, no Wendy or Mat—Michael.

Peter's hand fell to the hilt of a sword that wasn't there.

The Fairy had abandoned her apartment, and Peter knew it was serious because her precious furnishings were all gone. The genuine Queen Mab couch with club legs, the bed covered in delicate, pink star fruit blossoms, the Puss in Boots mirror, the Charming the Sixth chest of drawers, the Margery and Robin rugs. Only the Tiddly-winks chandelier remained.

Still, the island held firm. Peter wasn't whisked off to his next thrilling adventure. His aches, pains, and blooming bruises lingered longer than ever before. The side effects of the Fairy dust slowly dissipated. He was left for what felt like countless hours, days, months with nothing but quiet and loneliness to ponder his own misery and all that he had done to bring it on himself. As far as Neverland was concerned, Peter Pan had been long overdue for a serious and substantial time-out.

Longing for company, he retrieved his storybooks from the shelf. The fairy tales, the pirate legends, *The Wild & Wily West*. Peter perched on a bright red, stool-sized mushroom, spreading them out on the stump table. He opened each to the middle, slowly turning pages, no longer comforted by their familiarity. "Lies!" Peter shouted. "Lies, all lies!" He hurled the books off the table. They crashed into the walls, tearing pages and breaking spines.

He sobbed, "Enough."

If only he hadn't harmed so many who he could've loved instead. All his life, Peter had gloried in magic, yet he had been quick to cast aside Belle, who'd been so generous with her gifts. All his life, Peter had longed for a mother, yet he had caused countless kids the pain of separation from theirs. All his life, Peter had longed to play the hero, yet he had become the villain somehow.

If only Peter could write himself a new story! Perhaps not as a kind, patient, or tender soul. Perhaps he would always be a bit impulsive, even a tad self-absorbed, but that didn't mean a life of cruelty was his destiny. Perhaps he would never fully make amends, for not all harms could be undone. Yet with time enough, he could make a good-faith effort. Was it too late for Peter Pan . . . to be not quite so terrible? With enough effort, could he become a likable chap?

Unseen in the crevice alongside the hearth, the shadow contemplated the Lost boy. No matter the century behind him, Peter was still a child at heart, and however vile or wicked they had behaved in the past, every child possessed the ability to grow into a better person. Perhaps not a perfect person; perhaps a few would always be rascals. Still, the shadow had faith that hope and hard work could heal the heart of one selfish boy, that hope and hard work could heal the world.

A lone tear trickled down Peter's cheek, the first he'd

cried since the death of the pirate captain—not the current one (obviously) or the last one, but the one before that. Jameson.

As Peter raised his hand to wipe the tear away, he was enveloped in a loving embrace.

At that moment, Peter finally recognized the shadow gently holding him for what it was—a shifting reflection of his own fragile humanity. He said, "There you are, old friend!"

The rift between them vanished. And together, they wept.

CHAPTER

33

Though Lily and Wendy had reconciled, they were still Lily and Wendy, so it was only to be expected that they had different ideas about how to proceed. All they knew for sure was that Michael and their friends were already aboard the *Jolly Roger* or well on their way to being so.

"The pirates regularly return to the island," Lily said on a cliff overlooking the beach and the Neversea, grateful for all Daniel had told her on their first hike together through the fairy-tale woods. "They keep a small drove of donkeys near the shore, north of Merfolk Lagoon. So, they usually drop anchor there. We could head out in that direction and wait—"

"For how long?" Wendy tossed her a banana. "Anything could happen to Mikey and our friends while we're doing nothing!"

"Do you have a better idea?" Lily peeled the fruit, leading Wendy down the slope, where they were soundly ignored by several flamingos and two feuding crabs in a grudge match.

Wendy had tied vines around Nana Bear's paws, and looped them around her arms, carrying the plush toy like a backpack. "I'm thinking."

"We could follow Peter north," Lily mused aloud. "I do believe he wants this sword back, but if he can't talk Belle into helping us, maybe another Fairy—"

"The Fairies won't do us any good. They barely tolerate humans. Belle is the *only* Fairy who ever had anything to do with us, and she's given that up. Peter included. The last thing she said to me was: 'I have no further interest in humankind.'"

That tracked with what the Native kids had said about Fairies. Lily chose her footing carefully. The rocks were a bit slippery. She didn't want to fall. "Well, unless we wait for the pirate ship to come to us, we'll have to reach it by air or sea, and the obvious choice is—"

"Sea!" Wendy jumped down on the sand.

"I was going to say 'air,'" Lily replied. "I'm not going back in the water."

Wendy was gobsmacked. Could this really be the stepsister who was so afraid of flying? What had happened to her? "The Neversea isn't all bad," Wendy said. "A mermaid may have saved my life!"

"Good for you. Three Merfolk nearly drowned me and Daniel!" Lily frowned. "It's *Merfolk* for all of them. Singular and plural. They don't call themselves 'mermaids.'"

As the girls exchanged stories of their death-defying encounters, the flamingos took flight, startled by a trio of odd birds, about two feet tall, scampering to catch up with Lily and Wendy. They were young Neverbirds and, contrary to belief, not extinct.

"I think we should try talking to the Mer*folk* anyway," Wendy argued. "They could help us safely reach the ship, and it's not like we have a lot of options. If they say 'no,' at least we'll have—"

"The Merfolk despise the pirates," Lily replied, "and they think all humans are pirates."

"All humans are pirates!" a Neverbird repeated as the other two hopped alongside it.

"That wasn't you?" Lily whispered to Wendy, who slowly shook her head.

The girls turned to find the birds gazing up at them, expectantly. The apparent leader raised her proud beak. "Greetings, valiant ones! We witnessed your vanquishing of the Pan, Murderer of Neverbirds, including our beloved parents. What kind of fowl are you?"

"They talk," Lily murmured. "How can they be talking?"

Wendy said, "Don't look at me. You're the one who wants to be a zoologist."

At least the Neverbirds seemed friendly. "You're the one who wants to be a wizard." Which seemed equally, if not more so, on point.

"I'm Wendy." She crouched. "This is my uptight

stepsister, Lily. We are not fowl, er, birds. We're human beings. We're trying to rescue a bunch of human kids from the *Jolly Roger*."

"More heroism!" the spokesbird exclaimed. "How can we reward you?"

It occurred to Lily that, as locals, their new feathered friends might have a better handle on the situation than she and Wendy did. "Uh, do you have any advice for us?"

Flapping, they flittered about. "Merfolk! Merfolk! Merfolk rule the Neversea!'"

Wendy laughed. "That's four votes against one. Mermaid—*Merfolk* Lagoon it is."

Lily exhaled. "Okay, but I warned you." Addressing the birds, she said, "Mvto."

And Wendy added, "Yes, thank you."

As the young Neverbirds scampered off, the island was impressed by the respect the two human children had shown for three of its most precious winged inhabitants and subtly shortened the journey to hurry Lily and Wendy along their way to shelter.

CHAPTER

34

While Merfolk might be found patrolling, caretaking, or luxuriating in any of the local waters, there was only one location where they congregated on a regular basis— Shipwreck Rock, in the middle of their lagoon, reputed to be the most perilous place in Neverland.

Wendy had spied the rock from the air when she first flew above the island.

Lily had only seen it drawn on Clifford's maps.

Because darkness was upon them (and who knew how long that might last?), the girls spent the night in hammocks at the Native kids' treehouse.

Lily asked how Michael had fared among the Lost, and Wendy spoke with trepidation of his moments of forgetfulness. They assured each other that both the Native kids and the Lost boys would look after their little brother, as best they could, on the *Jolly Roger.*

"Frank and Ethan are pretty far gone," Wendy

qualified. "But I don't think they'd make things worse for Mikey." She tried not to dwell on the flying arrows that greeted them upon their arrival above the island.

With a sad smile, Lily said, "Imagine Mikey with real-life pirates. If they weren't so scary, this would be his dream come true."

"He kept asking for your mama," Wendy said. "He misses her so much."

Lily could tell from her stepsister's tone that Wendy missed Ms. Roberts-Darling, too.

Lily breathed slowly in, slowly out. She had braved the starry skies, the emerald ocean, and the mysterious caves. She had been dragged underwater by Merfolk and stalked by a ravenous crocodile. She had made new friends and found Wendy and together they had faced down Peter Pan. Lily had surprised herself by all that she had overcome, all that she had accomplished.

Yet her next words to Wendy were her greatest act of courage since their adventure began. "Wendy, if we somehow make it home, would you maybe . . . change your mind about not becoming my sister?"

Wendy was genuinely confused. "What do you mean? I never said I didn't want to be your sister." She shifted in the hammock. "We are stepsisters."

Lily fully understood that sisterhood—*family*—was about so much more than having official legal paperwork, but she also knew it could protect those relationships. And under the circumstances, having that kind of protection would go a long way toward reassuring her. "Technically, if Mama and Papa George get divorced, we won't be stepsisters anymore. We'll both still be Mikey's sisters, and I'll still be John's sister, but you and me—"

"And John and I," Wendy whispered. "We wouldn't be officially related anymore." Truth was, at the time of the offer of the adoption, she'd been so torn between her love for Ms. Roberts-Darling and her desire to honor her mum's memory that Wendy hadn't worked out what it all might mean for the rest of them. "Do you think Mom still wants me, now that she and Dad—"

"Yes." Lily knew her mama's heart, her mama's love. "Of course. Always." She took a breath and said a silent prayer. "Happy birthday, Wendy."

For a long while, the girls lay quiet in the hammocks.

Being in the treehouse reminded Lily of how much she'd come to care about Daniel, Terri, Strings, and Mateo. When she finally spoke again, it was to tell Wendy all about her new friends and the tiger cub, too. Then Wendy told Lily all about Frank and Ethan, K. D. and Oliver.

Wendy explained that Peter's relationship with Belle was complicated and wondered out loud if the blue electric guitar in the Home Under the Ground might belong to Strings. Lily explained that the elder Clifford had passed on his knowledge of the island to Daniel, who in turn had shared it with the rest of the Native kids, and that Terri and Mateo were lifelong friends. "Terri's from Indian Country, Oklahoma, so she's been extra welcoming to me."

The girls talked long into the night, like they used to in their shared bedroom at home. They talked about Mr. Darling and Ms. Roberts-Darling, about Lily's daddy and their big brother John, about Auntie Lillian and all their other aunties and uncles, their grandparents and oh so many cousins, neighbors, and friends who were no doubt fretting about what had happened to them. They reminisced about Spot's antics and named the chameleon on the treehouse ceiling "Chameleonardo DiCaprio."

Together, Lily and Wendy prayed for everyone they loved. They prayed that their friends—Native and Lost—were safe and that so were Michael and the little cub.

When Wendy woke at dawn, Lily was already studying a yellowed, hand-drawn map of cave tunnels on the wall. "What're you doing?" Wendy asked.

"Memorizing the passages, in case we need someplace to hide from the pirates."

Wendy climbed out of the hammock, moved to her side, and pointed to a long, winding tunnel leading not far from the treehouse across most of the island to a fork where it split off into two other tunnels—one of which opened at the beach north of Merfolk Lagoon and the other which dead-ended at a lavafall. Their route was clear.

Wendy tapped the lagoon. "This way sort of cuts across diagonally, and if somebody—"

"Clifford," Lily put in.

"If Clifford was able to map it, we should be able to retrace his steps."

Lily agreed up to a point. "Theoretically, it should be a much shorter route than traveling aboveground. Except we don't know what sort of shapes the tunnels take, and most of the hike would be in pitch-black darkness and . . . you brought your phone?"

Wendy had pulled it from her jeans pocket and turned it on. "No signal but . . ." She tapped the flashlight app, projecting a bright beam. "Almost fully charged. We've also got photos, a compass, and"—Wendy grinned, pleased with herself—"some sweet tunes, if you want to hear them."

"You brought your phone," Lily repeated. Wasn't she supposed to be the practical one?

Given the likelihood that the *Jolly Roger* was anchored off the northeast shore, the density of the forest, the uneven terrain, and the fact that the pirates were traveling with a rambunctious group of kids, one of whom was barely past toddlerhood, plus a tiger cub . . . That would slow down anybody.

If luck and the island were on their side, the stepsisters might still beat the pirates to the ship in time to somehow liberate the captives.

CHAPTER
35

Illuminating their rocky path with the flashlight app, Lily led Wendy into the darkness. It was the same tunnel where Daniel had taken Lily to break the news that there was no hope of rescue. "Small steps, watch out for pointy rocks."

"Are you sure there's not a bear living in the cave?" Wendy asked.

Lily smiled, remembering that she'd asked Daniel the same question. "There was no bear last time."

Wendy was too short to have to worry about scratching the top of her head on the ceiling. At least for the time being. The cave would likely narrow ahead. "You're sure this is the same tunnel?"

"Positive," Lily said as they came into view of the oblong light. She found a couple of footholds in the rock, handed off the phone, and carefully crawled through the opening.

Impressed by Lily's decisiveness, Wendy made quicker work of it. She jumped down, and her breath caught at the sight of the grotto, illuminated from above. Sunlight shimmered off the lavacicles above, the pool below.

"You returned." The Merfolk was seated at the water's edge. "I didn't expect that."

"I didn't either." Lily lowered her voice and turned to Wendy. "That's Ripley. She's one of the Merfolk I told you about. Don't get too close."

Wendy clicked the light off and took a quick photo but remained where she was.

The girl Wendy had been before Neverland would've been dazzled by a Merfolk, and she was still mightily fascinated. But the girl she was now decided to take a businesslike approach. "Hello, I'm Wendy Darling, and this is Lily Roberts. Pirates have kidnapped our—"

"It's no use," Lily said. "She thinks *we're* pirates. This is a waste of—"

Ever the optimist, Wendy countered, "Ripley may never be our friend, but she doesn't have to be our enemy."

"We don't need her help," Lily insisted. Having agreed to this subterranean route, she was hoping that they would manage to rescue their friends and little brother without having to approach the Merfolk for assistance. "We came this way because it's the cave entrance Daniel and I used before." She shuddered at the memory of having been dragged down into the sea. "Not because I'm looking to . . . reconnect with Ripley."

Wendy recognized the fear in Lily's voice and kept her own calm and steady. "If we smooth things over, we won't need to worry about her getting in our way."

"I'm not so sure about that," Lily said.

Ripley, who'd been hiding out from her bickering cousins in the grotto pool, was amused and intrigued. Moments before first encountering Lily, she'd overheard the girl's prior companion mention Clifford. Furthermore, most humans who had fallen victim to Meredith's and Cordelia's underwater hijinks didn't dare come so close to another Merfolk ever again. Yet here Lily was! And from the Neversea, Ripley had been moved into action by Wendy's valiant struggle as she dangled above the crocodile. These human girls had made quite the impression!

Wendy was growing frustrated with her stepsister. "Listen, I'm sorry about what the Merfolk did to you and Daniel, but at this very moment the pirates are taking Mikey and our friends to their ship. Their *ship*, Lily! As in on the Never*sea*!"

Lily was rubbing her temples. "I understand all that. You don't have to lecture—"

"I'm lecturing *you*? Lily, do you ever listen to yourself talk? You can be such a know-it-all! Think about Mikey!"

"I am, and I don't trust—"

"Attention, humans!" Ripley realized she was being derelict in her duties. "You are trespassing," she demanded in a rote voice. "Leave our waters be. Humans do not belong in the Neversea or on our island."

"Is it just me," Wendy began, "or was her heart not in that?"

"You might be right," Lily replied. Upon reflection, she recalled that it hadn't been Ripley herself who'd dragged her or Daniel under. It was the other two.

Indeed, Ripley was more inclined to be sympathetic to the girls. If they were facing off against pirates, then the stepsisters and Merfolk shared a common enemy. In an iridescent flash, Ripley tucked and slipped forward—*splash*—into the water and then with a sharp twist—*ka-splash*—she soaked them before vanishing into the water's shadowy depths.

Dripping, Lily said, "That was rude."

As Wendy guffawed, Lily added, "What's so funny?"

"We were splashed by a real live Merfolk. That's amazing."

"We could be drowned by a real live Merfolk, if we aren't careful." Lily pointed out Clifford's chart of the island population and sightings—or rather lack thereof. "Indians, boats, planes," she said. "He didn't count the Lost."

"If Clifford was hiding from Peter, it was probably hard for him to track their numbers." Wendy reached up as if to touch the writing and then drew back again.

"The way I figure it," Lily replied, "the veil of Fairy magic not only locks us in. It also hides the island and surrounding sea from the human eye, radar, satellites. Any ships or aircraft that encountered it would crash and sink into the water, possibly sight unseen."

"Here be dragons," Wendy breathed as they left through the grotto.

With every step, light slowly dimmed. "Daniel tried to break it to me gently," Lily said. "He didn't want me to get my hopes up. But I still think we can find a way home. We have to try."

"If we do reach the pirate ship before it sets sail . . ." Wendy began. "Then what?"

"We improvise. Gauge our options when we get to the eastern shore. Hopefully, the crew will spend at least another day on land, gathering food and tending to their livestock. It's not like they know we're trying to catch up to them."

Sometimes the cave tunnel seemed big enough to run a subway. At other times, they had to shimmy through, and rock sliced through Lily's red calico sleeve. They passed the phone, weapons, and Nana Bear back and forth as necessary. A stream ran much of the length, though it seemed to disappear at times beneath the rock. The air smelled musty, earthy. It felt damp.

The stepsisters made steady progress, wary of the sharp protrusions and the uneven terrain, clinging to the furthermost walls where the cave narrowed, crawling when they had to.

Over the soft sound of lapping water, they became slowly aware of a chorus of squeaking, chirping, an echo of fluttering. It filled the air. Lily yanked Wendy down. "Bats!"

"Do they have rabies?" Wendy yelled, covering her head. "I don't know," Lily replied. "Do you have rabies?" Wendy was trembling. "That's not funny."

Usually, it was Lily who was the worried one. It took her a moment to appreciate that Wendy was genuinely afraid. Lily decided not to mention that they'd probably already passed beneath countless bats, roosting upside down. "Don't worry, we'll be okay. I'm right here."

As the overhead onslaught subsided, the girls cautiously rose. Lily said, "From what I've read, you're more likely to get rabies from a dog, cat, skunk, or raccoon. Not that you should ever try to touch one, but bats don't deserve their bad reputation." She exhaled, thinking out loud. "It's probably nearing sunset, if the bats were leaving the cave."

For a while, the girls walked in silence—stumbling here and there, bumping into each other a couple of times. Wendy scratched the back of her right hand.

Neither could shake off the feeling that they were being followed, but both chose not to mention it. They couldn't hear any footfalls behind them or ahead.

Lily said, "I feel badly for Clifford, living alone on the island all those years. When we get home, we should ask for Mama's help to let his people know what became of him."

Wendy kept the beam of illumination from the flashlight app focused ahead and didn't notice when the top half of Ripley's head quietly reemerged in the stream right behind them. "Was he Oklahoma Seminole or

Florida Seminole?" Wendy asked. She was no expert on Native people, but living in an intertribal community, she'd picked up some common knowledge.

"Daniel said Florida. The way he talked about Clifford, Daniel really liked him."

Every time the girls mentioned Clifford's name, Ripley felt a pang of grief, a surge of concern for these two young humans, who apparently had some sort of tie to him, too. Though only her cousins were aware of it, Ripley had vowed to protect the girls, to protect all the kids that Peter brought to Neverland, largely out of respect for Clifford's memory.

What's that? You're curious about Clifford and his life on the island?

All right, that's only natural, I suppose. Allow me to indulge you.

Long ago, a Merfolk named Tallulah was caught in one of the *Jolly Roger*'s fishing nets.

At the time, Clifford was the only Native person in Neverland. Through his early twenties, he'd taken refuge from Pan on the pirate ship. Knowing the captain at the time had a fierce mean streak, he feared what might become of Tallulah. Clifford dived off the side into the sea and cut her free. The captain labeled him a "mutineer" and ordered a rain of gunfire upon them.

It was Tallulah's turn to be the rescuer. Holding Clifford's hand, she dived deep, blowing an air bubble so he could breathe, and swam them both to safety in the grotto.

Tallulah was a young mother, mourning the death of her husband, who'd fallen prey to a certain crocodile that we know well. In time, she and Clifford fell in love, and he helped raise Tallulah's children, who eventually grew up to become Ripley's father and aunts. Though for years Clifford and Tallulah hid their relationship from Merfolk outside the immediate family, he'd been like a grandfather to Ripley and her cousins.

When the couple finally confessed their affections to Merfolk Queen Guadalupe, she'd surprised everyone by welcoming him as a refugee. In return, Clifford taught the Merfolk English so they could warn off interlopers, eavesdrop on Pan and the pirates, and verbally spar with them in battle. After all, Her Majesty was quite the fan of verbal sparring.

In any case, that's how a Seminole man came to have three adopted Merfolk granddaughters, and Ripley was the one who'd loved him most.

"Lily, if we do make it home, what's going to happen to us?"

"Ease up. Hang on; take Daniel's knife." Lily and Nana Bear squeezed between the rocks. "It's a little tight right here." She exhaled. "Okay, now you pass the knife and sword through to me."

Wendy did. "Angle them up," she suggested, wiggling through.

Lily added, "What do you mean by 'happen to us'?"

"Our family. You and me. Like you said, we'll both always be Mikey's sisters, but . . . so what? What will that really mean? We'll see each other at his high school graduation, maybe his wedding someday."

Was Wendy seriously rethinking the offer of adoption? Lily wondered. It felt like too much to hope for, so she focused on the question at hand. How strange to think of Michael growing up, getting married. "Like, will we all do Christmases together? Or, when he's old enough, will he just travel back and forth between us?"

"Something like that," Wendy acknowledged. "What about John?"

The question hung in the damp air. The temporary marital separation between Mr. Darling and Ms. Roberts-Darling wasn't the only major transition in the family.

John would soon be off to college. He'd come home to Tulsa on school breaks—they were sure of it. His girlfriend Gracie's parents lived less than twenty minutes away. Then again, maybe he would spend Christmas with her family or go skiing with his friends in Northern New Mexico or take an out-of-state engineering internship over the summer. Maybe he and Gracie would break up, and he'd meet someone else from somewhere else.

After all, John was a high school graduate now. A grown-up. A young one, sure, but growing up changed everything. It could take away the people you loved.

No wonder Peter Pan hated it so.

"You're thinking too far ahead," Lily said. "For the time being, Mama will bring Mikey up to New York. They'll stay in a hotel, and I'll come stay with her . . . or you."

"With me. You'll stay with me. We've shared a bedroom for so long, I can hardly imagine what it'll be like, not having you around all the time."

"Me neither . . ." The cave tunnel was so, so dark, and they had no way of knowing for sure how much farther they had to go. "Wendy, we don't know for sure that Mama and Dad are getting divorced. I don't think they even know." Lily had no idea what else to say. Her thoughts could circle round and round on the what-ifs. She hated when that happened. "It's hard, not really knowing what'll happen next."

Wendy reached for her hand. "We should talk about it more."

Lily nodded. "We will."

Hours later, Ripley clung to the uneven, sharp edge of a glittering pool and watched the stepsisters exit the cave on the eastern shore. Although Lily and Wendy had been oblivious to her presence, Ripley understood them better now, almost as if they were all friends.

The *Jolly Roger* was a fearsome-looking, sinister craft, stained with cruelty, blood, and greed. A detestable vessel—destroyer of the innocent and slayer of the mighty kraken. Or so the legends claimed. Lily and Wendy arrived on the violet and black stone beach just in time to glimpse the ship—with nine young prisoners, plus an irate, small tiger—sailing out to sea.

CHAPTER
36

The Merfolk appeared to be lazily batting about a giant translucent bubble, a pastime that they found as soothing and relaxing as playful. Yet their persistent presence on Shipwreck Rock was also a show of strength against their enemies and a love letter to the island, which adored them.

That said, the Merfolk didn't especially concern themselves with the Lost or the Native kids. When it came to human children, they had never been as pernicious as the pirates or as pesky as Pan. While they objected to all human trespassers in principle, the adults of Mercourt weren't inclined to expend much energy on the very young.

If it weren't for the novelty of Lily and Wendy's visit, Her Majesty might not have deigned to respond to them at all.

Lily and Wendy had practiced their impassioned plea for assistance.

After all, they had to find *some* way to reach the captives before who knew what sorry fate befell them. Are you cautiously optimistic? Remember, Mer air bubbles had kept Lily alive underwater and Mer defenses had protected Wendy from the *tick-tock*ing crocodile.

The girls could imagine being safely escorted through the Neversea to the *Jolly Roger* and back to the island again. They could envision a dozen or so more Merfolk working together to secure Michael's and their friends' safe return to land.

They had to try requesting finned assistance, even if it was a long shot.

"Excuse us, please. My name is Lily Roberts, and this is my stepsister, Wendy Dar—"

"Leave this lagoon, foul pirates!" Merfolk Queen Guadalupe, Protector of the Neversea and Marine Creatures, commanded from the high point of the rock. She wore an indignant, haughty expression and a red-coral crown. "You are trespassing; leave our waters be. Humans do not belong in Neverland."

"We're not pirates!" Wendy called from the seashell-littered beach as her stepsister gently pulled her beyond arm's reach of the water's edge. "We're middle schoolers!"

"We're not foul either!" Lily exclaimed, though they could've both used a bath. "That's a horrible thing to say."

"Pirates pollute the sea," Meredith put in. "Pirates endanger our people."

An exquisite, full-bodied Merfolk named Halle leapt from the turquoise-green water, swirling in midair, only to splash down again. Then she gracefully raised herself up to perch with tremendous dignity on the smooth base of the rock. "For thousands of years—"

"There we go again," Cordelia said in Merfolk tongue, fanning herself.

"Hush," Ripley scolded, playfully dunking her cousin. "Show some respect."

Halle tossed a scathing look in Cordelia's direction. Human or not, these young visitors were a fresh audience. "For thousands of years, the Neversea and our island were in balance.

"Then one foggy morning, the *Jolly Roger* appeared off the southeast coast. Romy, a Merfolk princess, welcomed the crew with a lovely song. A song that rose and fell like the waves, a song of the moon and wonder. She couldn't have known that the captain's head was full of foolish, hateful stories. He recoiled at the sound of her voice. He slandered Romy, accused her of trying to lure the crew to watery deaths, and later had the gall to claim he'd taken her life in self-defense.

"From all the way across the island, the Fairy court heard our wails of fury and mourning and, in solidarity, they enchanted the Neversea and our island with the veil." With a thoughtful tilt of her head, Halle acknowledged, "We remain forever grateful for their protection."

As Ripley disappeared into the depths of the water, Halle was winding up the story. "Not long afterward, one foolish, impulsive Fairy brought a human boy—the Pan— to the island and, together, they fetched more human boys, who grew into—"

"More pirates, awful pirates!" shouted several Mer- folk. "Pirates, awful pirates!"

The stepsisters fell silent as they retreated the way they'd come.

Wendy, carrying Nana Bear on her back, was reluctant to stray too far from the *Jolly Roger*'s preferred spot to anchor. "What if we take the pirates' donkeys and offer a trade?"

"Well . . ." It wasn't the worst desperate idea that Lily had ever heard, though neither had any experience with donkey wrangling. Lily could barely make out the *Jolly Roger* on the near-dark horizon.

But Wendy caught sight of a much closer boat. "Lily, look at that!"

The canoe on the beach had been hollowed long ago from a fallen Nevertree by a Seminole teenager who would've preferred to work with cypress wood. It had decidedly *not* been there when the girls walked by less than an hour before.

Wendy circled the boat, inspecting the hull for any sign that it might not be seaworthy. Appearing quite sturdy, it had been positioned with the bow kissing the surf, but by whom?

A quick scan of the sky, balmy waves, and tropical landscape didn't offer any clues.

With a hardy push, she and Lily could be afloat and, under the cover of night, on their way to the *Jolly Roger.* Was the canoe big enough to transport nearly a dozen kids and a small tiger on a return voyage to land? Maybe if they huddled tight. Wendy could already imagine holding Michael on her lap and the feel of his curls beneath her chin.

Lily was trying to figure out how the canoe got there. She remembered Daniel mentioning Clifford's canoe, but she had been under the impression that it was long hidden in a cave—perhaps it had even washed out to sea years before.

Lily reached inside the boat. "Paddles." They'd been thoughtfully placed there, along with grappling hooks attached to two coiled ropes made of woven vines.

"But we don't know how to steer . . . What's that?" Wendy plucked up a small, oblong, glinting object from a seat. She held it up to the rising moonlight.

"What if the pirates are using this boat to bait us?" Lily said. "What if . . . oh."

The turquoise-green Merfolk scale shimmered.

From the water, Ripley chimed, "All aboard."

* * *

As the stars shined upon them, Ripley—with her tail serving as a propeller—guided the canoe as it cut through the Neversea toward the *Jolly Roger*. The stepsisters ducked low so as not to be seen. Lily, who was hugging Nana Bear, harbored serious doubts about having accepted the Merfolk's offer of assistance, but Wendy had climbed right in and that had settled it.

The plan was simple: Sneak aboard, hide until the pirates nodded off for the night, and then locate and spirit their friends and Michael to safety.

Gently rocked by the waves, Lily tried not to fret about sharks, sea serpents, or, most of all, saltwater crocodiles. She tried not to fret about whether she and Wendy were strong enough to toss up the grappling hooks and climb aboard the ship. Could they do so undetected? Did most of the pirates sleep on the lower deck? She would have to wait to find out.

As the canoe drew closer, the girls heard the crew singing.

"Yo ho, hey, shiver me timbers,
Avast ye, there she blows.
A pirate's life be joyful then
To Davy Jones he goes."

Lily whispered, "You do realize that Ripley could be trying to foist us off on the pirates. Once we reach the *Jolly Roger*, we have no idea how to—"

"We'll figure it out." Wendy reconsidered the bristling reception that she and her stepsister had received at Shipwreck Rock. "Who knows. Maybe the pirates are friendly."

"Hey, heave to, me hearties, heave to,
Hoist the skull and crossbones,
Sail true to the pirating code
Or bow to Davy Jones."

Wendy gazed up at the skull-and-crossbones flag.

"Yo ho, beware the perky plank,
Me buccaneer, me mate.
It calls to Davy Jones's locker
But first ye be shark's bait."

Lily whispered, "They don't sound friendly."

As Ripley steered the canoe, she wasn't bothered that Lily was suspicious of her motives. She recalled her adoptive grandfather, Clifford, telling her stories of the Seminole Nation, of Native and First Nations people, of kids who'd been misled or outright tricked into coming to the island. She'd deduced that same fate had befallen Lily and felt a kinship of sorts to her because of that connection.

Over the years, Clifford had spoken of his brief time with the pirates, too. He had described it as a time of conflict, a thirst for change. He had hoped that the friendlier, more kindhearted members of the crew would outlive their ferocious captain to sail gentler seas. But having spent the rest of his life in hiding, Clifford died without finding out what had become of them.

Ripley raised herself to peer into the canoe. "You're on your own from here. I'm already risking my queen's wrath by bringing you this far, and, for our own safety, she absolutely forbids Merfolk to swim any closer to the pirate ship. Good luck." With that, Ripley submerged.

"Thank you." Wendy reached for a paddle. Now that night had fallen, she could barely see the island in the full moonlight. "Too late for a backup plan?"

Meanwhile, Lily was wondering exactly how they'd sneak aboard, how long it might take before they were detected and captured or killed alongside Michael and the other kids, who might well have met their demise already. Out loud, she echoed Auntie Lillian, whispering, "Remember to breathe. In and out, slow as you please. Just breathe."

"Yo ho! Foul Captain Jameson,
He lost a duel to Pan.
They claim that dead men tell no tales—"

"There's a canoe approaching!" called a raspy voice from the crow's nest.

"Wendy?" Lily whispered, still hugging Nana Bear.

"A canoe!" another voice cried out. "A canoe!" repeated still another.

Wendy reached to hold her stepsister's hand. She almost whispered, "I love you," but it would've sounded too much like "goodbye."

"Where's me spyglass?" was the answer. "Get moving, ye buckos, and haul them interlopers on deck."

CHAPTER

37

Belle curtsied at the foot of the royal dais as Fairy Queen Mab weighed her apology.

"Please, ma'am," Belle implored, blinking back tears. "I've broken all ties with Peter Pan."

Her Majesty presided from a throne carved from thin branches and adorned with tiny red blossoms. The silent glow of a thousand attentive subjects illuminated the glistening treetops of the Fairy Wood. The colorful birds, the singing insects, the slithering animals, and the frolicking ones, too, all quieted out of respect. Even the cool, tropical wind held its breath.

"I fully appreciate what his rash actions have cost us." Belle dared to raise her chin.

Did she really? the queen mused. Belle was such an impetuous, impulsive child. Only a few hundred years old. Her human pet had hunted the lions to extinction. The Neverbirds and tigers had declined to a precious few. A rumored tiger cub had gone missing. Moreover, the overall tiger and Neverbird numbers were insufficient to successfully propagate the species on the island. Her Majesty had difficult decisions to make about their future.

The troublesome human boy had been Belle's responsibility. Belle had made the devastating choice to bring him as a babe to the island, despite what the first generation of pirates had taught them about humans' selfish, destructive ways. Albeit for his own amusement, Peter had defended her people from those same pirates. Yet at what cost? The Fairies could defend themselves.

Queen Mab was kind and patient, the downside of which was that she perhaps had been far too tolerant and forgiving all along. "Abandoning Peter Pan to his own devices may only exacerbate the already-tragic situation." She thumped her tiny, ruby-encrusted scepter on the dais. "Belle of Neverland, you are hereby exiled from the Fairy Wood."

Belle gasped. "Forever?"

Queen Mab believed in redemption. "For at least as long as he lives."

Belle spread her arms wide, palms up, as if imploring the stars for forgiveness, and, fluttering her glistening wings, rose above her Fairy kin. In a fit of pique, she executed a breathtaking pirouette, and then, leaving a trail of shimmering Fairy dust, retreated in the direction of the Home Under the Ground well aware that Peter had likely returned already.

How forgiving is your nature? Do you believe Peter deserved yet another chance?

What about Belle, whose heart nearly shattered at the thought of a life of loneliness? Unlike Peter, she wasn't known for a murderous streak, but he had been warned time and again.

If Peter's demise was her only path to redemption, so be it. Who would've guessed that, after all these years, Belle might be the one to put an end to Peter Pan?

CHAPTER
38

"Ahoy, lassies!" called a sun-weathered rogue as a handful of pirates approached the slowly drifting canoe in a dinghy. "We be coming to fetch ye."

"What're we going to do now?" Wendy asked, gripping her paddle.

"Beats me," Lily replied in a hollow voice.

"Easy, poppets," cooed a man in a red bandanna. "We have no intention of harming ye."

Even Lily hadn't expected to be foiled so soon. She and Wendy stood cautiously, setting the paddles aside in favor of Daniel's knife and Peter's sword.

"Take us to our brother," Wendy demanded.

For a long moment, the pirates regarded them by lantern and moonlight, and then burst out laughing so hard they nearly tipped the dinghy. "Hand over your weapons afore ye hurt yourselves, and off to your brother ye'll go."

For Lily, it had been one thing to threaten an unarmed

Peter on the cliff overlooking the beach. Perilous as he could be, any interaction with him felt a bit like playing a game.

It was something else entirely to take on five fully grown sea marauders.

Furthermore, Lily still desperately wanted to board that ship. If that's where Michael was, that's where she wanted to be.

"Deal," Lily said, surrendering the knife.

Raising a brow, Wendy followed her lead, turning over Peter's weapon. However counterintuitive it might've felt, Lily was one of the smartest people she knew, and no matter what, they were in this together. "If you say so."

One of their captors chuckled in satisfaction. "This sword looks familiar. I know just the place for it."

The pirates hauled Lily Roberts, Wendy Darling, and a certain plush toy bear onto the deck of the *Jolly Roger*. The crew was a sight to behold. They sported a mix of historic garb and more modern apparel, much of which looked a bit too small or had been modified with strategic patchwork and the realignment of seams. Some had shaved their heads; others had braided their hair. A few wore gold earrings. Nearly all were barefoot. They ranged in age from teens to elders, white folks, Black folks, and other people of color. In addition to pirate-flavored English, a half dozen spoke Spanish, five spoke Mandarin, two spoke French, and three spoke Hindi.

Peter had spirited them all away from their families, some to live as pirates from the start, others to join his Lost. Without a steady supply of dust, they had all grown together into a craggy, rough-hewn, and fresh-faced found family who had made a jolly home together at sea.

"Where are our friends?" Wendy demanded, standing shoulder to shoulder with her stepsister. "Where's Mikey? You promised to bring us to him."

"Soon enough," replied the pirate in the red bandanna. "He's dining at the captain's table."

"Mikey!" Lily and Wendy hollered. "Mikey!"

Blam. The broad, arched wooden door to the captain's cabin had slammed open. "What be all this ruckus?" *Blam.* The door swung shut again.

"Interlopers, Captain. They be demanding to see their brother and their mateys."

"Both," Lily whispered, Nana Bear at her hip. "We want our brother and friends, too."

"We, we want them all back," Wendy clarified, blinking. "We, uh . . ."

The stepsisters were awestruck by the magnificent pirate queen. She wore a white-plumed hat, a long-sleeve white linen shirt, and a series of long multicolored ribbons tied to her belt, creating a rainbow skirt flowing over her black pantaloons and below her knees.

"Ahoy, me name be Captain Esmerelda Smee, and if memory serves me right..." As she pointed at each of them in turn with her skull-head cane, a turquoise-and-gold macaw squeaked and flew from her shoulder to the main ratlines. "Ye must be Wendy . . . and Lily."

Was it a good or bad sign that the captain knew their names?

"So, you're here on me ship, looking for your mateys, eh?"

"Are you going to make us walk the, uh, perky plank?" Wendy asked, recalling Peter's storybook, which featured an illustration of a blindfolded captive at sword point, doing just that.

Do you recall Peter's yellowed storybooks, the ones he'd finally cast aside? While a handful of skills and traditions had been passed down, many from the original crew, the lessons the pirate book contained had been powerfully influential in framing the crew's self-image and how they conducted themselves. After all, the original crew of the *Jolly Roger* had long died off, and again, most of these sailors were one-time Lost kids—those who'd turned thirteen years old back when Peter simply banished teenagers from the Home Under the Ground and their younger mates who'd escaped a more grisly fate.

Which begged the question, were the legendary pirates of the Neversea as inclined to bloodshed as the illustrations suggested?

"Did you make *our brother* walk the plank?" Lily asked.

"Did I . . . ?" Captain Smee let out a loose belly laugh that her crew was quick to echo. "Well, I'll say, me fearsome reputation sure speaks for me."

Using the cane, she returned to her cabin, opened the door, and hollered, "Finish up your grub and come on out, sprogs. These lasses are fretting that we've harmed ye."

Michael was first out the door. "Sissies!" He took a half dozen running steps and flung himself in a three-way hug with Lily and Wendy. "Nana Bear, I missed you *so* much!"

Not far on his heels, Daniel and Terri, K. D. and Oliver, Strings and Mateo, Ethan and Frank spilled out after Michael, and, with shouts of joy, the celebration commenced.

"This calls for chanties and dancing," the captain ordered, adjusting her hat. Meanwhile, left behind in the cabin, the tiger cub snored and grunted softly at the foot of the bed.

As they feasted on pineapple, cured pork, and sweet potatoes, it didn't take Lily and Wendy long to ascertain that—no matter their wardrobe and posturing—the crew of the *Jolly Roger* was more fairly described as "sailors" than "pirates." Sailors who spent most of their days fishing, as evidenced by the enormous net being freshly deployed by crew members on deck.

Given their limited navigational range, imposed by the veil, and the lack of other ships, the crew hadn't engaged in any real pirating or plunder since the first generation. They did loot and kidnap. They had robbed food and resources from Neverland and made off with the Lost.

You could say they had all that in common with Peter. But he stole whatever struck his fancy and took kids from their families. At least the pirates were motivated by survival and offered sanctuary to many a Lost child that Peter might've disposed of via crocodile.

When Lily asked about the long-ago death of the Merfolk Princess Romy, several pirates expressed deep sympathy and an earnest desire to make amends. No one had any memory of the story itself, though a few older folks did recall affectionate tales of Clifford.

"Is it true that you hunt Fairies?" Wendy wanted to know. "That you wage war against them?"

"Prickly wee creatures." Captain Smee reached for a sapphire-colored velvet bag tied on her bejeweled belt, and extracted a glowing vial, no bigger than your pinkie finger and about as wide. "Handed down to me by me adoptive father, Captain Smee, Sr., may he rest in peace. I've been saving it for an emergency."

"Fairy dust," Wendy whispered. She was reminded of the stash Peter had kept in a thimble on his curio shelf in the Home Under the Ground.

"Aye," Smee said. "Not enough for the whole crew. We don't care about flying around the island, and it's the Fairies who want to wage war on us, not us against them."

That was news to Wendy and, she realized, it would be to Belle as well. "Then why—"

"We've only been trying to catch a Fairy long enough

to ask if its kin might help us *all* sail through the veil to waters beyond. But they be fast moving and not inclined to listen to our request."

Wendy reached for the glittering vial and held it, tantalized. She handed it to Lily, who shed a tear at the sight. Was there enough Fairy dust for the Roberts-Darling siblings to fly home to Tulsa? Perhaps, but that didn't matter. They weren't star navigators. They couldn't find their way without help, and they never would've considered leaving their new friends behind.

CHAPTER
39

Could Belle truly bring herself to harm Peter? Though not a child in years, he was still childlike, sort of perpetually eleven years old. She thought of his laugh, his whimsy, of all the adventures they'd had together, of how she'd loved him at first sight in that baby carriage.

He might be a blight on Neverland, but he was still family.

Then again, Peter had dispatched of how many of the Lost without a second thought? Or tried to anyway. Consider his bullying, boastful nature. Might it be that his own murderous reputation had been overstated, his misdeeds exaggerated, his human death toll heightened by myth? If so, he'd still committed countless wrongs, earning the Fairy queen's condemnation.

Defeated, yet still fuming, Belle barely glimmered as she retreated to the tree-knot hole on the edge of the

Fairy Wood where she had stashed her furniture and other belongings.

What were her other options?

How unbearable it was to contemplate a long, long, long life of exile. Perhaps an eternity. Certainly, Belle had traveled the world—far more gloriously than any Fairy in history—and yet even those memories, contaminated by Peter's misdeeds, were tied to her disgrace.

Should she bid farewell to the island and seek asylum with the Fairy cousins who resided in, say, Kensington Gardens, Royal Botanic Gardens, or the San Francisco Botanical Garden? (Yes, plenty of Fairies made their homes in more modest neighborhood gardens, arboretums, or natural woodlands, but Belle had always considered herself quite fancy.)

No, that wasn't an option. She had a duty, not only to the Fairy queendom but to the wild beasts, too. It was incumbent on her to somehow protect them. To redeem herself by containing the terror that was Peter. At least she'd cut off his supply of dust, although perhaps too late. If she didn't eliminate him completely, Belle still had to prevent him from doing more damage.

Belle glimpsed her splotchy, tearstained face in the Puss in Boots mirror. Her golden pixie haircut fell in disarray. The tropical red blossom at her waist had wilted. Her sparkling glow had nearly died out. That wasn't the Fairy she knew, the Fairy who'd traveled across oceans and learned new languages and faced off against vicious pirates and rebuked mindless midair drones and, let us not forget, modeled the most exquisite ensembles in all of Neverland.

Never mind if Queen Mab and their fellow winged ones didn't believe in her.

Never mind if Peter hadn't believed in her.

Never mind if *you* there, reading this storybook, don't believe in Fairies at all.

Drawing herself up, Belle realized something that made all the difference. She'd hold up her pointy chin—shine radiant like a star—and while she was at it, she'd reclaim the Tiddlywinks chandelier she'd left behind to build a new home. And why?

Because Belle of Neverland believed in herself.

The determined Fairy hovered above the hollowed tree trunk that had briefly served as an entrance and exit for Wendy and Michael. Smoke wafted from the cleverly disguised chimney, dissipated in the tropical breeze. Belle cocked her ear to listen for any sounds of life rising from within the Home Under the Ground. Could Peter and the Lost be sleeping?

No, she heard a quiet, unfamiliar sobbing. How odd.

It almost sounded like—could it be?

Belle flew down through the trunk and peeked from above at the large underground room. Basket beds gaped empty. Storybooks lay broken and scattered across the earthen floor.

So, Peter had another tantrum, she thought with a sigh. What of it?

And then . . . Oh my! Could that really be him, weeping on the pink, stool-sized mushroom to the side of the hearth? Yes! Yes, it *was* Peter. He wiped away a miraculous tear.

Belle was stunned. "I—I am here only to retrieve my Tiddlywinks chandelier."

His head remained bowed, as if in prayer. She flew to her apartment to retrieve her light fixture. Belle didn't know what to say. She certainly couldn't bring herself to punish such a pitiful creature. Still, she surmised, their bond had been broken. It might have been forever tasked upon her to contain Peter's destructive behavior, but never again could they return to the playfulness that had once flourished between them.

Finally, Peter raised his tear-streaked face to speak to Belle for what he imagined would be the last time. As she unhooked the tiny chain from her alcove apartment ceiling, he called out, "Belle, you have meant more to me than flying and adventures, more than my sword or my flute. I'll never forget you." It was the closest Peter Pan had ever come to a declaration of love.

The Fairy was so shocked that she dropped her precious chandelier. The frame broke, the crystals went all askew, and she didn't care. Oblivious to the wreckage, Belle zipped to her doorway and studied Peter's watery gaze. Where was his sword? Where was his swagger? Something about him was different. Something about the entire room had changed.

The fire in the hearth flickered, cast shadows from the stool-sized mushrooms, the long stump table, the bed baskets hanging on the walls. Fairies knew light, understood light, were themselves light embodied. Belle knew something was wildly amiss about the light and shadows.

Her delicate jaw dropped. *Peter's shadow!* Not separate, not mocking or rebelling, but fully reconnected. *There* it was! Peter's shadow loomed large in the Home Under the Ground. Over a century of companionship, Belle had come to know the shadow quite well. Never would it have returned to fully embrace Peter, if he hadn't somehow dramatically changed for the better.

Peter took a hitching breath. "I—I messed up everything. I hurt so many kids, so many people, even you." Peter knelt on the earthen floor. "I'm so sorry. If only there was some way to make it all better . . . I would do anything, I swear."

That didn't sound like the Peter she knew. Still, she wondered aloud, "Is this a trick?"

"No trick." Peter's shoulders sagged. "I don't blame you for doubting me. But you don't have to leave, Belle. I know how much you love your apartment. You take the Home Under the Ground. I'll find somewhere else to go."

Could it be? Peter Pan had expressed appreciation and regret, and he had apologized. He had reconciled with his shadow. He had selflessly sacrificed the only home he could remember.

"Holy hollyhocks!" Belle exclaimed. "You're not a lost soul after all!" It was so clear now. Belle could see the revived potential within him. Belle could see him as if anew.

Yet all was not well. His anguish lingered.

The boy was heartbroken, bereft.

That would never do. The Fairy knew just the ragtag crew to cheer him up. "When will the other boys return? Where are they off to?" As he gaped at her, Belle prodded, "Peter, Peter, you must rally! The other children, where are they? What's become of them?"

Peter Pan blinked three times. His shadow believed in him. Belle believed in him. Could that be enough? He wiped the tears from his eyes. "Captured by pirates," he said.

CHAPTER

40

The *Jolly Roger* had sailed the coast of the Fairy Wood to the spot off the western side of the island where the ocean floor was deep enough to get as close as possible to shore.

Captain Esmerelda Smee called out, "Pipe down those chanties. Pipe down your yammering.'" She squinted in the moonlight. "What happened to the canoe? I ordered ye scallywags to tie it off to be towed." A moment later, the captain exclaimed, "Oh me, what now?"

It was Belle, appearing above, more luminous than ever. "Horrid pirates!" she exclaimed. "Release the Lost immediately!"

Were you surprised by Belle's appearance or demands? The Lost and Native kids really weren't either, no matter that she'd disavowed humans not that long before. Strings, who was strumming a ukulele, didn't miss a chord. To them, at least one more encounter with Belle and, for that matter, Peter Pan, simply seemed inevitable. Meanwhile, the crew of the *Jolly Roger* was flummoxed. After countless futile searches for a Fairy to talk to, Belle had come to them.

"Mikey!" the Fairy exclaimed. "Are you unharmed? We are here to rescue you."

"Hi, Belle!" Michael cheerfully patted his chest as if confirming his general welfare. "I'm okay." He held up his favorite toy. "Nana Bear is okay, too."

All the children were having a grand old time, Belle realized, taking in the jovial scene. They didn't need rescuing, though Nana Bear was looking a bit worse for wear.

"Who be this 'we' that ye speak of?" Captain Smee demanded as the macaw on her shoulder ruffled its bright blue wings. "Are there more Fairies approaching?" Smee was not ignorant of the fact that Peter often traveled in the company of a Fairy, but she had never before seen Belle up close for long enough to get a really good look at her.

At the same time, Terri asked Daniel, "Did you hear that splashing?"

They made their way through the crowd starboard to investigate.

"What are you doing here, Belle?" Lily asked. "I heard you were done with humans."

Wendy shot her stepsister a sideways look that said it was a rude question, but she wanted to know the answer, too.

"Peter has reunited with his shadow," the Fairy explained. "Under the island's care, he has reflected upon, reconsidered, and come to regret his many misdeeds. He is no longer the monster he once was. Peter is now growing into the boy we'd all hope him to be." She made a show of studying her glittery fingernails. "I may have been premature in dismissing humanity."

That was a hearty nugget to digest. "And here ye be." Captain Esmerelda Smee spotted a ripe opportunity. "Perhaps it's all an unfortunate misunderstanding. If that's the case, Belle, I'd appreciate the chance to have a word with ye about safe passage to seas beyond the veil."

Belle wasn't interested in that. She stuck her tongue out first at the captain and then at Lily, her least favorite child of the Roberts-Darling family. Because Belle was still Belle after all.

Rwowowow. Mateo was peering out the cabin doorway with the cub on a leash. "Uh, hi," he said, addressing the Fairy. "Frank and Ethan were telling me how your people watch over the animals on the island. If I give this cub back to—"

"Sweet succory!" Belle swirled, spinning Fairy dust all over the tiger, which, in turn, seemed to regard her as a delightful plaything and batted at her with its front paws. "Yes, yes, my queen will be overcome with joy. This baby tiger is hope for us all—hope with stripes."

The cat began to rise in the air, then panicked, landing on its paws. *Rwowowow.*

Lily winked at her stepsister. "Belle likes the tiger a lot more than she did Spot."

Wendy suppressed a chuckle. "A whole lot more."

Mateo knelt by the tiger. "The cub likes to chase bugs and bat at feathers and, well, you can feed her goat's milk or little pieces of fish."

So earnest. It was all Belle could do not to pinch him. She could do far better than that. She knew exactly how to take care of every animal on the island. Such practices were a focus of Fairy faith, culture, and education.

Hoping the captain didn't mind her stepping in, Wendy slipped between the Fairy and the cub. "Belle, I have a favor to ask, a big one." She took an optimistic breath. "Could you please arrange for the delivery of enough Fairy dust to fly everyone on the *Jolly Roger* back to their homelands?"

What a dull request, Belle thought. "Silly girl, don't you think we Fairies have considered that before? Why do you think we chose to trap the original crew of the *Jolly Roger* in the first place? So they wouldn't share news of our existence to the outside world, bringing countless more humans!"

It made sense to Smee that this would be a concern. She held her hat over her heart. "As captain, ye have me word that not a soul on this ship will breathe a word of your existence."

The Lost, the crew, and the Native kids murmured in agreement.

Belle rolled her eyes. She was unconvinced.

Oliver had mixed feelings about going home, especially now that he was living on the *Jolly Roger* instead of in the Home Under the Ground. But he missed his mother, his Saint Bernard, Charlie, and his family farm. He decided everyone needed a reality check. "Listen, even if we posted every detail of Neverland all over the internet with photos and livestreaming videos, nobody would take us seriously. Humans don't believe in Fairies or Merfolk."

"Pfft, their loss!" Belle exclaimed. Then she paused on the thought, aghast. The Fairy flew over to Wendy's shoulder and quietly asked, "Is that true? Are humans really so ignorant?"

It sounded like a simple question, but it wasn't. Wendy was no expert on what every human being did or didn't believe in—people, cultures, and religions varied. None of the other kids were rushing to answer. As a white girl in a Native community, for example, she'd grown up knowing that some Indigenous beliefs were none of her business.

Wendy decided to hedge her bets. "I think Oliver's right that you don't have anything to worry about from any of us as long as the veil hides the island." As a show of good faith, she opened the photo file on her phone. The couple of pictures she'd shot weren't any good anyway. Belle looked like a bright splotch of light. Ripley had been mostly submerged in the grotto, and it had been too dark at Merfolk Lagoon to bother trying to take a photo. Wendy hit DELETE.

The Fairy considered Wendy an expert on the human world and trusted her judgment.

And yet transporting so many humans, most of them fully grown? That would require so much dust, dozens upon dozens of Fairies. None of whom were speaking to her. And Belle refused to enchant humans anymore, now that she'd seen the harm the dust could do to them.

Where was Peter anyway? the Fairy wondered. They had both agreed it was far too risky to expose him to more dust so he could fly alongside her. Peter had boasted that he could swim the distance, and Belle had no reason to think otherwise, though she was a bit concerned about the many toothy creatures of the sea. On the flight to the ship, though, she'd caught sight of an iridescent fluke tail in the water. Perhaps Peter had become distracted and decided to go play tricks on the Merfolk instead.

Captain Smee nudged, "I speak for the whole crew when I says we'd be much obliged if ye'd help us out."

The Fairy had heard enough simpering. "It's not my decision to make. However, when I present the tiger cub at the Fairy court, I shall pass on your request to my queen."

Might Queen Mab reconsider her exile, too? Belle barely dared to hope.

Rwowowow. Swallowing the lump in his throat, Mateo

offered her the woven-vine leash.

Belle curtsied and removed it from the cub's neck before flying round the tiger to lift it by the scruff. As all those on deck watched in wonder, the Fairy and bewildered young cat took to the night air over the moonlit waters toward the Fairy Wood.

CHAPTER

41

The quartermaster announced, "Captain Smee, that croc who devoured the last two captains be circling under the plank, hoping for a meal." As Lily and Wendy shuddered at the mention of the gigantic crocodile, the boatswain added, "I spied a mermaid's tail, too."

Smee waved off their worries. "It's in the water, ye yellow-bellied curs." It was a harsh insult on the face of it, but her tone was gently teasing. "We be on the ship. Between the giant squids and sharks and crocs and Mer-folk, ye all know better than to swim carefree in these waters. If ye wants a bath, ye can hike to a waterfall when we return to the island." Her lips curled with hope that Belle might fly back with her Fairy kin to guide them through the veil. "*If* we ever return to the island."

Unbeknownst to those above on deck, Peter Pan clung, dripping, to the fishing nets draped along the port side. "Thank you." He winked at Ripley, who'd dragged him safely through the waves. "I always knew you were in love with me." Because even though he had regained his soul, Peter was still Peter after all.

"I didn't realize it was you!" Ripley exclaimed. "Not at first!"

"You didn't let me drown after you found out."

At that moment, in defiance of Queen Guadalupe's orders, Ripley could've reached out to touch the *Jolly Roger*, and on impulse, she risked it. Ripley flattened her palm against the wooden hull, hoping no one would be the wiser. She felt defiant, independent, free.

Between us, Ripley had never quite fit in at home. Longing for adventure, she sank into the murky depths, diving with a stingray, dancing with angelfish, considering her own options as she waited for Lily, Wendy, and friends to embark on their escape from the pirates.

As for Peter, he scrambled up the netting. When he peeked over the hull, no one noticed. The captain, crew, and kids were captivated either by Belle's shimmering departure with the tiger cub or by the toothy *tick-tock*, *tick-tock*ing crocodile on the other side of the vessel.

"Back to your revelry, me scallywags." The captain prompted a new round of chanties, the rise of a fiddle, a fife, a concertina. "Break out the rum and bourbon, but none for the sprogs."

The master gunner—not that they had any vessels to target—showed Strings his mandolin, and he struck up a friendly conversation with Wendy about New York City.

A few crew members danced a jig. Others broke out dice and playing cards.

Strings's conversation turned to Arthur Conan Doyle's literary detective, and Oliver, Frank, and Ethan were wowed by his command of Sherlock Holmes trivia. Strings had a lot of ideas as to how he'd rewrite the character, and they all agreed that he should. Lily talked volleyball, Mateo talked basketball, and K. D. talked soccer. Daniel's laughter mixed with Terri's and Michael's. It was the first time that Daniel had really relaxed since he couldn't remember when.

And Wendy felt like the distance from Indian Country, Oklahoma, to New York City to even London suddenly didn't seem so insurmountable after all.

Frowning at the festivities, Peter spied his sword, hung as if to mock him over the door to Smee's cabin. How could this happen? Indians and pirates conspiring against him! They'd made off with his storyteller and the Lost, who didn't appear particularly heartbroken about it.

Brainwashed! Peter deduced. That had to be the explanation! He pulled himself on board, crouched low, crept fast. He'd set them right again. There was the Indian girl, her arm around his Wendy. And there was the girls' little brother alongside the biggest Indian boy. Of course they'd met before—Dawson or Daniel was his name. He was wearing the black leather jacket.

Peter watched as, at the Indian girl's direction, a Black pirate sporting a red scarf introduced himself as Monsieur

Barthe and presented Daniel with the long knife that Lily had wielded against him. The boy waved it off, at least for the time being, likely keeping Matt-Michael safe from the serrated blade.

A moment later, Peter's hand closed around the hilt of his sword. Now he was ready to return, victorious, to Neverland. For the Lost to accompany him to the Home Under the Ground, for the Indians to regroup to the south, for them all to engage in a glorious game of war come sunrise. Then again, Wendy and her stepsister appeared to be inseparable. Perhaps it would be better if everyone chose their own team for the play battle. At a crucial moment, Peter would surprise everyone by switching sides, and afterward, Belle could join them in a bountiful meal of clams, pink star fruit, mutton stew, and anything else they could imagine. Wendy would tell a story and help him write a love note to send in a bottle to Ripley.

It was overwhelming to find himself genuinely caring for others again.

If Belle remained true to her refusal of sharing Fairy dust, then those gathered there would be the last human residents of Neverland. Like the last tigers and Neverbirds. And they wouldn't live forever. Tragedy, Peter thought. All his doing. He swallowed hard to keep the tears from returning. The lions—the lions of Neverland— were already gone. The Peter he had been had celebrated that, taken credit for that, was at fault for that.

Giant feelings tromped around inside him. Frustration

rose to the top. An urge to take center stage, to claim the moment as his own. No, Peter had not reverted to a hopeless state of selfish cruelty, but even those of us who are striving to do better still make mistakes.

Peter's gaze fell on K. D., whose face appeared a bit green from the rollicking rhythm of the sea, and then on Oliver, who was quite literally being shown the ropes by the boatswain.

What had become of Frank and Ethan? Oh, there they were, respectfully mimicking a grizzled pirate old enough to be their great-grandfather (Did Peter recognize him? Any of them?), who was dancing a jig. Peter rubbed his forehead. Any more fun, the Lost might refuse to leave! It was almost as if they had forgotten all about him.

Peter leapt to his feet, standing on top of the cabin, and raised his sword high. "Captain Smee, restore the Lost to Neverland or I, Peter Pan, challenge you to a duel for their release!"

"Oh no, not this foolishness again!" The captain reluctantly drew her weapon. "I have no quarrel with ye, lad. But you're not the captain here, savvy? Ye won't be taking anyone off me ship."

"Then a duel it shall be!" Peter crowed, jumping down to lunge at his sworn enemy.

Lily and Wendy exchanged a wary look, unaware that Peter was mostly playacting. The ship's crew, the Native kids, and the Lost drew back from the confrontation, forming a loose ring of spectators around Peter and Smee, trusting the captain to handle the situation.

Daniel handed Michael, who was holding Nana Bear, off to Lily and Wendy, who each kissed the top of their little brother's head while Strings and the mandolin player wrenched open the hatch so Terri and Mateo could carry the four-year-old to safety below deck.

"You rascally geezer!" Peter cried. "How dare you steal my crew?"

"Peppers and tongues, ye insolent brat! It's high time someone taught ye a lesson."

Yet where Peter sought to pierce, Smee deflected. He rushed. She sidestepped. He swiped. She repelled. He'd jab, prod. She anticipated, eluded, evaded his zone of attack.

Peter fumed, struggling with balance, lacking sea legs. "*Fight* me, you . . ." He searched his mind. "Decrepit bilge rat!"

Blades whipped. Clanged. Starboard, port, and back again. Smee was used to moving on deck, while Peter struggled to duel while fully tethered by gravity. Yet the captain didn't gloat or press her advantage. She didn't take advantage of her superior strength. "Ye're a sprog. There's no honor to be had in scuttling ye."

"I'm not just any sprog. I'm Peter Pan!"

"Aye, we know, lad. We know." What Smee lacked in wrist, she compensated for with a longer reach. "Enough with the bragging already."

Peter toppled sideways into the arms of Smee's crew member. They tried to hold him back for his own good, but Peter was having none of it. "Bad form! Let me go!"

Smee repressed a sigh. "It's all right, me mateys. We shall let him get it out of his system." They released Peter, and the battle commenced again.

In the heat of the duel, did you wonder what had become of Wendy and Lily? They had the good sense to gather with the other kids—at least those not hunkered below deck—in the entry to the captain's cabin, ready if need be to slam the rounded door.

"What happens if Peter wins?" Wendy asked.

"He'll never be the boss of me," Lily replied.

Right then the captain's beloved macaw flew across her line of vision, and Pan seized the opportunity, knocking Smee's cutlass from her hand. It skittered across the deck, out of reach.

The crew held its breath. The Native kids held their breath. The Lost did, too.

They braced for bloodshed.

And another Peter, the one who'd parted ways with his shadow, that Peter no doubt would've gloried in running Smee's heart through. But this Peter, in a show of *good form*, gestured with his sword for her to retrieve her weapon.

With grand aplomb, the mystified pirate queen smiled and revealed her skull-head cane to be a sword cane instead.

"Who be ye, and what have ye done with Peter Pan?"

Tick tock. Alongside the ship, the crocodile circled, eyes up, teeth eager, in the dark, choppy waters.

"I'm Captain of the Lost," Peter cried, with a hop and skip onto the plank. No, he hadn't forgotten that he could no longer fly, but you know how Peter was. He'd become caught up in the game. "You had no right to steal my family!"

Tick tock. "Foolish scoundrel," the captain replied. "They joined me crew willingly."

Tick tock. Wendy was growing to understand Peter. Can you say the same? Like her, he had been taken from a loving home. Like her, he was longing for family.

Tick tock. Peter swayed on the plank. "Wendy, is that true? Did you join the pirates?"

She wondered why everyone kept asking her the hard questions. "Yes and no, Peter, but never mind all that now. You're not safe out there. Come back to the ship. Please."

He turned his attention to Oliver and K. D., Ethan and Frank, huddled in the cabin doorway. "Belle told me you were kidnapped. Lost, was she wrong? Did you *want* to go?" Did you want to leave me?

Tick tock. Monsieur Barthe explained, "Pan, we took them to save them from ye."

Tick tock. Frank said, "Peter, we don't want to live in the Home Under the Ground."

"We don't want to be pirates either," Ethan added, much to Captain Smee's dismay.

Tick tock. "Well, maybe for a few days," Oliver clarified. "But not forever."

"We want to go home, to our real homes," K. D. said. "My parents are Alex and Cory Anders and my baby sister is Jewel . . . Peter, listen to Wendy. Come back to the ship."

Tick tock. What were they saying? Peter felt abandoned, rejected. Despite his wrongdoings, he was still their leader. "Mutiny!" Peter shouted, stomping. He wobbled, off-balance. "Cripes!"

Tick tock. "Easy, lad," Smee called. "I have no wish for ye to come to any real harm."

"Come back!" shouted the kids, the crew, and the pirate captain, too. "Peter, come back!"

Tick tock. They were right. Peter had wandered out too far and, realizing it, lost his nerve, just as an upswell of restless waves rocked the *Jolly Roger.*

Tick tock. Shaking, he dropped the sword, which landed sideways in the crocodile's brutal jaws. *Crack.* With a brutal bite, *clack*, the steel blade broke in two.

Tick tock. Now defenseless, Peter knelt to grip on to the plank with both hands.

The crocodile bellowed, leapt—*ka-splash!* Fell short.

Lily and Wendy jostled forward, through the crowd. It was up to them to tell Peter the truth that might save his life. "You're half right," Lily called. "No one should steal kids. But Captain Smee isn't to blame for that. *You* are!"

Tick tock. Wendy was more sympathetic. "All families change. People come and go."

Tick tock. Catching on, Lily added, "They may move to live close by . . . or far away."

Tick tock. Wendy thought of her mum, who'd died when she was just a little girl. "Sometimes they live in your heart."

"And sometimes," Lily said, smiling at Wendy, "you promise to visit as often as possible and to text or video chat every day."

All of which sounded persuasive enough to those on board. Monsieur Barthe used his red scarf to wipe away tears. Terri and Mateo cautiously raised the hatch to peek out with Michael.

Tick tock. With a gulp, Peter began slowly crawling toward the ship. His hands and knees were shaking. Captain Smee considered trying to inch out on the plank to fetch him, but that might only make matters worse.

The ship rocked again. "Peter's going to fall!" Oliver cried, raising a lantern. "Peter, hold on!"

"Hold on!" shouted the kids, the crew, and the pirate captain, too.

Tick tock. Over the years, Pan's sword had skewered Smee on more than one occasion, and not every wound had healed true. Still, she'd grown to care about him. After all, when she was eleven years old—back when he'd mistaken her for a boy—Esmerelda Eugenia Smee had been what grown-ups called "quite the handful" herself.

Ignorant of the cost of Fairy magic, the captain slipped her free hand into the velvet bag tied to her belt and withdrew the glowing vial. She flicked off the cap and released a cascade of shimmering dust in Peter's direction. "Fly, lad! Fly to safety!"

Are you worried that might have been the dust that tipped the scales? Do you fear Peter might revert to a state of selfish, inhuman barbarism? Not to fret—Smee's generosity was to no avail.

A brilliant presence rose between them to fully absorb the dust, illuminating the entire deck.

Peter toppled in surprise, spinning feet over head down toward a gruesome, watery demise.

Tick tock. The crew gasped, the macaw squawked, and the kids shouted, "Peter!"

If a crocodile could speak, it would've crowed, *"Finally!"*

CHAPTER

42

A flutter of Fairies intercepted a wide-eyed, flailing Peter's fall, catching him in a fishing net, and unceremoniously dumping him with a *thud* on deck. "Ow! Was that necessary?"

Radiating golden light, they sprinkled dust on the ratlines, the masts, the sails, the main boom—on every inch of the *Jolly Roger* not occupied by a human being or the squawking, squealing, squeaking turquoise-and-gold macaw.

It was the largest glittery fey gathering beyond the Fairy Wood in well over a century.

Belle tossed a Fairy-powered blue electric guitar to Strings, who caught it one-handed, and a black top hat to Frank, who suddenly seemed more like his dapper self again.

When she had burst into the Fairy court with a healthy

tiger cub, sharing news of Captain Smee's offer to keep the island secret in exchange for passage beyond the veil, Queen Mab quickly agreed to the proposal and, in gratitude, magnanimously pardoned Belle. Her Majesty had faith that the arrangement would finally close the chapter on humans in Neverland forever.

"Hang on," Belle called as the ship aglow rose from the Neversea into the night air.

It was her happy thoughts, and those of her fellow Fairies—baby tiger, "free the forest," "farewell, pirates," "good riddance to Peter Pan!"—that fueled the *Jolly Roger*'s flight.

"We're out of here?" Wendy asked, daring to hope.

"We're going home?" Lily added, wanting to be clear.

"Indeed!" Belle exclaimed. "We're off! I made a mistake in bringing Peter here, and now—with help—I am making amends. Humans belong in the human world, not in Neverland." Wendy and Lily raised their palms, and Belle gave each of them a tiny flying high five.

"We're what?" Peter climbed to his feet. "No more Neverland? What'll become of me?"

"Oh, Peter," Belle began. "In exchange for Queen Mab's blessing, I had to promise her that you'd leave the island forever, too. 'Every last human,' I said."

In a show of good form, Captain Smee broke into a slow grin. "Ah, lad, I do enjoy a big personality. That's why the life of a pirate has always appealed to me." She bent so that they were nose to nose. "Peter Pan, ye be welcome to join me family."

What an unexpected offer! Peter's breath caught. "You would be my mother?"

"Aye. Captain and mother and your port in a stormy sea."

Again, Peter still had his foibles. None of us reach our potential in a snap. Yet now that he had his full humanity back, Peter couldn't help but notice qualities in Smee that might otherwise have escaped his attention. The pirate queen led without bullying, fell back to let Lily and Wendy raise their voices when they were needed most. Captain Smee wasn't the kind to hold a grudge, and she had gone out of her way to show him forgiveness, concern, and kindness.

Maybe there was something to be said about being a true grown-up in every sense of the word. Maybe that kind of grown-up—a loving parent, no less—was what he'd always longed for. Peter bowed with a flourish. "Captain Mum, I somewhat humbly accept."

"Somewhat?" Smee's face was all lit up with love. "All righty, lad, it's a start!"

Wendy imagined Peter's future growing up on the high seas. She made a mental note to lend him some high-quality, page-turning books, including several with girls as heroes, books like *Ella Enchanted*. While she was at it, Wendy would send some books by Native authors, too.

Meanwhile, Terri and Mateo helped Michael up on

deck. Foul as the stench below had been, they were all grateful for salty sea air again.

"Sissies!" Michael leapt back into their arms. As they hugged, Lily said, "Mikey, you've been so brave, even when you were scared. You're amazing."

After a few moments, Wendy booted her phone, waiting for GPS to kick in, and leaned toward her sister. "Oliver's got a mean stepdad. I'm worried about him. K. D. says his mom wants out, but she might need some help to do it."

"We'll go to my mama," Lily said. "If anyone can help, it's her."

"You mean, *our* mama," Wendy replied. "I've decided to go ahead with the adoption because, well, I love her so much, and so that, no matter what, it's completely official that you and I will always be sisters, so you and I and John and Mikey will always be family."

Overcome by emotion, Lily could only nod. She let go of a lingering hurt, reassured in a way that meant the world to her. Together, she and Wendy could face the uncertain days ahead.

"Yo ho, hey, ahoy, my hearties,
A-sailing we will go.
Who was it lost our treasure map?
Dear Davy Jones might know."

As the crew broke into song, the kids clustered behind Captain Smee and Peter Pan, who steered the *Jolly Roger*, bathed in Fairy light, through the sparkling heavens.

Michael traveled on the captain's broad shoulders and Nana Bear sat on her hat.

"Are all pirate songs so grim?" Peter exclaimed.

"You're one to natter, lad," Smee replied, chuckling.

With their arms slung around one another, the no-longer Lost—Ethan and Frank, Oliver and K. D.—gathered starboard of Wendy. The Native kids—Daniel and Terri, Mateo and Strings, who'd fired up the magic-powered guitar—gathered to port side of Lily.

"Still afraid of flying?" Wendy asked. "I can stay in Tulsa this summer."

"Still afraid," Lily responded. "But I'll ride a bus or train to New York, for you."

Like all families, the Roberts-Darlings would change over time. The girls might have to live far apart, and they'd always be very different people. But come what may, they'd remain true sisters forevermore.

EPILOGUE

As the glistening bow of the *Jolly Roger* pierced the veil, the curious, twinkling stars murmured that they'd never before witnessed such a spectacle, and being stars, they had seen quite a lot. So bedazzled were they that only a small, serious star noticed Ripley diving into the seafoam, beneath and beyond the veil. She was towing a glowing Nevertree canoe, carrying stories of her adoptive grandfather, in search of his people in a faraway land currently known as Florida.

AUTHOR'S NOTE

From its earliest days, the story of Neverland has been regularly retold and reinvented.

Creator J. M. Barrie himself first introduced Peter Pan on the page, then the stage, and from there returned to the page again, making changes along the way. You may also be familiar with on-screen versions of the story. While some elements—like the spiriting of children to the island and epic battles with pirates—reappear again and again, the plot has proven especially malleable. More recently, the characters have been significantly reimagined, too.

That said, *Sisters of the Neversea* draws its inspiration from Barrie's novel *Peter and Wendy* (1911), also known as *Peter Pan*.

I write a lot of original stories, but I am fascinated by how narratives can change over time. With *Peter and Wendy* (and many other versions), I found myself puzzled and, frankly, horrified by the existence of Native people on the island, especially when I was a kid.

How did they get there? I wondered. What Indigenous Nation(s) did they hail from? Why were they described in hurtful language? Why were they behaving so strangely? Weren't they heartbroken about being marooned so far from home? None of it made sense.

However, I was enchanted by Barrie's fairy character, Tinker Bell, who I first encountered when I was about Michael's age. My affection for her was separate from her relationship to Peter and Barrie's stories, prompted by her independent presence in pop culture.

That said, Barrie's legacy is threaded through children's literature and, for that matter, the history of live theater, cinema, and, as with Tinker Bell, popular culture, too.

One of the most interesting and powerful things about Story is that it invites future storytellers to build on it, to reinvent, and to talk back. Like any other kind of magic, stories can harm or offer hope, even healing. I had a lot to say about *Peter and Wendy*. I wondered how someone like me might reimagine his work, so I gave it a try.

I rethought a great deal of the worldbuilding, which is a word that writers use to describe how a fictional—at least imaginary, at most fantastical—place comes together. My Native characters are a lot different from Barrie's. So is the way I write characters of various genders and characters with disabilities. And the fantastical characters—like Merfolk and Fairies—too.

In this novel, Peter uses the word "Injuns" to refer to

Native people. Lily is right that the word is both disrespectful and outdated. Wendy was right to correct him for using it. It made sense to me, though, that Peter would have learned the word from *The Wild & Wily West* storybook. I made that book up. It doesn't exist in real life, but too many books like it have been published. They're full of lies and nonsense and harmful depictions of Native people. In fact, *Peter and Wendy* is one of those books.

The lands you may have heard called the "Old West" or "Wild West" were (and still are) home to hundreds of Native and First Nations like those represented by the fictional Native characters in this story. Native people were never "wild" like animals. They were, are, and always will be people of real-life, sophisticated Nations.

What to say instead of "Injuns"? If you can be tribally specific, do that. Use the word that people of the Nation prefer to be called. Sometimes, though, you may be talking about a lot of Nations. In those cases, I use "Native Nations" and "Native people." However, some Native people prefer to say "First Nations" or "Native American" or "American Indian" or "Indigenous" or "Indian." Native elders are more likely to say "Indian," and of course they can say whatever they want. "Indigenous" is more of an umbrella word, referring to people from around the globe in their ancestral homelands. To both Native and non-Native readers, I suggest learning more about Indigenous Nations from books authored by writers of those respective communities.

In other aspects of this story, I took more of Barrie's lead. The pirates in this novel, like those in his, draw their inspiration from storybook fiction, not real life.

That said, I did reflect on my own experience with anxiety to write Lily. I know what it's like for my skin to break out in hives and for my mind to spin with worry and to freeze up when I become overwhelmed. I also know what it's like to breathe through it, like Great Auntie Lillian suggested in this book.

Do you know what that's like, too? Everyone feels anxious sometimes, and for some of us, it can become too big to deal with by ourselves. It's good to talk about it with someone who can help. When I was your age, I talked to the elders in my family, and they helped me. I wish that I had gone to a mental health professional, too. You may want to ask your trusted grown-ups at home and at school if they can connect you to someone who can offer that kind of support.

Careful readers may notice a few interwoven threads of Barrie's language as well as passing references to *Ella Enchanted* by Gail Carson Levine (in part because Barrie's novel mentions the often retold "Cinderella," probably influenced by Charles Perrault's version); "The Elves and the Shoemaker" and "The Goose Girl," collected by the Brothers Grimm; "the Judgement of Solomon"; the character Sherlock Holmes, created by Sir Arthur Conan

Doyle; the character Spider-Man, introduced by Steve Ditko, Jack Kirby, and Stan Lee; *Treasure Island* by Robert Louis Stevenson; the philosophy of myth by Roland Barthes; Milton Glaser's *I* ♥ *NY* logo; and the hit song "Don't It Make My Brown Eyes Blue" written by Richard Leigh, recorded by Crystal Gayle.

Mvto—or thank you—for reading. I've written books for kids who're younger than you and kids who're older than you. But you're who I had in mind when I first decided to become a storyteller. It took a long time for us to connect, but I'm so grateful.

May the stars always watch over you all.

ACKNOWLEDGMENTS

I live in a state of gratitude, honored by the support of teachers and librarians, booksellers and signal boosters, my dear friends in Native children's-YA literature and the creative community more broadly, especially those in the Austin chapter of the Society of Children's Book Writers and Illustrators.

One of the tremendous blessings of my creative life is being a member of the MFA faculty in Writing for Children and Young Adults at Vermont College of Fine Arts. Like most teachers, I learn so much from my students. While I was drafting this story, I had the good fortune to attend Adina Baseler's and Michael Leali's joint graduate lecture, "Building Better Boys," which informed my conceptualization of Peter and various secondary characters. Likewise, Clara Martin Hammett's earlier lecture, "The Voice of Wonder: From Wonderland to The Great Green Room, Moments of Wonder in Children's Literature," influenced my voice and my framing of Belle and the Roberts-Darling siblings in particular.

I also learn a lot from my fellow teachers. I'm grateful to the VCFA WCYA faculty for helping me to brainstorm a title for the book. It was my colleague, friend, and sometimes coauthor Kekla Magoon who originally suggested *Sisters of the Neversea.*

While working on the novel, I also had support at home. I appreciate the efforts of my husband, Christopher T. Assaf, who did a read-aloud of the first, full submitted draft, and our longhaired Chihuahua, Gnocchi, who loyally napped at my side while I wrote and revised.

I also appreciate my booking agent, Carmen Oliver; my assistant, Gayleen Rabakukk; and the Cynsations team for their aid in facilitating the more public aspects of my writing life.

My thanks to my long-time literary agent, Ginger Knowlton, for continuing to make my storybook dreams come true, and to my beloved editor, Rosemary Brosnan, for her wisdom, thoughtful suggestions, patience, and heartfelt support when I said I wanted to shelve my work in progress to write this novel instead. I am also grateful to Ellen Oh and everyone at We Need Diverse Books, James Farrell of Curtis Brown as well as Veronica Ambrose (copyeditor), Nicole Moreno (production editor), Courtney Stevenson (editorial), Cat San Juan (designer), and everyone else at HarperChildren's for their behind-the-scenes efforts and enthusiasm.

My thanks to legendary illustrator Floyd Cooper for

cover art that beautifully captures the loving spirit of the younger Roberts-Darling siblings and the sense of adventure threaded through this novel. I am, as always, starstruck by Floyd's talent, achievements, and graciousness. It's been a tremendous honor to work with him and to be informed and inspired by his artistic vision, in bringing this story and its young heroes to life.

Finally, my thanks to the young readers out there, especially those of you who are like me and read the notes like this one at the back of their books. Maybe you are a nonfiction reader like Lily or a fantasy reader like Wendy (or both), and maybe you're also a storyteller or writer like me. It was kind of you to join the Roberts-Darling siblings on their journey to the Neversea. I appreciate your time and effort. Please keep reading and writing. Raise your voices. Share your visions. Believe in each other and in yourselves. I believe in young heroes like you.

CYNTHIA LEITICH SMITH is the *New York Times* bestselling, acclaimed author of books for all ages, including *Rain Is Not My Indian Name*, *Indian Shoes*, *Jingle Dancer*, and *Hearts Unbroken*, which won the American Indian Youth Literature Award; she is also the anthologist of *Ancestor Approved: Intertribal Stories for Kids*. Most recently, she was named the 2021 NSK Neustadt Laureate. Cynthia is the author-curator of Heartdrum, a Native-focused imprint at HarperCollins Children's Books, and serves as the Katherine Paterson Inaugural Endowed Chair on the faculty of the MFA program in Writing for Children and Young Adults at Vermont College of Fine Arts. She is a citizen of the Muscogee (Creek) Nation and lives in Austin, Texas. You can visit Cynthia online at www.cynthialeitichsmith.com.

FLOYD COOPER received a Coretta Scott King Award for *The Blacker the Berry* and a Coretta Scott King Honor for his illustrations in *Brown Honey in Broomwheat Tea*, both by Joyce Carol Thomas. Born and raised in Tulsa, Oklahoma, he received a degree in fine arts from the University of Oklahoma and, after graduating, worked as an artist for a major greeting card company. He now lives in Easton, Pennsylvania, with his wife and children. You can visit him online at www.floydcooper.com.

IN 2014, WE NEED DIVERSE BOOKS (WNDB) began as a simple hashtag on Twitter. The social media campaign soon grew into a 501(c)(3) nonprofit with a team that spans the globe. WNDB is supported by a network of writers, illustrators, agents, editors, teachers, librarians, and book lovers, all united under the same goal—to create a world where every child can see themselves in the pages of a book. You can learn more about WNDB programs at www.diversebooks.org.